The Emperor's Winding Sheet

the Emperor's Winding Sheet

JILL PATON WALSH

Front Street
Asheville, North Carolina

Copyright © 1974 by Jill Paton Walsh
All rights reserved
Printed in the United States of America
First Front Street paperback edition, 2004
Designed by Helen Robinson

Library of Congress Cataloging-in-Publication Data
Paton Walsh, Jill
The emperor's winding sheet
p. cm.
I.Title.
PZ7.P2735Em   [Fic]73-90970
ISBN 1-886910-88-X (pb)

for my mother and father

Chapter 1

From where the boy was, precariously perched in the bending branches of the little orange tree, a wide and lovely landscape could be seen. The orange tree stood in the garden of a great church, built at the foot of the steep little town, a town all of pink brick and rosy red stone, with narrow winding streets, steps all the way, that clung to the top of a precipitous conical hill, a foothill of the mountains through which the boy had come, in pain from hunger, in pain from cold, and driven by the terror behind him. The garden on its terrace hung suspended over the valley, a wide valley, like a great round dish, with the spacious plain shimmering all over with silver-green groves of trees, and rimmed by steep circling mountains capped with shining snow—oh yes, the snow was fair enough to see from here below, out of its biting grip! On the valley floor, some way away, sunk among the trees, were the white walls of another little town. Over it all a pale and fitful winter sunlight coolly shone. A fair prospect, though the boy was deaf and blind to it.

It was the bright fruit that had tempted him into the tree. He had seen the like before, and his belly ached to remember them, for he recalled his mother having made a fragrant sweet preserve from some of these very orange-apples, that had come wrapped and crated in a cargo Uncle Norton had brought safely home to Bristow haven, out of some port of Spain. Clinging now desperately in the unsafe boughs, he could not tell if it was the moving branches that made his head swim, or his hunger—or he was indeed half dead from starvation—or the homesick yearning for his mother's quiet kitchen in far-off England, with the smell of preserves boiling away thickly on the fire. It was most likely of all to be the hunger, yet he did not stretch out for the fruit, but tried mightily to remain still and quiet; for he had not known, when he scrambled up the garden wall from the street, when he clutched the branches of the tree, and wriggled into them, that there was anyone beneath; and now that he could see the purple-coated gentleman, the purple-coated gentleman might at any moment look up and see him; might especially look up if the boy tried to get back over the wall; so now what was he to do?

Sooner or later, he knew, he would have to beg somebody's charity, throw himself on somebody's mercy. He needed food, clothes, a little money, a chance to find a passage on a ship. But fear had taught him that he must see the face of the one to whom he surrendered, to make sure there was kindliness there. The gentleman beneath the tree looked splendid enough; surely he had the means to help, if he had the heart for it. But the boy could not see his face; and it's a hard matter to judge a stranger's kindliness when all you can see of him is the high-buttoned crown, and wide brim of a tall and curious hat. If only he would move enough for the boy to catch a glimpse of him!

The stranger continued, however, steadfastly to bend his gaze downward, and neither moved nor looked up. He was seated on a marble bench, with a carpet spread out before it in the shade of the tree, reading in a large volume laid open upon his silken knees. The pages of this book were of lilac-tinted vellum and the letters were written in palest, purest gold. But the beauty of the book, like the beauty of the landscape, was as nothing to the boy in his misery and his ragged hunger. Wretchedly he decided he had best wait till the man departed; but how long might a man not continue reading, who read in such a book as that? So at last his hunger overcame him, and with his spittle gushing in his mouth, he reached out and plucked an orange, and sank his famished teeth in it.

Bitter! It dried his teeth, it dried his tongue, it stung and burned the roof of his mouth and brought tears to his eyes. The tears dissolved the landscape and the tree, laden with its bright thankless fruit. His head began singing, droning on a single note, and his hands relaxed their hold on bending bough. Slowly at first, he slipped, and fell fainting, and landed in a ragged dirty heap upon the carpet at the purple-coated gentleman's feet.

WHEN HE CAME TO, NOT ONE, BUT THREE MEN WERE STANDING round him, looking down at him. Their elaborate robes rose like columns from where he lay, face upward, blinking at the light, and he could not at first make out their features, against the dazzling brightness of the sky. There was a plump smooth young man, with a beardless face, a stout looking man of middle age, wearing a belt with a fine cup fixed to it on a golden chain, and the interrupted reader himself, clad in his fine purple silk. And as the boy's eyes grew used to the light again, he saw that they were all dark; dark-haired, black-eyed, olive-skinned, so dark indeed that with a spasm of terror he thought for one moment they were Turks, till he saw swinging above him a golden cross, set all with jewels, hanging from a chain round the purple gentleman's neck, dangling as he bent down looking at the boy.

The three of them spoke together in a strange tongue, and pointed at him, at his eyes in particular, which were an honest English blue, and at his fair hair, dirty though it was, and called him Frank.

"I am not!" he said, weakly indignant. "I am *not!* I am an English merchant, come through sundry perils and disasters, and right glad to fall in at last with Christian gentlemen!"

"Inglis?" said Cup and chain man. "Nai, Frank."

This made the boy so angry, he sat up, and with head swimming declared again, "I am *not* French! I am an Englishman, an honest luckless merchant out of Bristow!"

"*Vrisko?*" they said. "*Vrisko! Vrethiki*," and they laughed.

The boy jerked his emaciated frame into a kneeling position, and frantically glanced from face to face, looking for that spark of pity he might be willing to trust. There was curiosity and amusement in the eyes of Cup and chain man. There was something in the eyes of the plump smooth man, but he had the careful guarded look that servants wear. Nothing for it then but to trust the inscrutable dark eyes of the richly clad reader; the boy thrust a bony arm out of his rags, and grabbed hold of the golden cross on its chain. "In the name of Christ Jesus," he said, pointing first to the cross, and then to his mouth and belly, "give me food or I die!"

The purple-clad man clapped his hands at once, and a monkish servant came running. He was given an order. Kneeling on the carpet before the marble bench the boy released his hold on the man's cross of gold, and waited. Back came the servant with a dish in his hands, which he gave to the boy. There was a round of crusty bread, a little cake of soft white cheese, and a handful of olives. "Thank you," he said, but seeing their grave faces blank at that, he managed "*Gratias ago*" and saw that that had been understood.

Someone—the smooth plump young man—began at once, talking rapidly in Latin, asking questions. But the boy scarcely understood. In the first place he was eating, cramming bread down his throat, while his agonized belly glowed and rumbled with relief and pleasure, and that took his attention off case endings and parts of speech; in the second place, though he had spent a good part of his childhood in the new grammar school, being beaten for mistakes in Latin, and beaten again for speaking English in the play hour to his friends, all that was both long ago and far away, and the man who questioned him spoke very elaborate Latin, and with a heavy unfamiliar accent.

But as the worst of his hunger was assuaged, the boy tried harder. To "Who are you?" he managed to answer that he was Piers Barber, and to "How did you come here?" that he had set out from England in the *Cog Anne*, a ship belonging to Richard Sturmy, the Bristow merchant.

That luckless ship had come to grief on some storm-beaten rocky shore, holed and foundered, and many good woolen cloths went with her, and many good English souls. The boy thought he was the only survivor; certainly he had clung to a spar in the water a whole day and a night and half a day again without seeing any other.

"But here, how did you get here?" the man insisted.

"A ship came. They pulled me from the water. But …"—a blankness shuttered the boy's eyes, and a muscle twitched in his cheek—"they landed to take fresh water, and I slipped my fetter and ran … and ran … I came over those mountains," and he pointed to the black tall steeps of the Taygetus, topped with snow.

But this explanation brought a flood of incredulous questions. They babbled to each other, gestured, looked toward the mountains, spoke to the Latin-speaker, who questioned the boy. How had he eaten? How survived the cold? Why had he been fettered? What had made him flee through so harsh a country?

The boy gazed up at them with empty shallow eyes. "I don't know," he said. "I can't remember."

The Latin-speaker crouched down to him, and took the boy's hand. "Why were you fettered?" he asked gently, framing the words slowly. "Who were they who rescued you from the water?" But the boy flinched back from him, jerking his hand away. His voice rose in a panic-stricken cry. "No!" he wailed. "No! I can't remember!"

The three strangers looked at one another. They spoke in their own tongue. "That sounds like pirates, Sire," said the cupbearer.

"This is only a child, surely," said the nobleman.

The boy tugged at the hem of the Latin-speaker's robe. "Tell me where I am," he said, "and into whose hands I have fallen." And he pointed at the purple-coated gentleman whom he had first seen, for about him he sensed the greatest dignity.

"This is the province of Morea," came the answer. "The town of Mistra. And the lord is Constantine Dragases Palaeologos, who is Despot here." The boy felt, and looked, none the wiser.

"Well, where's that, then?" he asked, pointing to the other town across the plain.

"That's Sparta," he was told. And, "Sparta?" thought the boy in astonishment, switched back in a moment to a distant classroom wherein he had sat upon a hard bench and conned his lines of Latin, telling of Helen there.

Just at that moment a distant clamor, that had been beating faintly in their ears, grew louder—the racket of men and horses, as though they had been riding up the hillside for some time, and now had turned the corner into the street of the garden; trumpets sounded, and the three men looked at each other meaningly. Cup and chain man ran out into the street. Looking up, the boy could see a procession of plumed tall hats moving along over the top of the wall. When Cup and chain man returned there was a trumpeter with him. The beardless man made an urgent gesture to the boy to withdraw, and he needed little telling, for the trumpeter was a lad no older than himself, clad all in scarlet with wide embroidered sleeves, raising a silver trumpet proudly to his lips. Torn to tatters as he was, and clutching his charity dish of bread and olives, the boy was shamed into slinking behind the tree at once. There he crouched down behind the marble bench and watched.

It looked like a pageant, or a masque. The sudden fullness of his belly was making him feel drowsy, and through the courtyards round the great church, marching through the scalloped shadows of its nestling domes, the newcomers moved with dreamlike ceremony. Through one courtyard and another, and out into the garden beyond, they came, and stood stiffly rank by rank on either side of the arch, like the rows of saints and seraphim that flank a cathedral door. Last came two gorgeous armed and embroidered men who, seeing the Despot, came and knelt on the grass before him. And now two pages advanced, carrying an ornate box between them, and set it before the Despot on the grass. Then one of the kneeling lords threw back the lid of the box, and brought out of it a shining crown. It was a domed crown, like a helmet all of gold, thick-set with jewels and enameling, with an encrusted cross standing upon the crest of it, and pendant strings of huge pearls hanging from the rim. The sunlight flashed upon it in a dozen different colors.

There was a silence. The agonized silence made by many men holding their breath. A hundred eyes were bent upon the Despot Constantine; they watched, they commanded. The boy shivered. He could feel the tension in the sunlit afternoon air, something fateful happening, some terrible bond being forged. Then the Despot reached out his hand, and lightly touched the crown. Voices rang out.

"By the wish of the Lady Empress, and of the people of the City, and all their governors and demarchs," intoned the Lord Alexios Lascaris, "we bring you this."

"God give me strength to wear it!" said the Lord Constantine.

The boy did not understand. But he knew that he had tumbled into something far out of his scope. Out of his depth altogether. "As soon as they all remove from this garden," he promised himself, "it's up over that wall again, and out of it for me. I'd be better begging in the streets, or trying my luck in that other little town." He remembered as clear as daylight his Uncle Norton saying grimly, "It's always dangerous to deal with kings."

But they weren't all going yet. Someone else came through the arch from the courtyard, an old man dressed in black, with a grizzled beard, who leaned upon a stick to walk. The boy sighed. "Yet more of these fantastical foreigners," he groaned to himself. For certainly the newcomer was a strange and striking figure. His face was wrinkled and creased as an old man's should be, but yet all lit up and shining from within, like the face of a child at a market sideshow.

He came forward, and spoke. "I have been sleeping over

my books these very minutes past," he declared. "Till trumpets roused me. I never drowsed thus when I was a young man ... ah well, time brings us all to such shifts in the end ... what was I saying? Ah yes! My dream. I was visited, my Lord, by an unusual dream. Hear it, good Constantine."

"You dreaming, Plethon?" said the Lord Constantine. "We will hear it indeed."

"I have dreamed, my Lord, that I saw an eagle, flying in the zenith of the heavens, with many lesser birds flocking around him. And he flew through a dark cloud, whereupon many of the lesser birds fell back, and left him. Still he flew, till only one small bird remained beside him; and they two flew through the dark cloud to the light beyond. Who can interpret this?"

"Who indeed!" said the Lord Constantine. He spoke gravely, but there was a tremor of something in his voice—fondness? amusement?—that the listening boy heard, and strained to understand. "What is going on? What are they talking about?" he wondered, baffled, longing for them to go away. "Dear friend," the Lord Constantine was saying, "what did your great Plato think of dreams and auguries? Since when did you dabble in such foolishness?"

Then another spoke—a churchman, for on his shoulders black crosses were embroidered on white bands. "Not foolishness, my Lord. God speaks to us in dreams. Did not Pharaoh dream, and Joseph auger it? Did not the blessed saint ..."

"Let the saints rest in peace, and auger my dream for me, good Father," said Plethon.

"The black cloud is the power of the infidel Turk," said the priest confidently. "And the dream means this. That as long as any, even one, is at the Lord Constantine's side, who is at his side at this moment, no harm will befall, and the City will not perish."

"My Lord, who could stay always at your side—which man now present could remain day and night beside you?" Plethon asked eagerly.

"Come, Plethon," said the Lord Constantine. "Can I spare my soldiers and diplomats, that I should make them into slaves of the bedchamber?"

"But I, my Lord, could be spared to go with you ..." the old man said.

"Ah," murmured the Lord Constantine, "now I understand. Dear friend, I thank you," he said gently to Plethon. "But I would not uproot you from your peaceful life, and your dear books of Plato, to share what lies in store for me."

At that the Lord Iagrus spoke. He was the second of the two who had brought the crown. "Have a care, my Lord. As to the truth of dreams ..." He shrugged his shoulders. "But it is true indeed that the people believe in them. They are swayed by every idle prophecy. Should it be known you have defied one, it will do little to your standing with the mob."

"Then I must heed it," said the Lord Constantine. "But still I will not trouble Plethon's calm old age. For it happens, by great good fortune, by the providence of God perhaps, that a person of no consequence at all has been hidden here all the while, not a yard from me, and him I shall take with me, and keep with me night and day." And smiling wryly, the Lord Constantine reached down behind the marble bench he had been sitting on so peacefully not an hour since, and with astonishing strength lifted the boy by a handful of his rags, and stood him upon the bench, flinching at his sudden exposure to so many staring eyes.

"This is my lucky find," said the Lord Constantine. "My Vrethiki. And I swear that Plethon's dream shall bind him to me."

Angry and bewildered, the boy stood looking at them all. They all looked well pleased at something, except the strange old man. He was looking straight at the Lord Constantine, and weeping openly, with love and grief written clearly on his face.

"Be satisfied," said the Lord Constantine to him, very softly. Thus the boy's fate was settled, and he had not understood a word of it.

Chapter 2

When the despot left the monastery garden, handing his gorgeous volume to the curator of books, speaking graciously to him but like a man who speaks while thinking of other things, mounting a white horse with splendid harnessings, riding away up the hill, the boy sidled along among the throng of his followers, hoping to get through the gate and make a dash for it down the street. But before he reached the street gate, the beardless man took him firmly by the hand and led him away, at a brisk trot to keep up with the Despot's horse, among the attendants and servants. The party gradually mounted the hill along a winding narrow road broken every few yards by flights of shallow steps. The Despot's horse picked his way gingerly, side-stepping a little, up these stairwayed streets, and the donkeys on which some of his party were mounted barged straight up them, heads down, but the boy, feeble and sickly as he was, stumbled and dragged the hand that was leading him.

No doubt that was partly through weariness; but he missed his footing most often through snatching sideways glances at his keeper, and not looking where he went. His captor had a man's stature, but the smooth and beardless visage of a boy. The unnaturally womanish look of his face reminded the boy of poor Jack Half-Wit, who begged through the streets of Bristow, chewing his words up and slobbering pitifully, but this man's face was neither coarse nor stupid, but handsome enough, and shrewd. Besides, it was he who had Latin enough to converse with the boy. Rather short of breath from scrambling up the steep slope so briskly, and distracted by the sight of the tall narrow houses, and the great many-arched façade of a huge building hanging, it seemed, in mid-air above them, the boy could not manage to inquire where he was being taken, let alone why. He did manage, "Who are you?" to his companion, who answered, "I am Stephanos Bulgaricos, Eunuch of the bedchamber, and many other things besides, to the Despot Constantine."

Then they turned off the street, through a wide tall archway cut and carved in honey-colored stone, into a wide courtyard, where the Despot dismounted, and a boy came running to lead away his horse. The Despot moved gravely and with even steps up a stairway to an inner room, but Stephanos drew the boy out through a side door, into an inner courtyard. There were people of all sorts thronging in it, soldiers, servants, boys and men, and kitchen girls, and, hurried though they looked, they all had time to stare at the boy, and chatter, and point at him.

Stephanos led the boy toward a certain door, but an indignant outburst from the slave who sat before it, and the voices of others chiming in, mocking and angry, dissuaded him. He looked at the boy and led him back toward the well which stood in the middle of the courtyard. A monkey-faced derisive serving lad ran to turn the wheel and raise the bucket. Stephanos took hold of the boy's rags by the scruff of his scruffy neck, and ripped them from him, letting them fall in a dirty heap, and leaving him standing mother-naked in the bitter winter sun, in front of all those staring eyes, and buffeted by gales of unfriendly laughter! Head held high, lips bitten hard together, his two hands held before him like a fig leaf, the boy smarted helplessly. The rope wheezed and creaked on the rumbling well wheel.

Suddenly a thunderous shout broke through all the other voices. A black-robed figure—the churchman who had spoken in the garden—had appeared in one of the upper windows overlooking the courtyard. "Silence, impudent blasphemers!" he cried. Looking up, the boy saw a fierce visage contorted into a terrible frown above a flowing grizzled beard. "Has it not been said of this child that the very Empire shall not fall while he is with us? Wretch though he is, the Lord God has chosen him for a sign of His abiding mercy, and who shall dare to mock?"

"Oh, what have I done?" thought the boy, cringing. It never entered his head that the man's anger was not for him, and whatever it was he had done, being naked made him feel five times worse about it. "Is it not the poor and humble who are most pleasing to the Lord?" the voice ranted on. "Mysterious are the ways of the Lord our God, and beyond our understanding. Even with such a broken reed as this wretched child He can strike down our enemies, and save us from the jaws of the infidel, His will be done, *Ameen!*"

During this outburst the bucket had been drawn, creaking and groaning, to the rim of the well, and as the speaker cried "*Ameen!*" and turned from the window arch above them, Stephanos unhooked the bucket, and tossed the water over the boy.

Gray shining snakes and slopping gobbets of water struck him, and glazed his goosy skin. The cold seized and bit him, and cut off his breath in gasps; on the dusty slabs of the courtyard a pinkish dark starfish stain spread out from his feet all round him. His teeth chattered violently in his head. But nobody laughed; shamed into silence they looked at him, and looked away. Stephanos led him once again toward the bathhouse door, and this time the doorkeeper let them in.

Within was a tall round room, lined with marble under a domed roof, with a pool of deep warm water set into the marble floor. A wraith-like twist of steam curled upward from the surface of the bath to the air vents of the dome. How gratefully the boy slid into the warm water! How he tingled and glowed as his blue pincushion skin smoothed flat and pink again. Pink, that is, except for the brown weathering on the back of his hands and over his face and neck, where the Mediterranean sun had marked him, and for certain darker, fading bruises and marks … Bobbing up and down in the bath, flopping and splashing round in the water like a seal, he warmed up enough to scrape some more Latin together, and came to the edge of the bath to look up at Stephanos, impassively sitting there, on a marble bench.

"What was that crown they brought him?"

"The crown of the Empire," said Stephanos, somberly.

"What Empire?" asked the boy.

"The Roman Empire," Stephanos replied.

"*But,*" the boy exclaimed, "the Roman Empire passed away these thousand years ago!"

"The Western Provinces," Stephanos replied, "have been occupied by the barbarians for some considerable time, it is true. But in the East the Empire still stands. Against all onslaughts it has survived till now. Till now," he repeated. "God knows how much longer." And at that the somber note sounded so clearly in his voice that a little chill tremor reached the boy through his bewilderment.

He climbed out of the bath, and Stephanos clapped his

hands. Two slaves came, bringing towels to rub him down.

"But if he's a *Roman* Emperor," the boy persisted, from the midst of the enveloping clouds of linen, and the hands of the slaves patting him dry, "why does he not speak Latin?"

"Greek is the language of the Romans, and has been since the time of the Emperor Heraclius," Stephanos told him.

"And this land is Greece?"

"It is the Morea; a province of the Empire."

"Of the *Roman* Empire?" The boy strove to find his feet among these mind-boggling answers.

"Yes. The Lord Constantine has governed it under Christ, and most valiantly striven to keep out the infidel, and with some success. He has governed this province well, though he must leave it now." Again came the chilling tone of sadness in the man's voice.

"But why must he leave it now?" the boy asked. "Where is he going?"

"To the City. Where else? Come, we must go to the wardrobe master to find you a garment." And wrapping the towel round the boy and taking his hand again, Stephanos led the boy away, through arches and arcades and little courts sunk deep in the high-storied palace walls, and up a narrow flight of stairs.

"THIS ONE?" SAID THE WARDROBE MASTER, HOLDING A PURPLE tunic up against the boy. "No, that's too long. Shame to cut it, it's the only silk one left. This one? No, all those are too small. It'll have to be this one. Can't be choosy."

He offered for Stephanos' approval a worn tunic of purple linen faded to a rusty red in stripes which marked the folds it had lain in on some other wearer.

"Can't I have this one?" asked the boy, finding a dark-green one about the right size, and made of coarse woolen cloth. The heat of the bath was wearing off rapidly.

"You have to have purple, for the Emperor's household," said the wardrobe master, in guttural Latin.

"But surely, I won't be ... I mean I'm not," said the boy, "I'm not his man, nor he my master. I was hoping he would send me home ... in Christian charity ... he will, won't he? Why not?" His voice grew increasingly desperate as he saw the expression with which the two men exchanged glances.

The wardrobe master put the purple tunic over his head, and Stephanos found a belt and put it round him. The belt was of heavy leather, embossed with a pattern of leaves, and it was far too long—by the time it was comfortably drawn through to fit the boy's slender girth, half its length was surplus, hanging free. Stephanos took a little dagger from his belt, and scratched a light mark where the buckle lay. Then, removing the belt, he went over to sit where the light of the window fell squarely on the floor, and began to trim it to size. The wardrobe master busied himself finding hose and boots, and neither of them looked at the boy while Stephanos, carefully wielding his little knife, said, "You could not go yet, child. You are in too starved a state for journeying. For the present you are taken into the Imperial household. You will be well cared for." And Stephanos put the belt round the boy's waist, and drew it tight, and buckled it.

YET THE BOY COULD SEE THAT THE LORD CONSTANTINE HAD no material need of another page. He lived simply enough in his grand palace, though to the boy's eyes he was surrounded by unbelievable luxury. The palace walls were plastered smoothly, and painted with splendid pictures, over which, to ease his boredom, the boy's eyes traveled through forests and

hunts and in among row upon row of sacred and royal person-
ages. The palace was furnished with couches, and cupboards,
and tables, all of outlandish design to honest English eyes.
Every day the Lord Constantine put on clean linen next
to his skin, and every day washed himself in warm water,
or descended to the bathhouse. But although he had these
almost sinfully extravagant personal luxuries, he did not seem
to enjoy them. Watching his body slave put his shirt over his
head, and straighten or twitch the fine cambric smooth over
his body before bringing the stiff silk tunic that went over
it, it seemed to the boy that the Lord Constantine suffered
these ministrations patiently, rather than wanting them. Far
from needing more help about his dressing than he already
had, he often, while they were fussing over some detail of the
garments laid out ready on the bed, dressed himself without
waiting for them. There was nothing for the boy to do. But
he studied the Lord Constantine, watching for the moment
when he might kneel to him, and beg for his release.

There was a restlessness about that great lord, a sense of
impermanence. He lived like a soldier who had taken the palace
as a billet for a short season—as though nothing in it belonged
to him, or was of his ordaining, and all would continue when
he was gone. He enjoyed the hunt, though most of his time at
Mistra was taken up with receiving people and signing documents for them. The boy managed to dislodge the secretary's
slave from the office of bringing pen and ink and wax seals
for all these grants of land and confirmations of privileges,
required, it seemed, in large numbers to set the province in
order before the Lord Constantine departed from it, and so
got himself one small thing to do; but the palace was full of
servants, built into it like the furniture, as well as those who
were the Lord Constantine's own—Stephanos, and Cup and

chain man, who was called Manuel, and who poured out every drop of wine or water that passed the Lord Constantine's lips, and now the boy himself—so the larger part of the boy's time was spent standing around, idly staring, and when the pictures on the wall-plaster lost their charm, gazing sullenly at the Lord Constantine, his jailer.

He was a man of middle age, fairly tall, very slender. His hair was dark, his skin sallow. He wore a short beard very neatly and closely trimmed to a point, but his hair was long, hanging over his collar in ringlets, which, somewhat to the watching boy's disgust, required the attentions of a barber with hot curling tongs every few days. His lean face wore a somber expression as soon as it was at rest. Although every day much time was spent going in procession with crowds of attendants to hear Mass said in this church or in that—at least the boy thought it was Mass, though most of it was hidden from sight behind gorgeous and complex screens—although they had always heard at least one, and sometimes as many as three services in three different churches in the course of the day, yet the Lord Constantine prayed again at bedtime, kneeling before an icon of the Virgin, in his nightshirt, with his black eyes shrouded by his drooping lids, murmuring, head bowed, for long minutes before he slept.

And the only thing expected of the boy, he soon discovered, was simply to walk behind the Despot everywhere he went, three or four paces behind him, and be seen to be there. He might as well have been a dog.

THE PLENTIFUL WHOLESOME FOOD OF THE PALACE BEGAN TO smooth over the grooves between his ribs, though at first he could eat only mouthfuls at a time. Stephanos made broth for him and Manuel brought him watered wine. He soon recovered enough to eat normally, and was full of curiosity, and rebellion. "Why do you carry that cup round on a chain?" he asked Manuel.

"To foil attempts of poisoners," said Manuel, in his limping, scanty Latin, rolling his eyes dramatically. "Cupbearer goes everywhere with Emperor; the Emperor drink no other cup. Cup chained to me; if Emperor poisoned they kill me at once. Only for ceremony, now, and all I'm for is taste and pour the wine."

"But might someone poison him?" asked the boy.

"He crowned Emperor soon," said Manuel. "More Emperors have died out of their beds than in them, I can tell you that."

"Why must I go to church with the Lord Constantine?" the boy demanded of Stephanos. "We've been to church three times already, and I'm sick of going. Why can't I just stay here?"

"He has sworn a great oath that all the people know about to keep you by his side," Stephanos said. "Now stop arguing and get down there, this very moment."

SO WHEN THEY RETURNED THE BOY CHALLENGED STEPHANOS. he had time to think, walking to the church and back, and he was furiously angry. Stephanos and Manuel were together, sitting in a window arch looking out over the town, when he found them.

"What do you mean he swore an oath to keep me with him?" the boy demanded. "You said he would send me home when I was well enough."

"I said only that you were too weak to go at once. I did not say what was to happen later ..." said Stephanos quietly.

"Why, you treacherous liar!" cried the boy.

"It was true you were too weak," said Stephanos. "Lower your voice, you will disturb the Lord Constantine.

"That's devilish!" the boy hissed, between clenched teeth. He was rigid from top to toe with rage. "You made a lie out of the truth! Do you think I would have stayed here so meekly if I'd known? I'd have run away long since!"

"Where would you have fled to?" asked Stephanos, his voice still steady and low. "Back through the mountains to the sea? Or northward to the lands held by the Turks? Or to a seaport perhaps? They belong to Venice or to Genoa; how would you fare among them?"

"I could hardly fare worse than here, if here I am a prisoner cruelly held!" the boy replied.

"*Cruelly* held?" said Stephanos. "*Cruelly?* And yet what I would call cruel is the sending of a child as young as you on perilous journeys over distant seas."

At that the boy's rigid posture gave place to trembling. Misery rose in his throat. "They couldn't help it!" he said. "My father was sick. Trade was bad. The Baltic was closed to us, and the Iceland run. My Uncle Norton found a venture for me on Richard Sturmy, his friend's, ship … he was not to know she would be shipwrecked." But he remembered his mother's alarm. Uncle Norton had come to see them, and stood before the fire in the hall, and rocked to and fro on his toes—a way he had, with his hands clasped behind his back, under his fur-trimmed cloak. "A fair opportunity for the boy," he had been saying. "… As you know, I have no ship of mine own in harbor at this time, but my right good friend Richard Sturmy hath an enterprise making ready. He is to take pilgrims to Jaffa in the Levant …"

"The Holy Land!" his mother had cried. "But there will be infidels, and surely, Brother, a risk of foul play from the men of Genoa, or Venice, for is not that trade all theirs?"

The boy had thought no more of his mother's alarm than if she had been fussing over him riding a dozen miles on some errand. But it all looked different to him now; his eyes brimmed with tears, and he turned his head away that Stephanos might not see them.

"... For the homeward journey," Uncle Norton had continued, "he hath cloth and wool and tin to take to Pisa, hard by Florence. Piers may take goods to trade on his own account, without charge or fee. This is a good offer, madam, made to you out of friendship. Others who embark with Master Sturmy must pay him a full tithe."

"Piers hath done well learning Latin," the boy's mother had said, "I wondered if we might put him to Oxford, or the Church."

"I have no money for it, Sister, if I would," said Uncle Norton. "God witness what I do now is by my reckoning the best I can devise for him, and I could no better were he my own son."

"Don't fret, Mother," the boy had said. "I'd rather far set sail than be a clerk at Oxford. I'll be all right."

But he had not been all right. And Uncle Norton's own son, his cousin Tom, was safe at home in England, while he was here; caught in some mysterious trap.

"Oh, help me!" he cried suddenly to Stephanos. "Talk to him! Make him send me home!"

"He cannot, child," said Stephanos. He took the boy's hand, and drew him down to sit between them in the high window, and he told the boy what had happened in the garden.

"It seems to me an idle, foolish fancy to put trust in dreams and prophecies," the boy said at last, when he had heard it.

"But if he does, why does he not take the old gentleman who dreamed the dream? Why did he lay this burden upon me?"

"Take Plethon with him?" said Stephanos, throwing up his hands. "God knows he has troubles enough without that! There are already in the City ten thousand shades of opinion upon every topic in theology; but a man who puts Plato before Christ, and praises all day and every day none but the ancient heathens—why, he would infuriate them all! The Emperor Manuel did well to persuade Plethon to leave the City, and study here in peace. My Lord Constantine must have thanked God for you, when he slipped out of the trap Plethon had laid for him, and got out of taking Plethon home!"

"It would be the death of the old man, anyway," said Manuel.

"But if it's just a trap ... just a bit of scheming," protested the boy, "why does anyone heed it? Why does it matter? Why must I lose my freedom for it?"

"It is like this, my son," said Stephanos. "The Lord Constantine dare not offend Plethon because he is a famous scholar, known and well loved in the West, from whence is our only hope of help against our enemies ... and he dare not take him to the City for fear of offending the Church, against which he already struggles in vain to make them submit to the Pope in Rome, and so get help from him ... and he dare not ignore the dream and the prophecy because whatever he thinks of it himself, the people are deeply moved by such things, and will blame him if he flouts them, and he must somehow make one people out of them, and make them fight."

The boy said nothing. "No wonder he calls you Vrethiki," said Stephanos.

"Why does he so?" demanded the boy angrily. "I am Piers Barber, an English apprentice merchant out of Bristow …"

"'*Vrisko*,' you kept saying. 'Find.' Our word for a lucky find is Vrethiki."

"So what, then, is to become of me?" asked the boy.

"You will stay with the Emperor. When he is crowned and goes to the Imperial City, you will go too, to keep the people's courage up, and be a talisman of hope to them."

"Well," said the boy. "Since you say I must, I must. But not willingly. I could wish my uncle had sent me on the Iceland run, or anywhere in the world but here, where I am no more Piers Barber, a free-born Englishman, but Vrethiki, the Emperor's most unwilling and resentful slave. I shall run away if I can, as a slave is like to do!"

"Few men are free," said Stephanos. "Try to resign yourself."

Chapter 3

How could he resign himself, when he was racked with homesickness? When he thought of England— and there was nothing to take his mind off it in all those long hours standing uselessly around, witnessing everything, understanding nothing—when he thought of England it was its greenness he remembered. Not that the land of the Morea was not green, but it was the wrong kind of green. The olive trees that carpeted the valley floor were a silver-gray aspen color, with a lovely shimmer like silken garments when the wind caressed them; but pale and cold. And the tall cypresses, elegant and lovely tapered towers, were green, but heavy green, with a bitter touch of blackness in them, and they, too, of a cold dark hue. The leaves of the orange trees were green, with that dusty dark greenness that overtakes English leaves in summer, but the boy was yearning for the bright yellow-green, fresh juicy green of an English meadow, the amazing tender emerald green of the young leaf sprouting and unwinding in the cool northern spring.

Flowers came; the Greek spring dawns early, and soon the land was extravagantly coverleted in flowers. Every dry stony crack put forth blooms, every blade of grass was divided from the next by flowery stems. Strange and beautiful, and quite unknown to him as many of them were, they gave him joy, but his heartache grew worse from them even so. Improvident and wildly spendthrift, this foreign spring wantonly used up the flowers for every season at once; fruit and blossom in the orchards side by side, daisies and violets to remind the boy of spring at home, and at the same time poppies and the wild rose to tug at his heart with thoughts of English summer. When the land began to put forth flowers, he thought he would never bear it.

As for the people at home, he remembered his Uncle Norton with venomous particularity, every hair, every wrinkle of his overbearing face; he remembered his Aunt Norton, whom memory could not deny was handsome, with almost equal resentment—she and her nasty present for making fruit preserves! He remembered his father lying in the rank close sickroom smell of the upstairs bedroom, and his mother …

All day long he pushed away, crushed and stamped on images of his mother when his mind suggested them, because they hurt too much. But then at night, at night, when he unrolled his straw pallet in the great high antechamber to the Lord Constantine's room, and lay down in the light from a little oil lamp whose sweet golden brightness did not reach the roof, so high it arched above him … then, when the lamp made of the painted figures on the walls a host of tremulous quivering ghosts, towering over and around him, their feet and hems bright, but their faces sinisterly occluded … then, before Stephanos came and lay down somewhere near him, then, when he really needed her, he could not find her face. Her nose he could remember, her eyes, her lips, the set of her head on her shoulders, her hair drawn back into her snood, but he could not make these fragments join together, and see her whole, even for an instant, and his pallet was often splotched with tears.

•

NOT ONLY HOMESICKNESS TROUBLED HIM; THERE WAS SOMETHING
in the air. The Lord Constantine had been offered, and
had accepted, a golden crown; yet there was no rejoicing.
There was an eerie gloomy tranquillity about everyone, a
quietness not as though they were at peace, but as though
they were crushed. And now and then he would hear that
note of aching sadness in a voice whose tone was clear to
him, though its words were not. Then, thinking over and
over what Stephanos had said, he found sinister phrases
in it ... *The Lord Constantine needed help from the West ...
wished his Church to bow to Rome and so get help from the
Pope ... against enemies ... the boy himself was to be talisman
of what hope there was ...* The boy recalled these words,
and flinched at them inwardly for day upon day before
he screwed up courage to face a clear answer, if he asked
Stephanos a clear question.

"What meant you, telling me of hope and danger, and help
from the West?" he asked at last. He was helping Stephanos and
Manuel sort and pack away the Lord Constantine's linen, his
cloak-pins and prayer books. "What danger are you all in?"

"The Turks," said Stephanos. "We are surrounded on
all sides by the infidel. Of the whole Empire this is the last
province left—this, and a few miles round the City, and the
City itself. The Sultan could crush us between finger and
thumb. He has tried once to take the City—and God raised
up a scourge for his back: the horde of Timur the Lame, who
fell upon his lands from the East, with a great mob of nomad
warriors, so that the Sultan had to leave the City, and hasten
away. But we know he will try again."

"Never say die," said Manuel. "The City has withstood so
many sieges before. Besides, the West will send help."

Looking swiftly toward Stephanos, the boy saw at once that he did not believe it, though he did not shake his head, or speak a word.

Trembling, the boy asked, "He is going to take me ... to somewhere ... with the *Turks* all around it?" His voice shook.

"Child," said Stephanos to him softly, "those pirates who took you from the water ... who fettered you ... they were Turks, were they not?"

"No!" wailed the boy. "No! I can't, I can't, I *don't* remember!" His eyes had that shallow, shuttered look in them, and he was clenching his hands.

"It does make it hard on you," said Stephanos. He reached out a hand, and squeezed the boy's taut shoulder.

"What's upset him?" asked Manuel in Greek. He often failed to understand the boy's school Latin.

"He is dismayed at the thought of going to the City," said Stephanos.

"There's no accounting for the barbarians," said Manuel.

ON THE EVE OF THE CORONATION OF THE LORD CONSTANTINE at Mistra, his prelates and companions assembled to hear from the Metropolitan bishop the details of the ceremony that faced them on the morrow. First, in his own hand the Emperor must write the Creed, and swear to uphold the Holy Church, and the teachings of the seven Councils. Someone suggested that it would look well in the West, and speed up what help might be coming, if the Emperor would write the Latin Creed instead of the Greek one. This set off a dispute which went on late into the night. Iagrus and Lascaris— they who had brought the crown—were summoned, then Plethon, then John Dalmata, and various holy monks from the monasteries of the town.

Standing wearily behind the Emperor, half asleep, leaning against a wall, Vrethiki waited. Supper was long overdue, and still they talked. First hungry, and then, as the accustomed hour for eating came and went, no longer hungry, but very tired of standing on the hard cold floor, Vrethiki, bored as always, watched. After some considerable time his aching knees gave way, and he slid to a sitting position on the floor. The hard wall behind him resisted the projection of his shoulder blades, and the cold flagstone chilled his buttocks through the worn thin fabric of his clothes. Even in his discomfort he wondered what agitated these strange gentlemen now. Could the Turks be coming? Hardly. Plethon—curse him for his dreams!—seemed to think it childish, whatever it was, or so the boy thought, watching his countenance. Iagrus and Lascaris thought it grave. The Metropolitan was deeply upset—his voice trembled, his hands shook, perhaps with anger, and he seemed near to tears. Emotion filled the room. And the Lord Constantine—who seemed to insist on hearing each man's opinion—he, Vrethiki thought, was filled with weariness and harassment. The boy thought, "What use is it to be Emperor, if you let these bigwigs bully you?"

It was very late when at last they reached agreement, gravely bowing themselves out, and the Despot rose at last from his chair in the council room, and went to his own quarters. He beckoned John Dalmata, a plainly clad, soldierly sort of man, to join him. A meal was laid waiting for him on a great table in the antechamber, a table large enough for the whole family of any Emperor who had one. He looked around at the faces of his overwatched attendants, and spoke. At once more stools were brought, and the plain loaves of bread, and cheeses, and bowls of olives that the servants ate were carried in on platters, and set round the table. Naming them one by one, the Lord Constantine asked them to sit and eat with him. Blushing, they took their places, at once discomforted and pleased. Vrethiki, called by name, was given a place at the Despot's left, with Stephanos beside him. John Dalmata sat on the Despot's right, and beside him a chaplain, who spoke a blessing. There was an uneasy silence, and no one began to eat.

"Come, friends," said the Lord Constantine gently. "Eat with me tonight, for we are all hungry. And once I am crowned and in the City, there will be no chance of this; I shall no longer be able to live like an honest soldier, whose household is his family. You all here have served me well and faithfully through many hardships, and more are to come; let us eat like friends while we still may." He passed the plate of cold fowl and the wine jelly that had been set before him, down the table for all to share. He asked for more wine to be brought, and watched to see that every plate was loaded and every cup was filled before he took a morsel of the bread and meat on his own golden dish.

Vrethiki seized his round of bread in both hands, gripped on the edge with his teeth, and tugged. He spat out the olive stones with a little plopping noise. His fellow dinners averted their eyes. The Lord Constantine beside him ate delicately, hardly like a man, thought Vrethiki; he broke his bread into fragments, and took them to his mouth held daintily between finger and thumb with the other fingers elegantly curved. What happened to the olive stones Vrethiki didn't see, and couldn't imagine; and the Despot ate, he noticed, hardly more than a bird.

Later, when the board was cleared and the bedding unrolled, and the Lord Constantine helped into his nightshirt and to bed, when the servants lay down in the antechamber, and Stephanos blew out the little lamp, Vrethiki lay eyes open in the darkness, wrestling with memories of his mother. He had got past sleepiness, just as earlier in the day he had got past hunger.

"Stephanos?" he murmured in the dark.

"What is it?" whispered Stephanos, and his hand found Vrethiki's. "Does the dark trouble you?"

"What were they all disputing over so long, that grieved the Lord Constantine so?"

"They could not agree whether he should write the Greek or the Latin Creed. It must be written in his own hand, and handed to the bishop who crowns him as a pledge of faith."

"Why couldn't they agree?"

Stephanos sighed, but he answered patiently, "The Lord Constantine's brother, the late Emperor John—God rest him—tried to unite the Eastern and the Western churches. He thought it would be good if there were but one Christendom; and he thought that the Pope would bring a Crusade to rescue the City, if the City were Catholic too. There was a great council at Florence to decide the matter. That is when I became an Imperial slave—for the Emperor John purchased me because I knew Latin, and took me with him to Italy. In the end there was agreement. All but two of the Greek churchmen signed it. But then they came home again, and the people in the City railed on them, and would not have it, and our brave churchmen mostly revoked their signed consent. So now it is like this. Plethon and some others say if the Emperor writes the Latin Creed it will be a gesture that might win good will in the West, while Iagrus and Lascaris, who have come straight from the City, say nothing would be more foolish: it would enrage the people, and cast doubt on the coronation in the eyes of the pious—bad enough that it is to be done outside the City, and by the Archbishop of Mistra not by the Patriarch. The Lord Constantine wishes to be loyal to his brother, who signed for uniting the churches, and at the same time to be loyal to the true and ancient faith. He does not know what to do."

"If it's a bad thing not to, why doesn't he go to the City and be crowned by the Patriarch?" said Vrethiki, trying to take this all in.

"First, because the Patriarch is being ignored by half his clergy, since he is one who supports the Union with the West. Second, because the Lord Constantine wants authority quickly."

"Oh," said the boy. "Stephanos? If you were the slave of the Emperor John, why are you Constantine's now?"

There was a pause. Then Stephanos said, "My master the Lord John had a wife whom he greatly loved. While he was in Florence she died of the plague. Nobody had courage to tell him; he learned of it only as he was entering his palace again, thinking to see her. Then he could not bear anything which reminded him of his long absence, and his bitter loss. In Florence I had been with him daily. He gave me away to his brother."

"Oh," said Vrethiki. "Stephanos, did you mind?"

"Go to sleep," said Stephanos.

The boy said nothing for a minute. Then after a while, "Stephanos? What difference is there between the Greek and Latin Creeds?"

"They have added to it in the West," muttered Stephanos wearily.

"What have they added?"

"The word *Filioque*, thus making the Holy Ghost proceed from the Son also instead of from the Father only ..."

"Mother of Christ!" exclaimed Manuel from the darkness beyond Stephanos. "Must we listen to this all night as well as all day?"

"*Filioque* …" thought Vrethiki, sleepy at last. "One word … added … but what difference does it make?"

Chapter 4

On the morning of the lord constantine's coronation as Emperor of the Romans, Stephanos came wearing a remarkably splendid tunic, purple embroidered in scarlet, and carrying a ceremonial garment for the boy. This garment was so stiff with round medallions, leaves, branches and birds embroidered in golden wire that it stood upright of its own volition upon the floor.

"I'm not wearing that!" said the boy indignantly. "It's a woman's sort of thing!

"Who asked you what you would wear?" said Stephanos. "No one asked you. This is what you must wear. You have to walk beside an Emperor today."

"No!" the boy cried. "What's wrong with my ordinary tunic? What's all that gold for?"

"Gold?" said Stephanos. "That's spun brass, child, you may be sure. You needn't think of running off in it, imagining it will pay your passage home. But with a little sunlight on it it looks good enough."

"I won't wear it!" said the boy. "I won't, I won't, I won't!"
"And why should I do everything they say?" he thought. "Am I a slave? Or did I willingly enter service here? Anyone has his pride—a dog has that. There must be something they

can't make me do!" But even while he made these fine statements in his head, his head was extinguished like a candle flame under the conical snuffer of the offending robe.

He howled! Not just with anger—though very angry he certainly was—but with pain. The front of the ancient livery was gorgeous with threads of gold, but the back had long since lost its quilted lining, and was as prickly as a thorn bush with cut ends of wire thread like a thousand needles. "Ow!" he wailed, and the more frantically he struggled the more cruelly it scraped and pricked his skin.

There was uproar. "Stand still, you ape, you donkey!" bellowed Stephanos, trying in alarm to keep the precious costume from damage by the flailing mass within. Half the servants in the hall, who were standing ready, robed and waiting, came running to his assistance. A dozen pairs of hands held the fierce cloth against its screaming victim. Roughly they seized his arms, and thrust them through the stiffly encrusted sleeves. His wrists emerged scratched and just perceptibly bleeding. Too late it occurred to him that it might possibly have been donned painlessly had he not struggled against it—too late, for he was already smarting from a hundred tiny wounds. He stood limply, sobbing, and scolding voices rose around him on all sides.

Then sudden silence. The Lord Constantine stood in the door, decked in purple and gold. He, too, was solid with embroidery and covered with gem stones, shining from head to foot. When he moved forward a step he staggered a little under the unaccustomed weight of it. He looked like an icon, stepping out of its frame. He moved stiffly. He shone. He made silence out of clamor.

"What is happening here?" he asked. Stephanos began to talk.

"Oh, I won't wear it, I won't," sobbed the boy. "It's like a shroud!"

"What does he say?" asked the Lord Constantine, looking at the boy, standing head high, stiff and gorgeous like a doll, with the tears pouring down his cheeks. His dark eyes rested on the boy as though seeing him for the first time. Stephanos translated. The Lord Constantine smiled, half a smile. His smile was as slow and stiff as the rest of his movements that morning, as though his heavy robes had encased and imprisoned even his solemn face. He spoke directly to the boy.

"He says, 'Look, my child, we are all here wearing them,'" said Stephanos gruffly, turning, as the Emperor walked slowly out of the room, to follow behind him, leading Vrethiki by the hand.

THE EMPEROR, CLAD IN A GREAT ROBE OF PURPLE SILK COVERED with eagles embroidered in golden medallions, stood bare-headed in the great hall of the palace of the Despots at Mistra, writing on a sheet of vellum on a lectern standing before him. At his side Vrethiki stood stiffly, offering a tray with ink and sand and pens upon it. On his other hand stood Iagrus, holding wax and the great seal. The hall was thronged with dignitaries and churchmen.

I, Constantine, the Emperor wrote, *in Christ Our Lord faithful King and Emperor of the Romans, with my own hand wrote and inscribed these words ...*

The pen scratched lightly over the creamy surface. The Emperor's hand was small and neat, penning the dancing unfamiliar letters.

I believe in God the Father Almighty, Creator of Heaven and earth. And in Jesus Christ His only Son, Our Lord, and in the Holy Spirit, Lord and Life giver, who proceeds from the Father—

The hand and pen stopped together. For a long moment the pen was held suspended a finger's breadth above the vellum. Then the Emperor wrote, *who with the Father and the Son is adored and glorified ... And in One, Holy, Catholic and Apostolic Church ... Furthermore, I fully confess and approve the Apostolic and divine traditions, and all the provisions and definitions of the Seven Ecumenical Councils ... Likewise I promise I will remain the faithful servant and true son of the Holy Church, I will abstain from killing and mutilation, and all such acts as far as possible. I will follow justice and truth. All this I promise to the Holy Church of God, this month of January, the sixth day thereof, the year of Our Lord MCDXLIX.*

Iagrus poured out the wax, and the Emperor pressed the seal into it. A little red drop was splashed onto Vrethiki's hand and burned him, so that his hand shook, and he came near to upsetting the ink.

The Metropolitan bishop stepped forward to receive the sealed confession, and bore it away, with his clergy two and two processing after him.

Suddenly the hall was full of soldiers. They came running, shouting, *"Ho, ho, Basileus!"* their armor clanging as they ran across the marble floor. They seized the Emperor, and dragged him toward the door, and out into the pale sunlit morning. For a moment the astonished boy thought there had been a revolution, a mutiny, but then he saw that though the Emperor resisted, it was with curiously little force, almost ceremoniously, as though it was expected of him. Outside, on the top of the steps, the soldiers stopped, with the Emperor held between two of them. The crowd outside roared and waved red scarves and ribbons so that the whole square undulated in shades of rippling scarlet. The soldiers put the Emperor on something—a great round dish—a shield—and raised him up on it, shoulder-high, and, shouting and clashing their swords, smacking the flat of the blades on their polished greaves, they carried him round the square, and back up the steps again. And here came Plethon, and Iagrus and Lascaris, and John Dalmata, all marching up the steps to stand in a ring, each with a hand touching the rim of the shield. The assembly in the hall, meanwhile, had pressed forward into the doorway to see, and Vrethiki among them stood gauping like a bumpkin at a Michaelmas fair, astonished and pleased.

Then they put the Emperor down. His horse was led up to the steps, and he mounted, and slowly made his way through the press of people in the square, with the entire household of the palace escorting him. Vrethiki walked behind the horse, suffering agony from each jostle and bump in the crowd, feeling like cheese in a grater as at each step the encrusted back and front of his stiff robe shifted against his flesh. He had great dignity of bearing, for the only escape from the pins and needles was to walk straight as a board with head held high.

The great concourse of people filled the little street like a river brimming to its banks. They flowed downhill toward the cathedral church. On the steps of the church the Emperor dismounted and turned to face the crowd. A man appeared beside him, wearing his household purple and carrying a wide basket full of little bundles tied in scarlet cloth. The Emperor made a sign to him, and he began to throw these bundles in all directions among the people. There was jumping and upraised arms to catch them, and a scramble for those which fell. The people laughed and shouted. The servant threw the bright little packets higher and higher, and wider, and one hit Vrethiki on the shoulder and slid into the wide fold of his sleeve. He clutched it.

Followed by his retinue, the Emperor entered the church, to stand under the painted dome and receive the holy oil, the gleaming crown, the body and blood of the Lord, the interminable blessings. As the ceremony droned on, Vrethiki fingered the little knot of cloth surreptitiously, and, when everyone round him had bowed low and the droning wail of the choir had risen to a climax, he untied it.

There on the red square of rag lay three golden coins, three silver, and three bronze. A great hope leaped in the boy's heart—money! A means of escape; the price of a donkey! In his mind's eye he was at once free of his gorgeous slavery, and riding away somewhere, looking for a friendly ship ... in danger perhaps, hungry and cold perhaps, but *free*, not dragged away to some doomed and beleaguered City ... He looked again at the coins. He had seen such before—they were bezants. That City of which these strange Greek Romans spoke must be Byzantium then—Constantinople. What did he know of Byzantium? Only that it was full of devious, cunning men. "And that," he thought bitterly, "I have already found true." At the thought he glanced sideways at Stephanos, and saw that he was weeping, openly letting tears fall.

Gleaming dimly in the angled shafts of light from the ring of windows round the dome, the crown was held high, and lowered onto Constantine's head. The choir's chant swelled suddenly and a clamor of bells broke overhead. Outside the people shouted. The Archbishop put into the Emperor's right hand a golden orb, with an upright cross upon it, and into his left a silken bag. But then, as he rose, and moved toward the door, suddenly he was surrounded by men in working clothes; men in dusty aprons, who blocked his path, and jostled round him. The boy, following with Stephanos just behind, stared in amazement. Nobody shooed them off.

In the pockets of their aprons were masons' tools; they showed the Emperor fragments of marble, Carian green, and porphyry. They showed him little models of stone monuments and sarcophagi. "Choose your coffin, Emperor!" they cried. "From whom will you choose your tomb? Come, Emperor, choose your tomb!"

The Emperor said, "I thank my honest stonemasons. But this choice, which for all my predecessors was an act of humility, would be for me an act of pride." He gestured them away, and they stepped back, and let him go out to the people who were calling for him outside. The whole populace of the little town was on the streets to escort him home again the full half mile; there were not so many of them as the good citizens of Bristow.

The Emperor went early to his bed that night. Vrethiki, helping Stephanos fold and put away the silken garments and shining regalia, stole a chance to peep inside the silken bag that the Emperor had received with the golden orb. It was full of common dust.

A FEW MORNINGS LATER THE NEW-CROWNED EMPEROR RODE up to the top of the hill to inspect his troops at the castle there that capped the conical town. High though his windowed palace towered above the cathedral where Vrethiki had first fallen at his feet, that palace spread its russet roof tiles far beneath them like plowed fields long before they rode through the castle gate. Vrethiki liked the castle long before they got there, though its massive gray masonry looked forbidding enough as they looked up at it from here and there along the winding road that ascended toward it. As they actually rode in, to the sudden clatter of horses' hoofs on the booming drawbridge, he realized why. It had a familiar look to it that spoke to him of home. It had a slightly pointed doorway arch, and long arrow slits for windows. It was like those many castles that the barons had made in England to hold the people down. He liked it better still inside. The ring of walls enclosed the hilltop, and within its circuit another smaller wall enclosed the final upthrust of the summit with a battlemented crown. There were horses, a cattle pen, and food store and water cisterns all safely within. Soldiers' quarters were in the towers, and in rooms in the thickness of the walls. Vrethiki and Stephanos climbed the inner wall, and, clutching their cloaks around them in the pull of the wind, looked out over the outer bailey at the rolling land of Lacedaemon and the tall Taygetus mountains with their dazzling cloak of snow.

Vrethiki shuddered a little, not at remembering coming through them, for that had gone from his memory like the suffering of a fever, forgotten the moment one is well. But he shuddered because he did not remember. Below them the Emperor sat on a dais with his troops standing to attention before him. He was speaking to them, for they were deciding who should come with him, and who should stay.

"This is a fine stronghold, Stephanos," said the boy, happily. "It is like the castles of my own country."

The wind that rolled over that wide landscape surged like a wave breaking on the crest of that high place, and his words were blown halfway to Parnassus before Stephanos answered them.

"Yes!" yelled Stephanos, into the wind. "It was built by a Frank."

A great sense of safety had embraced Vrethiki. Standing there you could see danger coming for forty miles or more, and wait for it bravely, ringed in by walls within walls. It had the feeling of that little island in the river on which he used to play in summer once; it had the self-sufficient feeling of his mother's pantry, stuffed with salt meat and vinegar apples and ropes of onions for the winter; it had the evening feeling of the fire well made up, the shutters barred, the doors fast bolted, and all safe within.

"Stephanos," said Vrethiki. "This is a fine fortress, and a pleasant town in goodly countryside. And there is a palace here. Why doesn't he stay and be an Emperor here?"

"The City belongs to him, and he to the City," said Stephanos. "This is just Mistra. How could there be an Emperor here?"

"Why not? In England the court is where the King is. And if the City is beset all round with ... Turks ..."

"There was an Emperor once who would have fled the City to save his life," Stephanos said. "His Empress came to him full of scorn for his cowardice and said, 'All men die, soon or late; but they say the Empire makes a splendid winding sheet.' He stayed. Only when the Crusaders came were the Emperors forced out of the City for a while ..."

"I come from a family of Crusaders," said the boy proudly. He remembered his ancestor lying peacefully cut in gray Purbeck marble in the parish church, legs crossed upon his little dog, covered in wavy lines for chain mail, with his great sword lying like a cross upon his breast.

But Stephanos was staring at him in pure horror. His bland smooth face was distorted with disgust; his eyes flashed fury and loathing. "So you are one of them!" he said. "One of that cursed brood!"

Vrethiki was stunned. He simply gaped at Stephanos' flushed and twisted face.

"Crusaders!" Stephanos cried. "Coming, as they said, against the infidel, but they dipped their greedy hands to the elbows in Christian blood! Coming in the name of Christ, but they sacked the seat of Christendom, and put a whore upon the altar of the Church of the Holy Wisdom! Coming in justice and truth, but they raped and sacked and plundered, and tore away the glories of the City to deck out Venice and the West! Thieves! Plunderers! Wastrels! Ruling the City like a pigsty, pawning the sacred vessels, selling the Most Holy Crown of Thorns, stripping the lead from the roofs of the very palaces to pay for their filthy vices! When we took back our City all was lost; nothing left of the wealth or glory, nothing to pit against the Turk. Indeed if the City falls into Turkish hands it will be not the Sultan only, but the Crusaders who have laid it low. And now, after so much ruin—now they have left us helpless before the enemy—will they come to our aid? Not without forcing the *Filioque*, and unleavened bread between our teeth!"

"But I have done nothing ..." stammered Vrethiki, "I know nothing of this ..."

"What else could one look for from that savage pack but an ignorant whelp like you?" screamed Stephanos, fists clenched, head thrown back, howling into the windy void over the battlements. "You and your stupid questions, your bottomless ignorance! Is there nothing you know? Is there nothing you understand? Must I tell over for you the whole history of God and man? Not a word of Greek about you, and your Latin so barbarous it would torment the ear of a saint—God help us, I do not know which is worse, our friends or our enemies!"

Turning his back on Vrethiki, he strode away along the parapet and plunged out of sight down the stairway of the nearest tower. A trumpet was calling the Emperor's escort together again, and, reeling from this storm of words and carefully keeping a distance behind, Vrethiki had to follow.

"But I thought he liked me," he lamented within himself. "Didn't he like me? Always kind, patiently answering ... but perhaps it was only from duty ... his face shows so little, it moves so little, like a shut window, like a still pool ... Oh, it's hateful here; I will run away, I will!"

Below, the soldiers had made their choice. The Emperor rode down the terraced city to his home. As they went, they left the sun behind them and descended into the heavy shadow cast by the height itself onto the lower slopes, onto the town below. A sharp chill lurked in the shadow. Fear lurked in the chill, and weighed upon the boy's aching heart. He was to be dragged away farther yet from home, to that hateful City, surrounded and doomed, to which all these people hastened and would not save themselves, like moths drawn to the flame. On the hilltop behind them stood the bright castle, still golden in the evening light; but marching down into the shadows, toward the danger, came most of the Emperor's soldiers, by their own choice.

Chapter 5

Abad time followed. in the bustle of the preparations for the Emperor's departure, Vrethiki kept casting about for a chance to slip away quietly, lose himself up a side turning, and get out of the town. But there was work for him now, errands in plenty, and Stephanos seemed to be always watching him. After the descent from the castle Stephanos had said not another unkind word to the boy, and seemed as placid, as gentle and as kind as before; but the boy no longer saw his manner as meaning liking, and took no comfort from it. Besides, those impassive brown eyes seemed always to be coldly watching him, as he sought for his moment to run.

A great cavalcade of men and donkeys, packhorses and carts, was assembled to go to Monemvasia on the coast, there to take ship for the City. Ships had been arranged with the Catalan Company, a fact which mightily disgusted Vrethiki, who remarked that even his Uncle Norton had a ship of his own, and a part share in another. Manuel replied that the Emperor did have some ships, but they were at the City. So the last days at Mistra went by, and the boy had not made good his escape. There was no doubt at all that Stephanos was keeping a watch on him, night and day.

The boy grew desperate. And so on the last evening at

Mistra, when the Emperor had taken leave of the people in the square outside his palace and came to his rooms to pray before sleeping, the boy chanced his last throw, and, flinging himself at the Emperor's feet, appealed to him directly.

"Don't take me; I beg you, set me free!" he said. "Oh, Lord Emperor, don't take me into danger in a quarrel that is none of mine."

The Emperor looked down thoughtfully at the boy's fair head, at the anxious blue eyes staring up at him. He called for Stephanos to translate the boy's words for him. The boy waited, still kneeling. He half expected the Emperor to be angry; he only seemed sad.

Stephanos said, "He would have me tell you that he cannot do what you ask. Necessity compels him to act as he would rather not. He says that surely in the necessities of life we should see the inscrutable will of God."

Vrethiki cried out despairingly, "I will see nobody's will in it but his! Is it God's will that princes should enslave helpless strangers?"

"I won't translate that!" cried Stephanos, his voice thick with anger. "How can you lay this burden upon him, when he has already so much to carry?"

The boy said nothing for a moment, wholly astonished by the idea that the Emperor needed defending—against him. In the silence, the Emperor gently touched a lock of the boy's hair, turned away, and went to his prayers.

"Vrethiki," said Stephanos, urgently. "Listen to me. Try to understand. What you cannot avoid in life, you must accept with dignity. Men are not judged by the fate God appoints for them, they are judged by the manner in which they meet that fate. What has happened to you has happened; you will only bruise yourself by fighting against it."

The boy did not reply. His face did not relent from its wild and sullen expression. He was still kneeling before the spot where the Emperor had stood.

"Listen, accept this danger with a quiet soul. God will see the sacrifice, will see the burden you bear quietly. He will judge. He will reward. But if you struggle, if you go unwillingly, you will lose the merit of it, and yet you must go, just the same. Find the courage to submit."

"Courage to submit?" exclaimed the boy. "I'd call that cowardice. I'd call that unmanliness. What I need is courage to fight to the last gasp of breath in my body. If life is going to batter me, the least I can do is go down fighting; I'll bite and kick to the end!"

"A fit end, then, for a barbarian! Rage as you like, I cannot help you. But if you dare to utter one word of appeal or complaint to my master again, I'll take a belt to your backside myself; understand?"

"Ah," said the boy, getting up. "Now the truth is out. That's your true colors." And he marched out. Behind him, Stephanos stood frozen with a dismayed expression on his face.

THE BRIDLE OF VRETHIKI'S HORSE WAS LOOPED OVER STEPHANOS' wrist all the way on the ride to Monemvasia. He said nothing. For all his angry words, he was overwhelmed by a glum crushed hopelessness. And once on shipboard, he was flooded with grief and homesickness. The last time he had joined a trim vessel, it had been riding at anchor in Bristow, loading tin and cloth, and full of English voices, and high hopes whose owners now were dead. The Catalan ship which carried the Emperor was a babel of half the tongues known to humanity. She was of a strange elaborate build above the water line, and carried her sail somewhat oddly rigged; but she creaked like the *Cog Anne*, she smelled of tar and salt like the *Cog Anne*, groaned like her as she swung into the wind. As Monemvasia fell away astern he remembered the smart wind that had borne them down the Bristow Channel, and his mother, dwindling to doll-size, waving and weeping on the receding quay. The Catalan sailors knew their business well, and he took pleasure in watching them handle sail and sheets, though before long he was needed below decks and could watch no more.

They were hardly afloat before the Emperor became seasick. Stephanos and Manuel were both pale, with that green-tinted pallor that seasickness brings. Vrethiki, rock-steady on his stout trading legs, with the Bristow Channel and the Biscay Bay behind him, scarcely felt the movement of the ship; and, grimly pleased at the sight of Stephanos' misery and the thought of for once getting the better of him, he went to take warm water and towels to the Emperor's bedside, and empty slop basins himself.

He had hardly got the Lord Constantine lying between clean sheets, and swabbed down the wooden boards beside his bed, and set a clean bowl ready for the next disaster, when Stephanos needed similar attention himself. The boy sniffed disgustedly at the acrid smell of the cabins, and recklessly poured wine into the water with which he mopped up the mess. The ship continued to pitch and roll easily on the swell; really it seemed to Vrethiki more like the rocking of a cradle than like the open sea; but it was hard work being the only member of the Imperial party on his feet. It was night before he finished tending everyone. The Emperor had refused to eat anything at all, but Stephanos had taken a few spoonfuls of soup that Vrethiki offered him on a spoon, and coaxed and wheedled him to swallow.

When all was done he went above decks. The clean salt air filled his lungs and lifted his spirits. He listened to rope and timber grumbling at each stress and strain, at the water frothing and slopping along the ship's side below him. He looked at the neatness with which every rope lay curled, and the tidy trim of the sails, and mentally saluted the captain. He looked up at the fantastically abundant stars—millions more of them than ever graced an English sky, clustered as thick as buttercups in a Bristow water meadow. He stood leaning on the gunwale for a long time before he found the strength to steel himself for the closed fetid air of the cabin beneath.

Things continued so for three days. On the second, grumbling and hectoring him in English, and telling him he would need his strength for the days to come, Vrethiki managed to feed the Emperor a bowlful of broth, a spoonful at a time. To Stephanos he said sharply in Latin, "Oh, come, sit up and eat, sir. Where's your manhood?" And Stephanos flinched, and struggled upright, and ate like a scolded child.

That evening when Vrethiki climbed up to take the air, the ship was moving through a narrow channel with a sloping wooded coast on either side. It looked like the Bristow Channel, only narrower. The green shores pricked his memory. "This is the Hellespont," a sailor told him. "Keep a sharp eye out for the shore—it's Turkish land."

"Which shore?" asked Vrethiki.

"Both," said the sailor. But nobody offered any resistance to the four ships, as they slipped up the middle of the channel in the gathering dark.

BEYOND THE NARROW CHANNEL LAY A TRANQUIL LANDLOCKED sea, on which the ship moved so swanlike that even the Emperor and his Eunuch recovered somewhat. Vrethiki carried food for them from the galleys, and acted as page again rather than nursemaid. The Emperor gave him a heavy silver coin, and a slow half-smile as a grave thank-you for caring for him. Vrethiki put the money in the little knot of rag with the coronation bounty, reflecting that though it would take more than gold to save his skin, and escape was beyond hoping for, there would surely be a use for it some time. On the evening of this smoother day he went up as usual to take the air, and found the ship almost motionless, sail flapping gently, deliberately letting slip the wind.

"Nearly there," said the coxswain, whose Italian was just comprehensible, when the boy asked, with gestures, why this was so. "And not wanting to land till morning."

Nothing broke the surface of the tranquil sea. Gently it rippled, glassy and smooth, and shining with opalescent radiance in the low-sloping light of a golden evening. Leaning on the rail, idly looking, dreaming, the boy nursed his anger in his heart like secret treasure. It gave him strength. But for all that, it was a fair fine evening. It seemed as though a translucent infinitely pale shawl of gray-blue silk had been cast over the surface of the sea, with a silver sequin or two scattered over it when he looked toward the light. And the sky too was radiant, clad in veil upon shimmering veil of golden and ivory silk. Along the skyline lay a band of brightest, purest sheen, a river of pale liquid gold, dividing sea and sky; and in one direction, in the distance, hovering above the molten horizon lay a cloudy shadow, a mirage of land, with a great round mass, a tall wide dome, rising at one end of it.

"La Città!" said the coxswain. "Ècco la Città; Santa Sofia! Ècco!"

It was the City, at last.

Chapter 6

The emperor slept peacefully enough that night, and his servants were undisturbed. The ship might have been tied up in some haven, so little did the cradling waters rock her. But very early in the morning Vrethiki woke to hear pulleys groan again at ropes rattling through them, and the loud canvas snap and bang as the wind stiffened it and the water began to chuckle and suck against the ship's side.

They were under way again. Quietly Vrethiki rose, and went above.

Lilac against a rose-pink sky lay the long promontory of the City, hovering dreamlike above the silver sea. It was much nearer now: a lovely complex shape, topped with slender columns, laden with swelling domes. As they drew nearer, and day brightened, Vrethiki half expected the vision to fade and vanish, so unearthly and insubstantial did it seem, but it solidified, and took on shape and detail in the gentle morning light. All round, it was ringed by towers, towers and battlemented walls, with the sea dancing and sparkling at the foot of them; above, rose arch upon arch, terraces, towers, columns and clustering domes. Pink and purple and honey-colored stones—gray domes, green domes, overtopped with shining crosses of gold-white marble clashing brilliant against the deepening blue sky! Vrethiki was mildly surprised to remember that he had thought Mistra a fine place, for he saw now at once that there was, there could be, no place in all the earth like this.

The sailors were putting in to a little harbor at the southern, western end of the City. Even so, looking back as they sailed smoothly along the southern shore, he could see that the City lay at the mouth of a channel no wider than the Hellespont. The jutting promontory on which it stood came within half a mile of the facing shore, and had he not a few minutes before looked up the open water of the channel beyond the tip of the City, he would hardly have known, looking back, there was a break in the land there at all.

"Over there," said his friend the coxswain, pointing to this other shore, "Turks." And he drew the side of his hand across his neck, in a cut-throat gesture.

A WIDE TENT OF SCARLET CLOTH WAS READY FOR THEM ON the shore. The Emperor was carried from the ship to this tent, and there put on his ceremonial robes, and his crown. Vrethiki, seeing what was coming, seized his penitential robe himself, and put it on on top of his scruffy everyday tunic, thus saving himself the pain of it next to his skin. The Emperor's horse was led into the tent, and he mounted it, and looked around for Vrethiki. A little brown pony was brought for Vrethiki, and he was told to ride three or four paces behind the Emperor. Then they drew back the curtains of the tent door, and the Emperor rode forth to the welcome of his people.

Beyond the tent a crowd were gathered, shouting and waving. A procession was drawn up ready, ranks of priests, and ranks of soldiers, to escort him. Fluttering pennants flickered at the points of the soldiers' spears. The sun flashed off their helmets and greaves. The route was lined with people all the way, standing in the rows of young green corn, beside the roadway, yelling and weeping, and holding out hands to the Emperor. The land sloped gently upward as they rode, and a low rolling crest cut off the view ahead, like the rise and fall of an English plain, never quite as flat as it seems from a hilltop viewpoint. Then as they moved onward, mounting this low incline, a line of walls and towers rose out of the ground ahead. On the facing slope, beyond a little valley, stood the walls of the City.

When he came on them so suddenly like that, it was their size which struck Vrethiki first. They were huge, the towers like a battle line of looming giants. Right and left they stretched, down to the shine and ultramarine of the sea on their right, and up the hill on their left, disappearing over the crest, all at regular intervals, like well-drilled battalions. The defenses were deep as well as high. First there was a moat, very deep, and walled and faced with buttressed masonry; then a wall, with battlements and towers, and, behind that and beyond, towering over it, another wall, a massive wall like a cliff, with gigantic towers standing one in each space between the towers of the outer wall. And all was made of well-squared, fine gray masonry, braced and trimmed with bands of dark-red brick.

"But the Turks will never get in!" thought Vrethiki, with a sudden lift of the heart.

The road they were riding on wound toward a point in the wall where the regular march of the towers was broken by a huge white bastion, a vast stark white slab of marble, rising even higher than the inner towers. In front of it was a flourish of arch, columns, stairways rising on either side, and every cranny and foothold of the walls here, every inch of battlement and step of stairs was swarming with citizens, shouting and waving. In the terraces between the walls there was also a band of small boys, who burst out singing as the Emperor rode over the causeway across the moat. Across the moat they went, up the sloping stairs, through the outer arch, and then Vrethiki saw that the mountainous white marble bastion had a vast brazen door in the middle of it.

"The Golden Gate," said Stephanos at his side, as they rode through. "This was here even before these walls were made, they say." He tendered the remark like a peace offering.

"How long ago was that?" asked Vrethiki, interested in spite of himself.

"The walls? They were made for the Emperor Theodosius, a thousand years ago. The triumphal arch? I don't know, but long before that …"

Beyond the great gate lay a little enclosure with smaller walls round it. It was full of soldiers, yelling and stamping, and waving pennants on their lances, and blowing outbursts on their bugles. The Emperor reined in his horse, and raised his arms to them in greeting before riding on.

On through the streets of the City, through the thronging crowd. Vrethiki had never seen such a street. It was lined with marble all the way, with marble and with porphyry. Great houses faced the street, not with windows, but with high blank walls, pierced by columned gateways, and over-topped by columns, by columns and roof gardens, and little gabled roofs and upper chambers, and casements and balconies. And from every upper window of every house along the way, from every door, over every wall and pillar, hung swaths of colored cloth. The people had draped their houses with robes and coverlets, with arras hangings, with carpets and with sheets, red, purple and gold, linen and wool and shining whispering silk, for the boisterous wind off the sea to sport with and wave like flags. The great road passed through squares, through forums. Huge columns stood there, shooting skyward, standing memorials to something Vrethiki had never heard of, no doubt ... and pedestals laden with statuary, bronze horsemen, marble statesmen, gilded saints. They came at last to the Hippodrome, a huge stadium, with an oval elongated cursus, down which the Emperor rode past tiers and tiers of joyful shouting people. At one end of it, to the right, rose the huge mass, the great buttressed bulk of that first dome Vrethiki had seen—the one so massive that it loomed in sight even from far out to sea.

The Catalan coxswain had called it Santa Sophia, but Stephanos now murmured, "The Church of the Holy Wisdom."

But although they rode toward it, to Vrethiki's surprise and faint disappointment they did not enter there. At the doors stood an old man who must be the Patriarch, robed in white, with black crosses on his pallium. The Emperor dismounted, and went to meet him, and knelt before him on the steps, but when the Patriarch had blessed him, the Emperor mounted again, and the procession moved on. And while the Emperor knelt thus, it was as if a cloud had slid across the sun; the crowd fell silent, and cheering ceased. You could hear the people's feet, shuffling on the paving. They muttered to one another. When the Patriarch stepped forward, someone hissed. And a cracked voice called crazily from far back in the crowd, "Woe to the City for Constantine!"

Stephanos clenched his teeth, and scowled toward the voice; but now the blessing was over, and the Emperor was riding away, and as though the cloud had passed the crowd was pleased again, and cheering. Children ran along beside the Emperor's horse, jumping, and calling with their high birds' voices. They pointed to Vrethiki, and gabbled at each other. The people threw branches of myrtle, branches of olive before the hoofs of his horse, and from windows sprinkled him with rose water as he passed. The street they were riding down now was taking them back in the general direction of the land walls, and after some long time, when it seemed to Vrethiki they had been riding for hours, when the sun was overhead, and the shadows deepening to velvet black, he saw the walls again ahead of them. The road ran down a little, and the land walls descended to meet the walls of a palace, which stood in the corner of the City at the angle between land walls and sea walls. Over the roofs of this palace lay a prospect of tranquil water and green hills.

They descended the slope, while the walls of the palace rose above them, and rode through the great bronze gates that stood wide to greet them, and into a garden, full of trees, and little marble basins planted with herbs. A fountain gushed from a conch in the hands of a bronze Neptune and brimmed a wide white basin full of clear water. Paths of flagstone led across beneath the trees. A bell struck three clear notes, and the great gates of the palace swung shut. The clamor of the crowd was shut out, and in the sudden hush Vrethiki heard the fountain trickling, and a small bird singing on a bush. Wearily the riders dismounted. From a doorway in one of the buildings that crowded haphazardly round the garden an old woman came forward, wearing a black damask robe of great richness, and walking with the help of a silver cane. Stepping forward swiftly to meet her, with hands held out toward her, the Emperor called her, "Mother."

VRETHIKI NOTICED ALMOST AT ONCE THAT STEPHANOS WAS an important person here. From the moment they entered the gates of the Palace of Blachernae, he was surrounded by slaves and servants, calling him sir, asking for instructions, running to carry them out. He went at once, trailing Vrethiki three paces behind him, to inspect the Emperor's apartments. Servants who had made them ready went with him, eager to show him what had been done. Stephanos approved the rooms, all three of them: a chamber hung with damasked silks, with a wide hearth and a good fire burning, and gilded couches, and a writing desk, a bedchamber, and a large anteroom, with the walls all painted, and the floor of colored marble, and a great wide throne at one end. All these rooms had large arched windows with glass in them, and so were both warm and light.

When Stephanos had seen over the Emperor's lodgings he saw to their own: a little chamber off the Imperial anteroom for him and Manuel. He had an extra bed brought in for Vrethiki before marching on to look at rooms for priests, wardrobe keepers, stewards, chaplains, captains, for everyone who had come with them from Mistra. Every three minutes it seemed messages were carried to him from the kitchens and cellars about arrangements for a banquet that night. He had no time at all for Vrethiki, who soon stopped following, and returned to the little room. Here he untied his bundle and put his few things in a small wooden chest that seemed to be for him, since it was beside his bed. Then he pressed his nose to the window, to look through the little thick squares of glass.

He could see the upper reach of the Golden Horn, lying shining between the arms of the sloping hills beyond the City, but all distorted and twisting in the glass, like a view through the heat of a bonfire, so he stood on the low wooden bed, and opened a little hinged casement, the better to see out. Below was a courtyard, in which soldiers came and went from the ground floor beneath him where they seemed to be billeted. He could hear the buzz of voices, and some laughter. A group of them were sitting around in a sunny corner, cleaning weapons and harness, and right below his window a man was rubbing down his horse and whistling at his work.

"Our king went forth to Normandy," said Vrethiki's mind to him, "With grace and might of chivalry, God for him wrought marvelously … That's an English tune!

No, it can't be; it must have Greek words too. Or Italian, or Serb, or something," he added, for a babel of tongues surrounded him.

Just then Manuel arrived, and began to unbuckle his ceremonial wear. He put the encrusted belt and the Emperor's drinking cup on its chain down on the bed.

"So, how like you the City now?" he asked, slyly. "Still pining for Mistra?"

"Oh, Manuel!" cried Vrethiki, his head reeling to think of the walls, of the size, of the great domes, of the wild crowds, of the splendor. "Oh, what a City!"

"Oh, City, City, eye of Cities," declaimed Manuel, flinging his arms wide, and flapping the wings of the damasked eagle on his gown, "Oh, City, City, head of all Cities! Oh, City, City, center of the four corners of the world! Oh, City, City, pride of the Christians, and ruin of the barbarians! Oh, City, City, second paradise, planted in the west—"

"Yes!" said Vrethiki. "Yes!"

"THIS PLACE!" HE TOLD HIMSELF, STANDING BEHIND THE Emperor's throne at the great banquet that night. "The crown and jewel of all the world; a man hasn't lived till he's seen it!"

He was in a semicircular row of the Emperor's servants,

ranged behind the throne. Behind them again, in a larger half circle, stood a contingent of soldiers, all in white and shining bronze: the Imperial guard, the Varangians. The Emperor sat on a wide throne like a couch, gilded and carved and inlaid with mother-of-pearl, and laden with cushions. Beside him, on his right, lay a copy of the Gospels written in gold on lilac vellum and propped open with an ivory pointer set with emeralds and pearls. The Emperor's crown blazed on his head; from the lower rim of it dangling strings of rubies and huge misty pearls hung down among his long dark curls. Before him stood a great table spread with white damasked linen, scattered with sprigs of sweet herbs and flower petals, and loaded heavily with fish and fowl on dishes all of gold. Vrethiki had never seen such food—there were roast sucking pigs, and swans, and peacock, and wild duck, and innumerable huge fishes with gray and silver scales, set upright as though swimming upon the platters in shoals. And there was fruit too, in golden baskets—apples and melons, figs, dates and raisins, and dishes of little bright green nuts, and there was cheese, and artichokes, and hard-boiled eggs painted purple and standing in little eggcups of bright blue enamel. So beautiful was all this food that it did not look real enough to stir Vrethiki's hunger.

Nobody sat down at that table; instead, the Emperor's guests thronged the hall, standing, and Stephanos called their names out, one by one, and then they came forward, the servants loaded plates for them, and they went back to their places and ate, standing, while others were called upon. And each man, as his name was called, shouted a greeting to the Emperor in his own tongue. Such a list of grand names, and lordly offices! "Peré Julia—Consul of the Catalans in the City! Girolamo Minotto—Bailey of the Venetians in the

City! Giovanni Lomellino—Podestà of Pera—the colony of the Genoese across the Golden Horn!" Vrethiki saw, with a twitch of curiosity, how these last two gentlemen looked daggers at each other. There were Greek names too. "Lukas Notaras—Megadux! Theophilus Palaeologos, cousin to the Emperor! John Dalmata, Commander in the Imperial army! Orhan, Prince of the Turks, rightful heir of the Ottoman throne!"

Startled the boy looked up to see a Turk, fully armed and wearing barbarian robes complete with turban, suddenly appearing at the table. But he joined his hands, and touched them to his forehead respectfully, and greeted the Emperor in elegant Greek.

As more and more guests came forward to receive meat and drink, more and more servants were busied carrying platters to and fro, refilling goblets, removing empty dishes, and Manuel, standing by the table pouring out the ruby wine, called Vrethiki to come and help him. Vrethiki moved through the throng, carrying golden goblets, full to a guest, or empty back for more. He moved in a daze, moonstruck by the splendor around him. Those shining walls of polished porphyry, in which the lamps, reflected, floated in wine-dark gleaming pools! Oh, the height and brilliance of the ceiling, which seemed to be made of a great glittering sheet of starry gold; gold everywhere, blazing on the Emperor's shining crown, darkly rich on the Emperor's table, heavy and precious in the goblets cupped in Vrethiki's trembling hands!

Stephanos called out another name—"John Inglis, Captain of the Varangian guard!" and John Inglis cried suddenly, in English, "Hail to thee, Emperor, long life, good health, and victory!" and hearing his own tongue spoken, Vrethiki stopped short, thunderstruck, and dropped the cup he was carrying.

He expected it to ring upon the floor, to sound like a bell as it rolled away. Instead it made a tinkling crash—it shattered on the marble at his feet, and he stood looking stupidly, mouth open, at the scatter of shivered fragments on the floor. The thickness of the pieces showed translucent, gray-green. The gold was paper-thin, cracked and flaking. The golden goblet had been made of painted glass.

As Vrethiki took this in, staring where he stood, a little curved fragment lay rocking on the floor, cradling a drop of the dark dregs of the wine. Then servants came running up, and the telltale splinters were hastily swept away.

Now Vrethiki looked round him with different eyes. How many of the jewels were also glass? They looked suspiciously regular, the colors clear and harsh ... on many of the golden dishes could he not now see a dark band on the rim, where the gold was wearing thin, showing the glass beneath? And there were carefully stitched and mended patches on the tablecloth ... and cracks on the panels of the purple walls, filled in with plaster and carefully painted over, but not quite matching. And now he noticed a green patch on a corner of the ceiling, where the roof had let in rainwater, and green mold grew on the golden surface ... Even on the Emperor's crown, couldn't he see faint lines and creases, as though it were made of leather, gilded leather, instead of solid gold?

"This is all false!" cried Vrethiki to himself. "This is all faked and painted, all for show, like what the mummers wear, or the maypole dancers! And the Emperor sits there, enthroned, dolled up in frippery frumpery like a player king! To think I was taken in by it!" Tears of rage and disappointment ran down his cheeks, and Stephanos, thinking to comfort him, whispered that the cup he had broken was of no consequence, no value at all.

AND IF THE MAGNIFICENCE OF THE EMPEROR'S COURT HAD faded all at once, like fairy gold, so too, Vrethiki found, had the glory of the City. Riding at first light through the streets, escorting the Emperor to pray in the Church of the Holy Apostles, through a City bereft of colored hangings and of surging crowds, how different it all seemed! Grass thrust up between the paving slabs of the streets; ruined houses lay in tumbledown heaps. The marble and the porphyry, the tall columns, the bronze statues, all were there, but the columns leaned a little, the houses were shabby, there was ruin everywhere, on every side. A boy was pasturing sheep on the grassy mantle worn by the bones of a fallen house; up every side street Vrethiki could see plowed fields, with the spring corn tenderly fingering through the furrows, or orchards, just now with their swelling buds pale-tipped with the promise of blossom, and there were even little copses and straggling clumps of wild rosebush growing along the way. They passed a fallen cistern, some of its arches still standing at ground level, bare of vaulting; the great square, sunken deep, that had once held water was dry now, and the rich silt in the bottom of it was carefully hoed and planted with lettuces. They passed a princely house still lived in, but in a different manner from before. The great bronze gates to the courtyard of this house stood hanging askew on broken hinges, jammed open, dark with tarnish, and through them Vrethiki caught sight of a goat tethered to a marble angel standing in the basin of a cracked fountain, and hens pecking in the dust.

The City had shrunk to a number of little settlements, with almost empty countryside between them, except along the main streets. As though conscious of their isolation, some districts even had walls and fences of their own around them. And yet, across a valley in the spine of the City, a vast ancient aqueduct went marching in gray grandeur, its huge two-storied arches still carrying water to still unbroken cisterns; from almost anywhere in the City the encircling sparkling blue water of the sea, to the south, or the Golden Horn, to the north, shone at the end of every prospect. The Church of the Holy Apostles when they reached it, though its windows were cracked, and though the roof let rainwater in, and though pigeons flew in the dome and fouled the floor with droppings, was yet the most splendid church Vrethiki had ever seen, adorned with pictures made all of fragments of gleaming glass, so that it shone with a dazzling golden light …

The boy's feelings were churned up intolerably by all this glory and dereliction. "Oh!" he cried inwardly, "what splendor there once was here! And yet there's nothing left— nearly nothing—it's all ruined and cracked. It could no more withstand attack than an empty husk can withstand a wind … the Turks will storm it … they will get in …" And fear choked off his thoughts, and left him sullen and afraid again. For surely, he knew, his own fate and the fate of this impossible City were now the same.

SEEING HIM DOWNHEARTED, HIS BLUE EYES STARING LISTLESSLY, Stephanos, riding homeward beside him, began to talk to him.

"You see that column there? The one with its top knocked off? There's a story about that one. It was said to be the stoicheion of the Tsar Symeon, King of the Bulgars. Some people believe that everyone has a stoicheion—some material object bound up with his destiny ... there was an Emperor once who thought his stoicheion was a bronze lion that stood in the Hippodrome ... he had it polished and burnished every day, and set a guard on it day and night, so that nobody could so much as scratch it ... well, as I was saying, Tsar Symeon was a danger to the City in his time, and a wise old monk told the citizens that Symeon's stoicheion was that very column, within the City, so then the people broke the capital off the column, and the Tsar Symeon fell dead!"

But Vrethiki could scarcely raise a smile for this absurdity. He was thinking that the people they had seen in the streets that morning were in as wretched a condition as the fabric of the City: poorly clad, and plying humble trades. There were hawkers with jars of water or lettuces on handcarts, shouting their wares; there was a group of boys with baskets on their backs, standing idly on a street corner, waiting for employment as porters; there was a gypsy boy with a tambourine, and a young bear wearing ribbons led on a chain behind him, ready to dance for a coin. Among these poorer folk Vrethiki saw one or two with ears or noses cropped, or lacking a right hand. Only once had they seen a prosperous sight—a curtained litter, carried by well-dressed slaves, taking a princely lady to her morning prayers.

Then as they rode, suddenly a cracked voice from a window cried to them, "Woe to the City for Constantine!"

The Emperor reined in his horse below the window, and his party clattered to a halt behind him. "Come now, old mother," said the Emperor, looking up at the latticed shutter. "You have said those words to me once already. Say what you will, and have done"

"I say you should have been Demetrios, you should have been Thomas!" came the screeching answer. "Was it not prophesied, long ago, that the last Emperor would bear the same name as the first?"

The Emperor was silent a moment. Then, "God's will be done," he said, and moved on.

When Stephanos translated this exchange to Vrethiki, it plunged him into yet deeper gloom. Not even a wet nurse would give credit to such a farrago of superstition, he thought. And Stephanos, glancing at the boy's face, turned aside for a moment as they passed a little street market. When he caught up with them again, he had brought a present for the boy—a little songbird in a wicker cage.

"Here, perhaps his songs will gladden you," he said, giving the cage to Vrethiki, as they dismounted at the palace gate.

But Vrethiki's face grew darker still. "I'm not an Emperor," he said, "I don't need creatures caged!" And opening the basketwork door, he shook the bird out into the open air. It fell to the ground, and fluttered in the dust. And then it flew, but not into the trees of the palace gardens—instead it flapped desperately round the cage in Vrethiki's hands, pressing against the wicker bars with beating wings, trying to get back in. Bewildered, Vrethiki covered the cage with his cloak, and then, lost, the bird flew upward, wheeling and circling overhead, till at last it winged away toward the green country outside the City.

Watching all this with a wry little smile, Stephanos said, "You see, it is not simple, my little Crusader. Nothing is simple."

Chapter 7

A nd yet for many months there was a simple pattern to the days. At dawn Stephanos rose, and went to wake the Emperor, knocking three times on his door. The Emperor dressed, and came to the throne room, where he prayed before an icon of the Virgin, half covered with silver and studded with gems, that hung on the wall. Then he sat on the left of his wide throne, with the Gospel book beside him, and Stephanos and Manuel brought his breakfast to him, and stood by while he ate, and Vrethiki ran to fetch more bread, or more figs if they were needed. When the Emperor had eaten, the three of them bore away table and dishes, and moved the Gospels to a lectern standing near, and the Emperor moved to the right side of his throne, for in council he was to act as Christ on earth. Vrethiki shifted the footstool for him. Then Stephanos ushered in the notable men who wished to see the Emperor, and handed him a list of the day's affairs. While the morning's work began, the servants retired and hastily ate their own breakfast.

All morning the Emperor received his ministers, and his officials. They prostrated themselves before him, and then rose, and stood, and discussed affairs of state. Vrethiki opened and shut the chamber door as the great men came and went.

Watching their faces and gestures, and catching now and then a word or two in their latinate Greek, he tried hard to discern any business that had to do with the defense of the City; he could never forget that his life depended on such frail hope as these grave and somber men might be able to provide. Fear still haunted him. He did not remember what it was the Turkish sailors had done to him; still his mind refused to let him remember. But sometimes nightmarish fragments came back to him, and for a fleeting moment he recalled their hawkish noses, their dark brows, and full cruel crimson lips; or the marks on private parts of his body he had carried when he fled from them ... he was more afraid of them than death. A thread of anxiety ran constantly through his bored and drifting mind as he listened to the great men talking.

When they had finished, the Emperor would sign the documents they laid before him, while Vrethiki held the tray of pens and ink. Then he would lay aside crown and stiff ceremonial robe, and the Patriarch, who often stayed when the other princes had left, did likewise, and the two men sat down together for lunch. The Emperor embraced the Patriarch like an equal when he left. But Vrethiki didn't like him. He had shifty eyes. He seldom looked the Emperor straight in the face. Then at three o'clock the palace gates were shut, and the Emperor went to visit his mother's bedside, for she had fallen sick, and so Vrethiki was free till the evening. That rule about being at the Emperor's side seemed to be only for public Occasions; within the palace he was free.

Sometimes Stephanos would tell him what had happened in the morning's discussions ... that the wiry gray-headed newcomer, for instance, whom the Emperor had been so glad to see, was Phrantzes, his dear friend and Chief Secretary, who had been away in Trebizond, trying for a Comnene princess for his master to marry. He had come straight home as fast as he could when the news reached Trebizond that the Sultan was dead. "He says," Stephanos related, "that the Emperor of Trebizond was fool enough to rejoice that his old enemy was dead."

"Isn't it good news then?" the boy asked.

"Hardly. The old Sultan was a wise man, and weary of fighting. His untried son is a different kettle of fish."

Or, the boy would learn, the Emperor was at his wits' end about the man called Scholarios. The citizens all hated the Union of their Church with Rome, and Scholarios preached against it every Sunday, whipping the people's feelings to a frenzy. The Emperor kept asking the Patriarch to deal with him, but nothing had been done.

"It's my belief," said Manuel darkly, "that the Patriarch is afraid to face him." So the Emperor had appealed to Rome, both for help against the Turks, and for learned clerics who could preach and explain the Union of the Churches, and make it acceptable to his people. "We don't have a home-grown Holiness capable of dealing with Scholarios," added Manuel. "He would make circles round the Archangel Michael in debate."

"Yet he signed for union in Florence," said Stephanos.

But though Stephanos was willing enough to translate, Vrethiki learned still more from another source—from the Englishmen in the Varangian guard. He found his way to their courtyard, below his window, the very first chance he had, looking for the English voice he had heard in the throne room. There was John Inglis, the captain, and four others, among a band of Danes and Russians, and Bulgars, and Serbs and Swedes and Germans, and even one Icelander, and four Spaniards, and a Turk. The Englishmen didn't mind Vrethiki sitting talking to them, especially if he was helping to clean harness and polish weapons, or mixing bran for the horses at the same time. And their talk was not all solemnized by being in Latin, as Stephanos' was. Besides, since those last days in Mistra, he had not been quite at ease with Stephanos .

It was from John Inglis that Vrethiki learned that the shifty-eyed Patriarch had fled to Rome, and was there complaining bitterly to the Pope that the Emperor would do nothing to enforce the Union of the Churches ... that the whole City thought the Emperor would do nothing while his mother was alive, because she opposed it and Scholarios was her dear friend, but luckily she was dying fast ... that the soldiers all took it for granted that the City was sunk without Western aid, and the West would help only if the City accepted the Union of the Churches ... nothing to cheer him in any of it.

But, he thought, lying in bed at night, such fine bold men as his new friends were would surely not be "resigning themselves" like Stephanos. He nursed a wild hope, thinking about them.

It came crashing the moment he mentioned it. "John," he said, in a low voice, urgently. "When you escape from here ..."

"Escape?" said John. "What from? We are not prisoners here. We could go whenever we wished."

"Oh," said the boy, astonished. "I thought you must be prisoners."

"No, lad," said John. "We came here freely, and could just as freely go."

"When you go, then—oh, please take me!"

"We won't be going; not for a long while yet."

"Oh," said Vrethiki again. "I thought you'd go—if you could—before the battle starts."

"What?" yelled John, suddenly purple in the face. "You thought I'd take a man's money to fight, and then rat off before the battle? If you were my size, boy, I'd break half the bones in your body for saying that! How dare you? Soldier of fortune I may be, but I'm yet a man of honor! And paid to fight, but I'll fight well for my pay!"

"Oh, I'm sorry. I didn't mean ... I didn't think ..."

"No. Well, you want to be careful what you say."

"Oh, but John, don't you mind losing? Don't you mind fighting on the wrong side?" cried the boy, his panic breaking through.

John paused a long while before he answered. He bent his head over the harness he was oiling across his knee. "I've been a soldier since I was a boy," he said, "not so much older than you. I fought for my own king in France, sometimes win, sometimes lose. I fought faithfully and well, to the best of my might. But when we burned Joan the Maid, there, that finished me. That finished me, boy. I don't mind fighting for a loser, so long as I'm fighting for the right. I couldn't fight longer for King Henry once I'd have hated him to win ... I came looking for a king whose battle was on his own lands. That's not much of a title to rightness, I grant you, but it's a start. I've been here ever since.

"So you're not going home?" said the boy disconsolately.

"No," said John. "Now be off with you."

BUT WHEN THE BOY CAME BACK A DAY OR TWO LATER, JOHN seemed to bear no grudges. He gave him a pile of bridles to clean and rub, and the talk was as free as before.

"John," said Vrethiki, "who are Demetrios and Thomas?"

"They are the Emperor's good-for-nothing brothers," said

John. "And we escaped having one or the other for Emperor only by the skin of our teeth! The Lady Empress saw to that; she may not be in favor of Rome, but she had a clear idea which of her sons she favored, thank God. Why? Are they coming to the City?"

"I just heard someone tell the Emperor he should have been one of them."

"They were both against the Union, especially Demetrios," said John. "So of course there were maniacs here with religion on the brain willing to support them. Either of them would sell his sister to the Turks, let alone the City. We are better far with Constantine."

"He's a good soldier; he leads men from the front," said Martin Freeland, John's second-in-command. "He's a man men would die for."

The boy stared at them with disbelief written all over his face.

"I'll tell you this," said John. "The Emperor's crown may be paste and paint, but his courage is real enough, even though he does surround himself with old men instead of good-hearted young captains."

"Does he?" Vrethiki wondered, and then said, "Stephanos is a young man."

"He's forty at least, if you call him a man," John said.

"But his beard hasn't grown yet .

"He's a eunuch, boy," said Martin. "That means he's had his balls chopped; he'll never grow a beard, nor pleasure a woman neither."

"That's not what I've heard," said another Englishman. "Do you know the story of the eunuch and the bailiff's wife?"

"No, what's that, then?" said Martin, interested.

"Belt up!" said John sternly. "Your barrack talk's not fit for the ears of a green youngster." And Vrethiki crept off, feeling queasy, to look for other company.

Other company was to be had: there were page boys and children about the palace, though the girls were kept closely watched, and indoors for the most part. Vrethiki remembered his cousin Alys, riding her pony on the green hillside, with her curls stretched out on the wind behind her, and felt sorry for the shy pale Roman girls. But the boys would play tag, or archery, or dice, and a number of games with boards and counters. Vrethiki knew only one of these games from home, and that one he could beat them at; he called it Nine Men's Morris.

Sometimes the Emperor went hunting in the fair forests that lay on the hills outside the City. Vrethiki liked the long rides beside fresh tinkling streams, under the leafy trees. And once or twice they went in the Emperor's barge across the calm waters of the Marmara to the islands—those that lay like shadows on the southern skyline from the City—and he and his court refreshed themselves, walking in the shady woods and cool breezes of those lovely places. Thus the long heat of summer passed away.

IN THE AUTUMN THE AGED LADY EMPRESS DIED. SHE DIED, and was mourned for, sung over and buried. Vrethiki, with the Emperor, walked barefoot and bareheaded in her long cortege. The Emperor did not forget her. His cheeks seemed hollower, his dark eyes larger than before; he ate even less, and seemed so dejected that even Vrethiki felt a twinge or two of being sorry for him. It was then that he could see which of the men who visited the Emperor were important to him: John Dalmata, the soldier who had come with them from Mistra, Theophilus, the Emperor's young and handsome cousin, with his wry lopsided smile, who kissed him on both cheeks on coming and going, and the anxious, faithful secretary, Phrantzes; these men could raise a smile, a little liveliness on their master's countenance. With everyone else he kept his frozen dignity.

"He has no hope," thought Vrethiki despairingly.

IT WAS THE DEPTH OF WINTER WHEN THE NEW SULTAN BEGAN to move against the City. He began to build a great castle on the Emperor's shore of the Bosporus, a mere six miles from the City. First, soldiers arrived, and then masons. Driving out the people from the little fishing villages that nestled on the slopes of the winding woody shore, they smashed and dismantled houses and churches, and hauled the stone away to build their walls. There were agonized meetings, the Emperor sent protests, sent embassies. The ambassadors returned to the Emperor, tight-lipped and white-faced. The Sultan had threatened to have them flayed alive if they came to him with such messages again.

Now there was panic in the City. The people ran hither and thither, carting reliquaries full of ancient bones around the streets, carrying icons from one church to another in procession, praying and singing, wringing their hands and asking heaven for help. Vrethiki was swept with that agonized irritation that overtakes someone who sees a person wake up to obvious danger too late. Stephanos calmly assessed the political advantage. "Now that the Empress Helena is dead, and the people are terrified, the Emperor can afford at last to silence Scholanos."

"Who is Scholarios?" asked Vrethiki.

"I've told you that before, surely," said Stephanos.

"I'm sorry ... all those strange long names ... I can't keep them all in my head."

"Well, he is one to remember. Now that our brave Patriarch has fled to safety, Scholarios is the religious leader of the people. He's the one who signed the Union in Florence, and now preaches against it."

"Because of Filioque in the Creed?"

"Because of that and other things."

THE EMPEROR WENT TO SEE SCHOLARIOS BY NIGHT. HE WENT with only Phrantzes, who brought a roll of parchment with him, and Stephanos and Vrethiki, and two soldiers to carry a lamp for them to ride by, and hold their horses at the gate of the house.

Scholarios received them in his room, a little room, white-washed, and furnished with a table, a stool, a wooden bed, an icon, and a shelf of books. Scholarios himself wore coarse-weave clothes. His face was tense, the eyes narrow and deepset. "What do you want with me, Emperor?" he said, fiercely.

"Your help, Scholarios," said the Emperor.

"If you have come to silence me, you come in vain," said Scholarios.

"You of all men," said the Emperor quietly. "How long were you secretary to my brother, and Judge General? Many years; you know what state the affairs of the Empire are in. I can appeal to you as a man who knows the arts of statesman-ship, who understands necessity."

"You misjudge me, Emperor, if you think I put necessity before truth."

"Ah, truth," said the Emperor. "Old friend, how often have you yourself not praised the Fathers of the Western church? Twenty years ago you were already writing to me praising the works of Aquinas. You recommended my brother to go to Florence; you spoke in favor of Union. How is it that now, in our moment of need, you have changed your tune?"

Scholarios looked him straight in the eye. "I was led astray by their specious arguments," he said. "Dazzled and led astray. God will forgive me my error because I have recanted it. But you, Emperor ..."

"What of me?" said the Emperor, and there was an edge to his voice. Vrethiki pricked up his ears. He was staring at the long row of Aquinas in Latin that stood upon the shelf.

"I will give you a copy of my tractate," said Scholarios. He held out to the Emperor a pamphlet, titled in Latin and Greek On the Character of Religious Peace, that it should be a Dogmatic Union, and not a Peace of Expediency.

"Thank you," said the Emperor, and gestured to Vrethiki, who took the pamphlet for him. "My friend, everyone knows you are by far the most learned among the Romans. In all Byzantium, there has never been a man to match you for brilliance. You say there should be a true union of doctrine; I thought that had been achieved, and that you had said so."

"I was wrong. I have withdrawn my error. But you, Emperor, do evil, do wrong, in seeking to buy help from the West by professing vile Western heretical beliefs in which you are not sincere!"

His voice got louder as he spoke, till he was almost shouting, and his fists were clenched. "This man is cracked," thought Vrethiki, staring at the fixed glaring eyes.

"I not sincere?" said the Emperor. "What of this?" and Phrantzes unrolled on the table in front of him the parchment he had been carrying. There was a Greek text, and a Latin one. Vrethiki edged up to the table and looked. I declare that I submit myself to the decision of this Council ... Wherefore

I consent to this opinion, The Holy Spirit proceeds from the Father and the Son, or from the Father through the Son, as from one principle and one cause …

It bore Scholarios' signature.

Scholarios said nothing. Instead he picked up a sheet of parchment, and laid it down on the table between them, beside his own confession. It was in the Emperor's writing. It was the Creed he had written at Mistra. "If you sincerely believe the West," said Scholarios, "where is the word Filioque in your creed?"

The Emperor bowed his head. Then at last, "I shall have to have at least your silence," he said. "At least your promise not to inflame the people. The Sultan is building a castle against us, and I must have Western help."

"Necessity!" Scholarios almost spat the word. "Expediency. Pah!"

"You are to go to the Monastery of the Pantocrator," said the Emperor, grimly. "You are confined there by my orders. You are forbidden to preach. Moreover, my command is secret; you are not to say that you are forced to retire. But God, I hope, will one day reconcile us in Heaven, where all these dark doctrines will be made clear."

"There will be no Heaven for those who desert the true and ancient faith for a little worldly advantage!" said Scholarios.

The Emperor turned on his heel, and they abruptly plunged out into the cool night air.

"How on earth did he get that creed?" hissed Stephanos to Phrantzes.

"Nearly the whole Church is in league with him," Phrantzes lamented.

"Oh, I wish I understood what this is about!" wailed

Vrethiki to himself. "Why does that one word matter? If I were Emperor, I wouldn't let anyone talk to me as that maniac did to him ... and as for riding away weeping—I think he's weeping, he does keep wiping his cheeks—I don't care what John Inglis says, I think he's soft!"

JOHN WOULDN'T AGREE. "YOU'RE WRONG, BOY," HE SAID, and would say no more. But about the Sultan's castle he was more illuminating. He drew a map for Vrethiki in the dust of the courtyard. "Look, here's the Bosporus—this narrow length of water like a river, though river it is not. Up here at the northern end of it is the Black Sea, and the trade route to Russia and Georgia, and Trebizond, and also the way that any help from thence must come. Now just here, at the narrowest point, the Turks already have a castle—they call it Andalu Hissar—and now opposite, on our shore, they are building another castle. They will be able to close the Bosporus to ships whenever they please. And they will have a strong point on our flank, and cover for crossing to our shore with great armies."

"But surely," said Vrethiki, "they have been crossing to and fro whenever they pleased anyway."

"True enough. Still, this looks bad to me," said John, with a certain glum zest. "And I'll tell you what's worst about it. He's chosen his site well, chosen with a soldier's eye. And his men, they say, are well organized, well fed, and working like fiends. He's going to be a good general, that one, and we could have done with a little incompetence. Ah well. So it goes."

THE CASTLE WAS ADVANCING WELL WHEN A HUNGARIAN called Urban arrived in the City, and demanded an audience with the Emperor. The Emperor received him in the throne room, in the presence of a dozen or so of his advisers, those that made up his council. Vrethiki, standing a little behind the Emperor's throne, was far from bored for once, for the conversation was in Latin, with Stephanos interpreting, since the Hungarian spoke no Greek. He was a stumpy little man, very splendidly dressed in Western fashion with doublet and hose, and short cloak, but though his garments were grand, his hands were dirty, blackened with ingrained grime, the nails broken and split. His face was pockmarked with a scatter of little white scars, and the end of one of his eyebrows was burned off. He bowed low to the Emperor.

"I am a gunsmith, sir. I have come because I hear you have a war on your hands. Seeking employment."

"What can you do, gunsmith, that others cannot?" asked John Dalmata.

"I am a maker of great cannon, sir. I can cast guns to throw balls weighing a thousand pounds or more, and throw them a quarter mile. Naturally, I can also make smaller artillery. I can supply every need."

The councilors talked together. They could scarcely credit such claims.

"I am not afraid to be put to the proof, sirs," said Urban, seeing their disbelief. "And I am a man of my word. What I promise I can perform. It was not a gun of my making," he added, touching his hideous pitted cheek, "that exploded and gave me this. No gun of mine has failed me to this day."

"Do we need heavy artillery?" the Emperor asked John Dalmata. "It is walls we have to defend."

"Guns could be mounted on your walls, sir," offered the gunsmith. "I have seen a cannonball mow down a hundred men."

"Ask him what he wants to work for us," said the Emperor.

"A thousand ducats a year, paid in Venetian gold. In addition I shall need twenty workmen, and a hundred and fifty tons of bronze for casting."

"It is too much," said Phrantzes. "We cannot pay him."

"Will you take less?" asked John Dalmata.

"Not I. I know my worth. You will not employ me then?"

"We cannot, at that price."

Urban shrugged his shoulders. "Ah well," he said. "I came to the Christian party first. But there are two sides to every quarrel. I can take my skill elsewhere. You may live to regret this, gentlemen."

"We are not afraid of artillery, behind such walls as ours," said Theophilus.

"As God's my witness, gentlemen," said the gunsmith grimly, "though your walls were mighty as the walls of Babylon, I can make a gun to bring them down in ruins!" He waited a moment; but nobody made a sign of being ready to change his mind. "I bid you good day," he said, and strutted out.

A day or so later, Vrethiki told all this over to his friends in the guard room, and found himself the center of eager attention. Every word he said was rapidly translated for the benefit of those Varangians who spoke no English.

"Come, boy," said John eagerly. "What did he say his gun would do?"

"Bring down the walls of Babylon."

"No, no, I mean what weight of shot? And how far?"

"I can't remember …"

"Try, boy!"

"A thousand pounds, I think ... and yes ... a quarter mile."

Someone whistled. "Blood of the saints!" cried Varangian John. "And the Emperor let this man depart in peace?"

"What else could he do? The man wanted more than he could pay him."

"Why, dammit," cried John in fury, "if he couldn't be kept by fair means, he should have been kept by foul ... he should have been thrown into a dungeon, or even waylaid on his way out of the City by someone with a long-blade knife; anything to stop him reaching the Sultan!" The soldiers all looked grave. They murmured grimly to each other, assessing the impact of that gun. John said bitterly, "When I said we could do with a little incompetence, I meant it on their side, rather than on ours."

But Vrethiki, for all that he was ready enough to think ill of the Emperor, and his heart took a familiar downturn at any bad news for the City, could still see that John was wishing his master had stooped to murder. He sighed. Even the Englishmen in this strange place seemed hard to understand. Though doubtless the ugly little gunsmith was a less tender victim than Joan the Maid.

Chapter 8

What use is it to keep arguing over hearsay?" cried the Emperor, sweeping a pile of rough maps, none agreeing with another, off the table in front of him. "We must go and see it for ourselves."

"But it's not safe, Sire. Not for you. We could send someone." That was Phrantzes.

"I need to see for myself," said the Emperor.

Very early in the morning, therefore, in the gray light before dawn, they embarked on a little galley that lay waiting for them in the Golden Horn. John Dalmata came, and another captain called Cantacuzenos, and Theophilus Palaeologos, and the Emperor with Vrethiki. The galley was rowed by forty oarsmen and had no need to wait upon the wind. She plashed gently through the smooth waters of that great harbor, moving along the north shore of the City, while the City itself lay as a long purple shadow against the rising sun. At first the water was fiery with the blaze of dawn; as the sun rose, and the galley rounded the point under the walls of Genoese Galata, and slipped out of the Horn, the sheen on the water thinned to silver in the brightening day, and the City lay far behind, fading to rose and lilac. They moved steadily up the winding waters of the Bosporus, with lookouts fore and aft. They were flying no flag, and the Emperor wore a huge black shabby cloak over his purple garments.

They had been moving up the Bosporus some half hour when they saw it. They came to a place where a high ridge juts into the narrows, and the Bosporus takes a zigzag round it. On the receding shore, at the mouth of a little stream, the Turks had long ago built a castle; now as the tall ridge on the Roman shore came into view, they could see it topped with towers. One huge tower crowned the slope, another stood far below on the waterline. They were linked with a massive battlemented wall, climbing down the line of the ridge between them.

"There, Sire," said the galley captain.

"Draw nearer," said the Emperor, staring ahead. The rowers dipped their oars, and the galley nosed cautiously forward. As it did so, more massive towers came into view. Along the waterline stood a line of four towers, the outer two massive beyond belief, and a curtain wall, nearly completed, was rising between them. Behind the shore, the castle straggled and sprawled irregularly up the rugged land, widening out to encircle enough steeply sloping space for a small town. At every turn of the walls a tower was rising. The watchers from the boat could see the encampment of the builders—a patchwork of tents and shacks within the castle. Silently they took it in. Nobody builds such a vast structure as that to serve a small purpose, nor does a man build so vastly at such incredible speed—for these walls were nearly at their tops, these towers were all but finished already—unless he is in haste. Vrethiki shivered.

That creamy new masonry, standing among the steep woods of the shore in the wispy mists of the morning, had been made to last for a thousand years—as though the land it stood on were already the Sultan's land, and would remain so for ages to come.

And remembering the talk among the soldiers about the shot range of guns, Vrethiki eyed the water between one shore and another, on which, oars idle, they were so peacefully now afloat. This was the narrowest point of the strange channel that divided continents; with a castle on either shore, there was no doubt the Sultan could reach any ship, could stop anything passing if he wanted to.

"Yes," said the Emperor. "I see."

Turning the galley, glad to escape seemingly unnoticed from the shore, they rowed away down the channel again, back to the City. The water was choppy now, swaying and sparkling with wind and current, and deepening to ultramarine under a blue morning sky.

Riding back through the City they crossed the path of a procession of people who were clambering a steep-stepped path up a rocky hill, toward a cluster of rust-pink domes just visible on the crest against the sky.

"Where's that?" asked Vrethiki, pointing.

"The Monastery of Christ Pantocrator," one of the soldiers told him.

"I lock Scholarios away, and the people beat a path to his door," said the Emperor grimly.

When they reached the palace, he strode through the gardens and ran up the steps to his door. He cast off the black cloak that had covered him from Turkish eyes, and threw it on the marble floor before a servant could advance to take it from him. He sat upon his throne, and beat his fists on the lectern in front of him, shouting for his councilors. His dark eyes flashed, and his voice shook. Whatever it was he was ordering, thought Vrethiki, wide-eyed, his advisers liked it very little. They argued, pleaded, talked, looked sideways their dismay at one another. Phrantzes began to write, to the

Emperor's dictation, but every so often he raised his head, and disputed over some phrase. The Emperor insisted. The letter was written. The councilors departed.

"What has he done?" whispered Vrethiki to Stephanos. They were standing side by side at one end of the throne room; the Emperor paced up and down below the windows, still agitated and angry.

"He has sent to the Sultan"—Stephanos broke off as the Emperor approached them, and resumed as he turned his back and paced away again—"to ask for his guarantee that he will not use the new castle to attack the City."

"What good will that do?" asked Vrethiki.

"None," said Stephanos, choosing his moment to reply. "None. Tomorrow he will see that. Today he is angry at the insolent outrage committed on his lands. Who can blame him?"

But when the Sultan replied the Emperor blamed himself.

THAT WAS THE DAY THAT DON FRANCISCO DE TOLEDO ARRIVED. he had brought with him a small party of Spaniards willing to fight the Turk. He came to see the Emperor. When the Emperor received him he did not bow low, but strutting forward seized the Emperor by the shoulders, and kissed him on one cheek and then the other, and then, standing, began upon a long farrago of names, all to prove that he was the Emperor's distant relative—some sort of cousin. An outraged murmur rose from the assembled company at this unheard-of familiarity. Lukas Notaras cried out to the upstart to bow down, to know his place. The Emperor was clearly very surprised at his guest's behavior. He stared fixedly at the Spaniard. He was a little man, all hung about with festoons of lace, and jewels, and silken fringes, and carrying a hat with a huge curled feather in it. His beard and mustache were tricked into an elaborate array of points. He seemed not at all abashed by the uproar he was causing but stood pertly before the throne of the Emperor as though he really were simply calling upon a cousin of his in some far barbarian country.

In the long pause the Emperor's astonishment made, he said in Greek, with a stumbling lilting accent, "I have come to offer my sword, Cousin Emperor."

The Emperor said, "A man who is cousin enough to come and fight for me is surely my cousin indeed." And moving forward, he returned Don Francisco's embrace. And then, suddenly, Don Francisco was on his knees at the Emperor's feet, kissing the Emperor's hand.

"He's good at that," thought Vrethiki, watching sullenly from his corner. "He knows how to win people. That cocky absurd little man will fight to the death for him now—and a lot of help that will be! But I won't be won. I'm not so soft. I shan't forget he keeps me here against my will, in danger, in a quarrel that is none of mine, for the sake of a sideshow Empire, all paint and paste and ruin. I hate him."

A common soldier entered, bowing, and said he was on duty at the Charisian Gate, and a party of Turks had brought something to him, and told him to take it to the Emperor. There were two more soldiers with him, carrying a leather sack.

"Open it," said the Emperor. Out tumbled two severed heads upon the floor. One lay on its left ear, fixing the Emperor with open staring eyes; the other rolled a little distance on the floor, spilling a spotted trail of gouts of blood. A gasp, then a wail of dismay arose. Don Francisco, at whose feet the rolling head had come to rest, staggered backward, retching into a handkerchief. A whiff of the butcher smell of them reached Vrethiki, and he felt his gorge rising. The Emperor stood stock still, gazing into the glazed eyes of the man whom yesterday he had sent unwilling to the Sultan, with letters asking for peace.

THE EMPEROR HAD ASKED THE POPE FOR HELP. THE POPE SENT Cardinal Isadore, and two hundred bowmen. They were only two hundred, but they made a goodly show, marching from the Golden Gate down the street called the Mese to the Hippodrome, and from there to their quarters on the wall by Blachernae. They were bravely clad in Papal colors, yellow and white, and armed with breastplates and helms of steel, each carrying a crossbow, and a quiver full of arrows on his back. The sight of them cheered the citizens immensely, and brought the crowd in the street round to the Emperor's way of thinking, at least for a day or two, though there was still a small group faithful enough to climb the hill of the Pantocrator, and read the note that Scholarios had pinned to the door of his cell there: Woe to those who put their trust in the West, rather than in God!

The Cardinal was a courteous and reasonable man, though he had come to insist on an immediate end to argument and the proclaiming of the Union of the Churches, and he made himself plain enough, but he had brought with him a fierce little man from Chios, the Arch-bishop Leonard, who made so many and such extreme demands that Lukas Notaras, the Megadux, told him, "Half of this would have the people rioting in the streets."

"Less than this," the Archbishop replied, "and the streets will be in the hands of the Turks!"

"Peace, gentlemen," said the Emperor. "Cardinal, I

thought the Council of Florence allowed us our own form of worship."

"Both Liturgies are equal, my Lord," said the Cardinal. "So both must be used. You must say a Latin Mass in the Great Church, and proclaim the Union there. The Pope asks only that."

So it was decided.

VRETHIKI COULD SEE THAT HE WOULD HAVE TO WEAR HIS best robe again, so he went and fetched it himself from the wardrobe master the day before. He turned it inside out, laid it across his knees, and spent hours feeling for the sharp ends of wire thread and bending them back with his fingernails, so they lay flat, or jabbed back into the thickness of the purple silk, away from his skin. Then in the morning, when Stephanos woke him, he put it on without a single prick, unflinching, and smoothed it down.

The fabric was woven all over with medallions between the leaves and branches, and in each medallion was a boy driving a four-horse chariot. Vrethiki rather liked it, if truth were told. And the new day that was just then fingering the rooftops and domes of the City promised at least a ride through the streets, and ceremony to look at, instead of the endless voices of the Emperor's council room, and, at last, a look inside the famous Church of the Holy Wisdom. But Vrethiki stamped on his lightheartedness. "I should not be here," he told himself. The anger muscle of his heart was getting tired, but he worked up his rage. "He keeps me prisoner against my will. I am no better off than a young calf driven to the slaughter. I hate him." Having carefully put himself into a sullen mood, he felt safe again. "Why should I care?" he asked himself fiercely, taking his place at the

Emperor's side and three paces behind him, when the procession mounted and formed up within the palace. "I'm not a Roman, or a Greek. And a lot of difference that will make to a Turk!"

THEY ENTERED THE GREAT CHURCH THROUGH A HUGE rectangular door. It led into a hall, in which the Emperor's party halted, while he dismounted. Another vast door faced them, and beyond it another huge hall, running transversely across the church, gleaming darkly with golden mosaic and walled with panels of marble. Here again the party halted. This time a priest came forward, and the Emperor took off his crown, and gave it to him. From this second great hall a third door of towering height led onward; beyond it there was so much light that Vrethiki thought it gave into the open air, except that he could see, seemingly a long way off ahead of them, the sanctuary screen and, beyond it, the altar.

From that first blinkered glance of a long forward view, Vrethiki unconsciously expected a long church, a marching avenue of columns like the nave of the cathedral at Bristow. Stepping through, on the threshold of the door, he was quite unprepared for the vast width of it—far to his left and right rose the great complex walls—and yet he had seen rightly when he saw that it was very long. Then, looking upward, he was dazzled by the height of it, for the eye of a worshipper on the threshold soared straight to the apex of a vast flattened dome, all pierced with a ring of windows, and shedding angled light—a golden arc, hovering overhead like a dawn; so immense, so brilliantly light, so sky-shaped a building could not seem like inside anywhere to Vrethiki; and yet it did not seem like outside either, with its dance of encircling columns, cool green, dark porphyry, with its enclosing, billowing, cloudy golden domes and half-domes. It was like some paradisal pavilion—the majestic tent of the Almighty, pitched across the sky. Head in air, gazing round him, Vrethiki blundered up the church, losing his place behind the Emperor, tripping on someone's trailing cloak, and then scurrying to catch up.

"It does look like a tent," he thought in a little while. "It seems to float, it seems to have no weight." For where were the massive piers to carry the downthrust? Where were huge columns tensed to carry great loads? Instead he could see only lovely walls, paneled in polished marble, pink and green and yellow, veined and suffused with streaks of creamy white, and bordered with vine-leaf tendrils carved in crisp white glittering stone. The columns were not firmly braced, but seemed delicately suspended, and carried their leafy capitals and the arches above them, all fretted into leaves and flowers and inlaid with purple roundels, as lightly as a dancer wearing a garland. Between the columns were glimpses of aisles and galleries, more light, more surfaces of gold, as though the whole walls were a windowed curtain made of silk rather than stone.

Yet with all this to look at, the boy's eyes were drawn upward, rising to the dome. The rim of the dome seemed not quite to touch the tops of the four arches on which it rested; it seemed suspended above them. And under the floating dome, the shining, folded, feathered wings of four dreaming Seraphim drifted shimmering in the angles of the arches.

The Liturgy was halfway over before Vrethiki came to earth again, and took note of what was happening round him. It was a Latin Mass they were saying. They were saying it to a half-empty church. And most of those present were weeping, weeping and wringing their hands. A wail went up when the Pope's name was spoken, cries of grief when the priest held up the white disk of unleavened bread. And when Cardinal

Isadore mounted the ambo, and began to preach, there were those in the audience who held their hands over their ears.

"Dearly Beloved Brethren," said Cardinal Isadore, and then paused for the priest at his side to read the same words in Greek. "I come to you as one who has been chosen by the Lord to gather all His sheep once more into a single fold. I am the legate of the Pope in Rome, and yet I am a Greek like yourselves. Look, brethren, at the great golden roof that stretches above us. It is made of a myriad million tiny pieces of golden glass. Each one of those innumerable pieces is set at a different angle from those around it, so that the whole may sparkle like the stars in the heavens. Even so, beloved brethren, we need not all be in all things the same to be pleasing to God our Father. Our differences may even serve to show forth His glory, if they arise from love of Him, and not from hatred of each other. Let each of us be sure that it is the light of God's truth that his beliefs reflect, and God in His holy wisdom will unite each different facet in a single eternal refulgence. His will be done. Amen."

And, "What does it matter?" thought Vrethiki. "What does any of it matter, compared to this? Churches at home are like hands, human hands laid together in prayer and pointing upward, but this church is like a swelling joy, like the ecstasy of the heart. Compared to this what does a Filioque matter, or a morsel of leaven in bread? Compared to this what do life and death matter, even mine? All that is as nothing, in the eternal wisdom of God."

Such a dreamlike peaceful expression lingered on the boy's face as they departed after the Mass that the Emperor noticed it as he stopped to put on his crown in the outer hall. "God is with you today, my son," he said. "Stay closely by my side."

•

WHEN THE SULTAN HAD FINISHED HIS CASTLE ON THE bosporus, he announced that no ship should pass it without stopping for his permission. A Venetian galley bringing silk from Trebizond was the first to defy him. His cannon sank it, and his men hauled the sailors out of the fast-running Bosporus current. The crew were decapitated, and the captain impaled.

Varangian John told Vrethiki about impaling. "They skewer them, like a chicken on a spit," he said. "A sharp pole driven in between the legs, and out between the shoulder blades, and set upright in the ground for poor devils to die on. They say the Venetian captain took two days to go. Some take longer. I'll tell you another thing, young Piers. The gun that did the damage was cast by our friend Urban. I told you he should have been dealt with. The Turks have a name for that new castle of theirs. They're calling it the gorge-cutter."

"How do you know that?" asked Vrethiki, astonished.

"Ways and means," said John cryptically. "The Sultan may have made a mistake, though, blasting off his shiny new gun. The Venetians can hardly overlook it—or at least we must hope they can't."

The Emperor hoped so too. He assembled all the Venetians in the City to meet him in council. Among them were the captains of six merchant ships lying in the Golden Horn, four of them bound for Trebizond and unable to proceed for fear of the Sultan's guns, and two on a homeward run, having come down the Bosporus just in time. The Bailey of the Venetians in the City, an elderly man called Minotto, promised the Emperor that he would remain in the City, that every able-bodied Venetian would bear arms in the City's defense, and that he would send urgent messages home to ask for a fleet to come swiftly to their aid. The Emperor spoke to each of the captains in turn, asking them to stay and help the citizens in their struggle. They consulted together, briefly. Trevisano was the one who gave their answer. "We stay," he said. "For the honor of God, and all Christendom."

The Emperor turned next to Pera. Over the Golden Horn, opposite the tip of the City, stood that Genoese colony which the Genoese called Galata. It was snugly ringed with its own walls, with its own warships drawn up below them. Nearly all the trade with the Black Sea and beyond was in their hands; they sucked the City dry of wealth. Their ruler, the Podestà, was evasive, careful never to give a straight answer. He would promise the Emperor nothing. Yet it was from Genoa that the best help was to come.

His name was Justiniani Longo. It was January when he put in to the Golden Horn with two ships, and the news of his arrival took the City by storm. Varangian John was cock-a-hoop about him: "A man of our own kind, lads, a soldier of fortune, who has never yet fought without glory, and best of all is famous, is renowned above all in the art of defending cities and dealing with siege warfare. Let's hope the Emperor knows what a bird has flown to him, knows how to treat such a man!"

"You should tell him yourself, if you think he might not know," said Vrethiki.

"Not I," said John. "But you could. You tell him."

Vrethiki told Stephanos.

Justiniani was a thickset, stocky fellow, very light on his feet. He presented himself wearing armor—a full suit of gray plated steel, and a short pleated cloak that fell from his shoulders just to his buttocks. He was wearing a huge wide-brimmed hat when he entered, but he swept it off as he came forward to the throne. His black hair had a streak of pure white, growing on his brow and swept back over his head like a plume. A splash of white grew also in his beard, a little off-center. He drew his sword, and, coming forward, knelt, and laid the blade on the Emperor's knees.

"Are you sent from Genoa?" asked the Emperor.

"Not sent, Lord Emperor. I am here on my own behalf, as a private citizen." He must have noticed the dismay on the councilors' faces. Standing, he said, "Genoa will do nothing for you officially. They are afraid of offending the Turks, in case that's bad for trade. They won't help either directly, or through Pera. The Podesta at Galata has orders to stay neutral. I blush for my countrymen, but I tell you the truth."

"Have you any other news for us?" the Emperor asked. "What will Venice do?"

"I have heard they are sending ships. But I saw nothing of them on my way here."

"And the Pope?"

"He is sending letters and embassies everywhere. Something will come of them perhaps ..." Justiniani looked straight at the Emperor. "Your Imperial Majesty would do well not to count on it, I think."

Vrethiki stared raptly at this famous man. There was a perky, sparrowcock look to him, as though he brought with him a breath of the fresh wind that had blown him here.

The Emperor handed him back his sword. Those dark eyes of his were bent on his visitor, weighing him up.

"Will you take me into your service, Sire?" said Justiniani.

"You can be my commander in chief at the land walls," said the Emperor. "If we win, I will give you Lemnos."

"That's generous," said Justiniani. Vrethiki could see that it was, from the angry look on Lukas Notaras' face.

"I must say honestly," said the Emperor in a cool level voice, "that I do not expect to have to make that offer good, unless we have help from the West. From somewhere in the West, and substantial help. Change your mind if you will." The Genoese looked at his new master with a slight twist of the mouth, and a twinkle in his eyes. "Come, Sire," he said. "War is a fickle thing. Here's seven hundred well-armed men with me. There must be some Venetian dogs here who can be made to bite as well as bark, and you have your own loyal citizens. Perhaps we can beat the bloody infidel, perhaps not; but for certain we can give him a good fight of it!" He broke into a cheerful grin. "I'll go and look at these walls you've given me," he said, and bowed, and marched out, with his sword lifting a fold of the cloak swinging behind him like a dog's tail.

"My Lord, you cannot, you absolutely cannot make him a commander," said Lukas Notaras. "The Venetians will never obey a Genoese. The commands must all go to us Romans."

"He's a soldier, Lukas, and you are not," said the Emperor. "Besides, I like him," he murmured under his breath.

At the dinner in honor of Justiniani and his captains which the Emperor gave next night, Justiniani said cheerfully, "A lot needs doing to those walls. First of all, the moat needs clearing, and flooding with water again as far as the lie of the land permits. There's a good stout fellow called Trevisano who's undertaken that, with his men."

The Emperor eyed Lukas Notaras across a bowl of figs. Trevisano was a Venetian.

IT SEEMED JUSTINIANI HAD REALLY BROUGHT A NEW WIND with him. Suddenly there was work, things to do, precautions and preparations. It seemed to Vrethiki that finding things to do had brought the horrible threat nearer, made it more real to everyone, and yet mysteriously dispersed the stagnant atmosphere of fear. The Emperor went riding with his new commander up and down the land walls, studying weak points and strong points. The citizens made work gangs to labor at clearing the great fosse of rubbish, at mending the walls, at carting stone balls for ballista and cannon, making stockpiles at well-chosen points. Justiniani had no trouble getting men to work for him. He smiled freely, praised freely, was not above lending a hand in a task he had ordered, generous with praise and always cheerful; he made even hard labor like carting stone seem worth while in a hopeful cause. Vrethiki's heart warmed to him; he thought him splendid. Riding the walls Vrethiki saw even the Emperor in a new light. The moment he got up on those windy parapets, talking strategy, he lost his ceremoniousness; he became a brisk and practical sort of man, with a good eye for cracked masonry, and so little hobbled by ancient piety he was willing, without batting an eyelid, to order the ripping up of tombstones or the dismantling of ruined chapels to be used as repair material.

Vrethiki soon knew the weak points and strong points on the walls as well as anyone. For anyone could see where the trouble would be. Halfway along the land walls a little river called the Lycus ran into the City from the countryside, and made its way to the Marmara shore. It was ducted under the walls in a huge conduit, but along its flat valley floor the walls faced an open plain on which attackers could marshal, and where they had room to place their guns.

It was riding along this section of wall one morning with the Emperor that Justiniani suddenly seemed to notice Vrethiki.

"Your master has a weakness, after all," he said to Stephanos who was riding at his side, taking notes of work that needed doing. "He has that lovely slave boy always at his side."

Stephanos flushed with anger, and answered smoothly, rapidly, in a fiercely muttered undertone. Justiniani apologized, gracefully. A moment later he tried again, asking Vrethiki himself where he came from.

"Bristow? Ah—Inglese!" he said, smiling. "Thence the sunny hair, and summer eyes. So you too have come looking for battles and glory. We are rash bold fellows, you and I."

Vrethiki glowed with pleasure, but somehow he couldn't just accept such praise, given on a misunderstanding. "I'm not so brave as that," he said. "I'd be far hence if I were free to go. But a fool dream binds me here." And he told Justiniani about the *Cog Anne*, and the shipwreck, and Mistra, and Plethon.

"So here you are," said Justiniani when he had done. "And being here, you will fight with the best of us, eh?"

"I'll keep my place by my master," said Vrethiki. "But as to fighting, I've only tooth and nail to do it with."

The next day one of Justiniani's swaggering soldiers came to the Emperor's apartments, bearing a parcel addressed L'Inglese. Inside the linen wrapper was an Italian dagger—a steel blade some twelve inches long, with niello inlay on the hilt, and a handsome scabbard of gilded leather work. Vrethiki ran his finger down the blade till he cut himself; wore it at his belt all day, taking it out of its scabbard every other minute, and laid it close beside his pillow at night. It was to be a long time before the boy exchanged words again with the great Genoese. But from that day onward he worshipped him.

Chapter 9

The emperor took luka notaras, Minotto, the Venetian, and the Turk, Orhan, with him on that morning's ride, round the circuit of the sea walls. The sea walls were simpler than the land walls. They were a single line of towers, girding the shore, with a great wall linking them, and a parapet and catwalk, and battlements along the top. Flights of steps ran up to the strong points from within, at regular intervals. In the northern run of the walls there were many gates, and outside them, on the beaches, was a great clutter of fishermen's boats and shacks. But the Emperor planned to shut off the great curving arm of water from Turkish attack with a boom floated across the mouth, between the tip of the City and Pera. "With God's help, we shall not need to defend this stretch," he was saying.

"A token force, perhaps," said Orhan.

"Nevertheless, if they did get through to attack here," said Notaras, "the walls are at their lowest here, and it was here that the Crusaders got in ..."

"You can defend this part," said the Emperor. "Your house is in this district, Notaras, and the fleet is in your charge, so it is as well you should be near it. You can garrison this wall, and hold your troops in reserve for bringing reinforcements as needed."

Farther along the wall they drew nearer the mouth of the Golden Horn. They could see Pera, with its fortified towers and walls, perched on the slopes of the point opposite. They began to discuss the placing of the boom to close the channel. Obviously the nearer the tip of the City it could be placed, the more wall could be protected from attack. While they talked Vrethiki stood looking over the parapet. On his left lay Pera, for the City projected farther than the northern shore into the deep waters of the Bosporus. Ahead of him the Bosporus stretched away northward, with the Sultan's castles out of sight round the bend. On his right the Asian shore, wooded, hazy in the sunshine, with a few Turkish villages visible and, at the nearest point, the pitched roof and minaret of a little mosque. It was so near! Vrethiki measured the distance with his eye. The gulf between friend and enemy, between infidel and Christian, was only this choppy mile or so of dark-blue water; and as the party moved on, turning southward round the point, Vrethiki almost thought he could hear, on a gust of the breeze, the wailing singsong call to an alien prayer.

The party rode onward swiftly, under the ruins of an older Imperial palace, crumbling away on rising terraces above them, and moved round the curve of the walls to the southern shore. The Emperor was not much worried by attacks on this section of the walls, for the current ran so fiercely and swiftly round the point that it would take astonishing seamanship to bring an assault to bear there. But the southern wall had numerous small harbors set into it, and each one needed careful looking at, in case it was a weak point. All would need garrisons. On their left as they rode stretched the bright sparkling sea, with its scatter of shadowy island in the haze.

They had ridden nearly to where the sea wall joined the

land wall again, on the southern shore, when they came to a little church, close within the wall. There was a garden round the church, with cypresses growing. And under the trees was a table, and a party of fishermen and shepherds seated, and eating, with a bride and groom. The Emperor reined in his horse, and looked down at this scene a moment. At once he had been seen. An old man wearing a shepherd's fluffy cloak came running up the flight of steps to the top of the wall, flung himself on his knees, and invited the Emperor to honor him by drinking a cup of the wedding wine.

The Emperor smiled. He dismounted, and climbed down into the garden. Stephanos and Vrethiki went with him, but his noblemen stayed where they were. The Emperor sat on a stool in the porch of the little church. He sipped wine, and ate a piece of grilled fish that they brought him, wrapped in vine leaves. The priest of the church, bowing gravely, told him that the young bridegroom was Basil, a fisherman, and his bride was Zoë, the shepherd's daughter. Zoë kept her face veiled, but Basil came forward, and greeted the Emperor. He was awkward and shy, not knowing what to say, or how to bow. A wrinkled old woman wearing black brought another piece of fish, "for the lucky child." Vrethiki ate it happily. It was pink and firm and salty, and pungent with some good spice.

Just then the musicians arrived, with shawms, and a psaltery, and a tambour. Basil led his bride forward to dance for the Emperor. She spun and glided, he leaped and stamped, a simple dance like a mayday romp in England. The Emperor watched and smiled. Vrethiki saw with surprise that he tapped with his silken foot to the joyful beat of the dance. At last Basil dropped to one knee, with his arms flung upward. He was a little breathless, and the sweat glistened on his smooth young face. Zoë, too, stopped spinning, and the fluttering ribbons on her headdress floated to rest. The Emperor rose.

"Fight as bravely as you dance, my son," he said.

Rejoining the others at the top of the wall, and seeing Notaras' cold disapproving face, he said, "You should have come down, Lukas, the wine was drinkable."

"Is this a time to marry?" said Lukas as they rode away.

"Soon it may be too late," replied the Emperor.

"HOW MANY MEN DO WE HAVE TO MAN THAT CIRCUIT OF walls?" asked the Emperor. "We need an accurate count. You see to that, Phrantzes. Get the demarch of each district to bring you a list of every able-bodied man in his district, and all the weapons they can muster. They must do it secretly, not comparing tallies with each other, but bringing the results straight to you. And, Phrantzes old friend, this is for your ears only, take the accounts to your own house, and sit down alone within your own four walls, and make a total, and let nobody know it but you and me."

THE SPRING HAD COME ROUND AGAIN. IT HAD HARDLY SEEMED like winter to Vrethiki, only storms, rainfall on gusty mild winds, and once a light scatter of snow that had been blown into corners and crevices by the wind, and melted almost as soon as it came. More often the rain was like a mist, a grayness in the air, a fine drizzle faintly caressing the skin. Bright sunlight had shone in between.

But that had been winter, for now it was spring, with an outburst of birds singing on every bush, and an outburst of sudden flowers scrambling all over the ruins, creeping in dusty corners on the streets, waving like fragile flags from parapets, from cracks in masonry. Storks came back, and built nests on the rooftops; spring plowing was halfway done in the City's fields, and the shepherds were busy with lambing in the flocks that wandered grazing through ruins and copses. The gardeners gathered a first crop of sweet green salad and sold it through the streets on handcarts. The sun shone, briefly interrupted by warm showers, and the air was bright and sweet like wine.

The flowers and birds were not the only ones to flourish unconcerned. Down in the Petrion quarter, where the palace household bought its fish on the teeming shore, the price of turbot was up because some of the fishermen needed new nets. "The old nets will not last above another month or so," a fisherman told Vrethiki and Manuel.

"Pray God they will have to," muttered Manuel. But the Emperor liked turbot. Manuel haggled a little, but in the end he paid. There was still a thronging market in the City, full of Genoese traders from Pera, the stalls laden with produce from the farms, with dried figs, with bales of silk, with leather-work and wool. Among the other merchandise, armaments: swords old and new, greaves, helmets, straps and bows were on sale, and yet the crowds were denser by the shining bales of silk. A strange-looking man in a long blue robe with sun and stars sewn on it in golden sequins, and flasks of brightly colored liquors on his stall, was selling painless poison in little phials, "to bring an end swiftly like a child falling asleep." But nobody seemed to need his wares, and he changed tune abruptly when a priest came by, and offered a marvelous cure for lumbago instead.

Vrethiki stared as he stood, waiting patiently, holding the fish basket, while Manuel was explaining loudly to a friend that he, Manuel, was buying produce only so that most of the Emperor's household could serve as soldiers; he himself was thinking of asking the Emperor to let him go ... The alchemist drew near to Vrethiki, and whispered to him. "No sweet death for you, eh, my young lamb? For you I've a better thing ... look at this ..." He opened a little box, and took out a jar of alabaster. He lifted the lid of this jar, and showed Vrethiki a cloudy, gray translucent ointment within. It emitted a pungent oily smell. "This, now, most wonderfully heals wounds—closes open gashes, stems the flow of blood, and brings the skin to heal over instantly ..."

"I haven't any money," said Vrethiki, backing away. The man's long beard had been oiled with some strong sweet-smelling preparation. The wrinkles that lent a little wisdom to his face had been painted on. "Money?" hissed the fellow, grabbing Vrethiki's arm. "Why, such a sweet child as you should not bleed for lack of such a trifle as money ... Here, young master, yours in exchange for your dagger ..." and still holding Vrethiki with one hand, he began to unbuckle the dagger with the other.

"No!" cried Vrethiki, struggling in the man's grip. "No, no, no!" And Manuel turned round, and came to Vrethiki's aid. "Get off, away with you, or I'll report you to the market archon!" he cried, waving a clenched fist under the ruffian's nose. "After your dagger, was he?" he said to Vrethiki, mockingly. "It sounded as though he was murdering you at the least!"

They made their way homeward. First they had to struggle round the press of women at the silk stalls, and there they saw Theophilus Palaeologos, standing waiting for his wife. "Will there be time to have the dress made up?" he said, smiling wryly toward her curtained litter, to which bale after bale was being carried for her approval. "You well may wonder. The world is coming to an end, and my wife is still buying new clothes!"

Out on the Adrianople road, going toward Blachernae, they came upon a procession. "There seems to be one every day!" thought Vrethiki, and this one was going to St. Saviour in Chora, just within the walls, to beg the Lord God that the citizens might at least be allowed to celebrate Easter in peace.

THE DAY OF PALMS CAME. THE CITY WAS FULL OF TERRIFIED rumors about the size of the Sultan's fleet, that was sailing up from the Hellespont. Even so the streets were decked with green branches, myrtle, laurel and olive on every column, every post along the road the Emperor took. He carried a cross in his right hand, and a mantle of acacia-leaf damask wrapped round his left, in which he held a candle. A great procession of priests and noblemen escorted him, on foot, to the Church of the Holy Wisdom. And when, after the Liturgy, he left the church, a little boy in a white garment came running, and seized a branch with a loud cry, and then all the people took branches, and waved them, and trooped home like a garden on the move.

Maundy Thursday came. They brought twelve paupers to the Emperor's throne room, clad in new white tunics. The Emperor tied a towel round his waist, poured water into a basin, and knelt on the floor. A reader declaimed in a loud voice the passage of St. John in which it is told how Christ washed the feet of His disciples. The Emperor washed and dried and kissed the right foot of each poor man in turn. Then he gave them three golden coins each, put off the towel, and went to hear the Liturgy. And he neither slept nor ate that day, or the night following, for twelve readings from the Bible were intoned in the Church of the Holy Wisdom, and during each of these the Emperor stood before the altar, holding a great candle. And between the readings he withdrew to his own part of the gallery and rested, while glimmering portraits of earlier Emperors stared down on him. A great marble door divided the Emperor's part of the gallery from the rest, and while the Emperor was within, Vrethiki stood at this door, holding the candle ready for his master to take again as the next reading began. The candle stood half as high again as the boy himself.

Dawn was breaking before they returned to Blachernae; and even then some ineffably holy icon was being brought in procession, with banners and singing, to the palace, and the Emperor had to stand in the gate and receive it, as though it were an ambassador, or a prince of high rank.

On Holy Saturday the Emperor sat enthroned in the Great Church, while the priests brought armfuls of laurel, and white lilies, white daisies, piling them in a great mound all round his chair. A huge heap of white and green surrounded him. Then someone cried "Christ is risen!" and the Emperor and his attendants picked up leaves and blooms and threw them left and right at the congregation, and the people ran forward, and taking handfuls of the flowers and branches pelted each other with them, hurling them everywhere in showers, laughing like children in a pillow fight, and shouting "Christ is risen, is risen!" with all their might. And when the service was finished the church floor was littered all over with petals and leaves.

Easter Sunday came; and before dawn the Emperor and people were gathered in the Great Church holding candles. Singing, they lit the candles one by one, passing the flame from candle to candle, till the whole church was flooded with starry light. Then the Emperor withdrew to the gallery, and the whole of his court followed him there, and coming they knelt before him each in turn, and saying "Christ is risen from the dead!" they kissed his right foot, his right hand, and his right cheek. Each great man in turn greeted him thus; men of lesser rank drew near, and bowed the knee, and then retired. The Venetians in the City kept this respectful distance, but Justiniani kissed the Emperor thrice like one of his own people, and so did the other Genoese. Only when this was over could the Emperor ride home, and break the fast he had been keeping since Maundy Thursday morn.

And when they reached Blachernae there was news as well as breakfast waiting. An advance guard of Turks had appeared some five miles from the walls; the Varangian captain had taken his men and led them on a skirmishing party, to see if he could delay them.

By nightfall he had returned. He had lost none of his own men. He had taken some hundred lives of theirs. But he could no more delay them than he could have dammed up a torrent in spate.

Chapter 10

It was on the morning of easter Monday, therefore, an hour after daybreak, that the Emperor ordered the gates of the City to be shut, the bridges over the moat to be hewn down. That same day a party of engineers from Genoa and the crews of four ships fixed the great boom across the Golden Horn. This was a huge chain, stretched from a tower of the City wall at one end to a tower of the walls of Pera at the other. There was some doubt whether the men of Pera would permit it to be fixed, but the engineer, Soligo, managed to fix it working from without, not needing to ask leave to enter Pera to do it; so he was allowed to make it fast. Along the length of the chain wooden rafts were anchored to float it and support it, and between one raft and another ten ships were drawn up, moored to the boom, and ready to defend it against any attempt to cut it and break through.

Each hour of the morning news came in to the Emperor. The boom had been fixed; the Turks were massing before the walls; the Sultan was pitching his great tent among the anissaries, his crack troops, in the Lycus valley, opposite the weakest stretch of the walls; ships were in sight off the City, making up the Bosporus.

Vrethiki was in agony that morning. Not since those few

moments of tranquillity and joy the Great Church had given him had he been able to work up the familiar brew of rage and resentment against the Emperor. Without it he was like a hermit crab wrenched from its shell: flinching and exposed. That morning he wasn't exactly afraid; that could be dealt with by fingering his dagger, and thinking how brave and capable Justiniani was; but he was still trembling in the joints and lurching in the stomach with something; like the excitement that had made him sick the night before he embarked on the *Cog Anne*. At the thought of being sick in the Emperor's throne room he quailed and gulped; and when the news of the approaching ships came in, and the Emperor dispatched Stephanos hot-foot to the sea walls to make an accurate count of them, Vrethiki went too, unasked, and burst out into fresh air just in time to quell his sickness.

The ships were galleys, making upstream under oar. They were keeping over toward the Asian shore, and although the beat of the drums they rowed to came faintly across the blue channel, Vrethiki could not make out much about them, so far away, and looked at against the light. The count went on and on, Stephanos and three soldiers each making a separate tally, one to check against another: so many biremes and triremes, and sloops and cutters. It soon became clear that there was a vast number of all kinds, and gloom descended on the watchers on the walls.

Vrethiki still felt queasy. The heat of the sun and the height of the walls were making him feel sick again. He left the vantage point, and descending the walls, wandered away alone into a quarter of the City he had not been in before. On these terraced slopes the ancient palace of the Emperors once had been. Now it lay ruined, courtyard after courtyard fallen and overgrown. Here and there a church stood, still precariously kept up. In one great fallen room there was a mosaic floor, with a bear on it, pawing and nosing an apple that rolled before him. Open to the air, and muddy, and covered with weeds, this floor was only visible in patches, here and there. A little way from the bear Vrethiki found two fat boys in short tunics, playing with wheeled hoops. He wandered on. All the rooms and courts of this palace overlooked the sea: the shimmering hazy Marmara with its cloudy dark islands, and the bright deep sparkling Bosporus. "If I were Emperor, here's where I'd like to live," Vrethiki said.

He was somewhere in the heart of the labyrinthine ruin now. On his right rose the great bulk of the Church of the Holy Wisdom; ahead, the massive curved tiered arches of the Hippodrome, crumbling at the top like a row of bad teeth, but below still grand and solid. A light cool breeze blew off the encircling sea. He was standing in a place that had once been rich; there were columns, some fallen, three still standing, of Thessalian marble, cool and green as shallow water. Broken marble lay around. A wide flight of steps led down from what must have been a columned portico, and a little way from the foot of the steps was the round marble parapet of a well. Vrethiki leaned on the parapet, and looked down. The black shaft was impenetrable at first. But as his eyes dilated he could see far down into the dark. Set in the green mossy masonry of the shaft wall there was a row of iron bolts—footholds to climb down there. "Ugh!" said Vrethiki, shuddering at the thought. And then he saw, far far below, a tiny spark of light. He could not think what it could be. He moved round the rim of the well a bit, and at once the spark was extinguished. He moved again. Whatever it was could be seen from only one angle. Of course—the well must be dry, and something shiny was lying at the foot of it, catching a stray gleam of sun. Vrethiki tossed a lump of stone down, and listened. No splash; only, seconds later than he had expected it, a just perceptible thud.

"Dry as dust," he said. "I wonder what it is down there." And then he heard his name called, and here was Stephanos coming. The last of the ships had passed upstream, and they must return to the Emperor with news.

"This is finer than Blachernae," Vrethiki said. "Why did the Emperors move?"

"It's long ago," said Stephanos abstractedly. "How would I know?" He was glancing anxiously at his lists as he walked.

"You seem to know such a lot of things …" murmured the boy.

"Well, then, let me think," said Stephanos, suddenly pleased, "What do I know about this place? There was a throne room somewhere here, built for the Emperor Theophilus, that had a throne mounted on golden lions, so made that they opened their mouths and roared. And the throne rose upward toward the roof, levitating the Emperor far above the heads of his prostrate visitors. And in the room itself there was an avenue of golden and silver trees, with fruit and flowers made of gemstones, and little golden birds, which flapped their wings and sang."

Vrethiki gaped. "What happened to it all?" he asked.

"The Crusaders looted it, I suppose," Stephanos said. "Anything that was left. The Emperors had already gone to the other palace. And when we got the City back it was too late to save this place because they had sold the lead off the roof to pay their debts, and it was all too far decayed. Come now, we must make haste back with this news, little comfort though it will bring."

•

LATER THE WHOLE COURT, ALL THE EMPEROR'S ADVISERS, RODE the length of the land walls, to see the enemy. The Turkish battalions were drawn up before the walls, patterning the land with lines of tents, with banners and standards from end to end of the walls, and as far as the eye could see. As far as they could see across the rolling hills outside the City stretched the hordes of the enemy, and how far beyond who could say? Standards stood planted before each unit, topped with plaques of brass, and bearing horsetail plumes. The Turks' bright armor, their fluted, pointed helmets, glittered in the slanting evening light. The Sultan's tent, of red cloth with golden fringes, stood shining, with all its tent poles fluttering banners on the wind. Already they were building an earth wall in front of their camp, running the length of the land walls, just beyond the moat. And the party on the walls could see them bringing up great guns; huge guns. All along the wall the black muzzles of their artillery pointed at the City; in the Lycus valley guns were being massed, row upon row. And one cannon was being dragged into position that was taking fifteen pairs of oxen to bring forward into place. It was still golden from the casting, not tarnished green yet.

"Urban's work, no doubt," muttered Stephanos to Manuel. It made the culverins and catapults mounted on the walls look like toys.

The Emperor rode on the wall, looking. The fiery light of sunset cast a lurid glare over the gaily clad horde and their gear. Then darkness came, swiftly, as always surprising Vrethiki, and making him wistful for the long gray evenings of a northern land. Still the Emperor rode the walls in the darkness. The plain was murmurous; a whisper of myriad noises ceaselessly jumbled reached their ears. A horse neighed. A voice called. The camp-fires of the countless enemy were lit one by one, a scatter of scarlet sparks on the invisible fields. Far across the land they clustered as thickly as the stars in the brilliant sky above.

Chapter 11

In the emperor's anteroom a fire basket was lit and glowing gently beneath the lamps. Phrantzes awaited him, his brow knitted up into a despairing frown. There were papers in the secretary's hands. The Emperor tossed off his cloak, which Stephanos bore away. He came and held his hands out to the comforting glow of the burning wood. He stamped his feet on the floor, shaking off the chill of the cold night ride.

"I see it is bad," he said to Phrantzes. "Let me know it."

Phrantzes whispered in a hollow voice, like a man who finds it painful to speak, "Six thousand, nine hundred and eighty-three."

The Emperor started. "What?" he cried. "How is that possible? That cannot be all!"

"The number of all the citizens thought to be capable of bearing arms, including monks and priests, is four thousand, nine hundred and eighty-three," said Phrantzes heavily. "As to the foreigners, it's hard to be certain, since I could not compel them to make an exact return. But they number roughly two thousand."

The Emperor was silent. At last, "How many do you reckon come against us?" he asked.

"As near as we can tell, a hundred thousand fighting men,

and more supporters. My Lord, if you would retire to a place of safety, there to continue, at least in name ..."

"I would not," said the Emperor. "But listen, old friend. On your loyalty, let nobody know that figure. Only you and I and these four walls must know it." Then he turned to Stephanos, who murmured, "My Lord, you know I am trustworthy ..."

The Emperor nodded, and laid his hand for a moment on Stephanos' shoulder.

"The boy," said Phrantzes. "I have seen him often gossiping with the Varangians."

"But he speaks no Greek," said the Emperor.

And luckily for Vrethiki's fragile peace of mind, it was true he had not understood.

"A CIRCUIT OF FOURTEEN MILES," SAID JUSTINIANI, IN THE war council. "And how many men to defend them?" No one made answer. "Not above ten thousand, anyway," he went on briskly. "In my opinion we cannot man both inner and outer walls, and must therefore fight on the outer one."

"A few bowmen, and some catapults on the inner wall perhaps," said John Dalmata. "They would be worth sparing from the main force to pick off any very forward Turk."

"And fighting between the walls," remarked Justiniani, "will allow us to lock the inner wall behind the men. That will stiffen their courage. The odds are very long, Lord Emperor. Be it so; the longer the odds, the greater our glory will be!" and he grinned, unseasonably.

The Emperor began allotting places. He himself with his own troops, the Varangians, took the Lycus valley, where the battle would be fiercest, with Justiniani on his right, on the slopes rising and then falling to Blachernae. Nowhere were there Venetians fighting next to Genoese, yet the men of various nations were carefully mingled, so that they might see clearly how one depended upon all.

"We must take up these positions by tomorrow," said the Emperor. "The Sultan will not join battle till he has offered us the choice of surrender, for his law forbids it. Nevertheless, we would do well to be ready from tomorrow. And Trevisano, will you take your gallant sailors and the Lion banner of St. Mark and march the length of the walls, that the Sultan may see there are Venetians as well as Romans among his enemies?"

"Gladly, Lord Emperor," said Trevisano.

At nightfall came the Sultan's message under flag of truce. He would spare the people's lives and property if they would surrender willingly to him. This offer the Emperor and his council refused.

VERY EARLY IN THE MORNING, VRETHIKI STIRRED IN HIS BED. Something had woken him. What? He could hear nothing now except the startled calling of a bird a little distance off. Pale light and a clear lemon sky showed through the window. Dawn. But he had woken dreaming of something—a nightmare, for he had woken sweating, for a moment relieved to find it was a dream, and then for a fleeting second had thought it real. What was it? His father falling in an upstairs room, the day the sickness came upon him. They had heard the heavy thud upon the ceiling boards; they had run up the stairs, and flung open the door. His father had been lying with a purple twisted face upon the floor, with his arms thrown up, and the coin he had been counting scattered all around him ... Or had it been that terrible moment when the *Cog Anne* was beating through wind and rain, running for shelter to a port called Modon. They saw, or thought they saw, the lighthouse, the great fiery flare set up to warn them, a little way ahead, but to the right, when it should have been on the left. And then suddenly a great jarring shock ran through the ship from end to end, and she keeled over swiftly in the furious seething waters ... How had he come to imagine the dream was real?

Then it came again. A noise so deep and low it could scarcely be called a noise, for he hardly heard it; but it made a tangible tremor on the morning air. He ran to the window, and climbed up to look out. It came again, a deepthroated boom, rolling down the slopes in truncated fragments of shuddering low sound, and then a sudden clamor of bells cut through it—bells not rung with the slow rhythm of prayer, but wildly jangled from churches far and wide on a hundred different brazen notes all over the City. The Turks had begun their cannonade, and the alarm was sounding.

The Emperor ate his breakfast standing, while Stephanos and Manuel strapped on his armor. He wore a golden breastplate and greaves and armguards, and a purple cloak, as an Emperor might have done who was a true Roman from a thousand years ago. The moment his armor was secured he put down the round of bread half-eaten, swilled down a draft of wine, and strode out to mount his white Arab mare, and ride to see the impact of the guns.

They were not, after all, firing the great mass of guns in the Lycus valley; not yet. They were firing nearer, on the height, blasting at the Charisian Gate, where Justiniani was posted. First a flash of white fire could be seen, followed a moment after by the ear-splitting noise of the explosion; then the wall quaked, and instantly, while the horse shied and picked up their feet in fear, came the thud and crack of the ball hitting the walls and shattering into a thousand splinters. Thick filthy black smoke billowed from the guns and rolled toward the walls, enveloping everything. The Emperor calmed his horse, patting her silken neck, murmuring to her, and urged her forward. As they mounted the slope and drew nearer, the gun was fired again. Flash, bang, tremor and thud rolled into one reached them all together now, and the smoke cloud that followed made them cough and weep.

"They are shaking the walls!" said the Emperor to Justiniani, dismay in his voice.

"Somewhat. When they hit them, Sire," said Justiniani. His face was blackened with smuts from the gunsmoke, and the sulfurous smell of it hung about his garments. When he grinned up at his master, his pink tongue and white teeth showed vividly, like the smile of a swarthy-skinned Turk. "Watch," he said.

Another gun was being made ready to fire. The morning wind had rolled away the smoke from the earlier discharge, though a plume of it still dribbled from the cannon's muzzle. A team of Turks was charging and loading the fourth gun in their battery. From the parapet of the inner wall, above the Emperor's head, a bowman took careful aim. His arrow transfixed the man who brought a torch to light the fuse. Another man came. The gun fired. The ball hit the ground.

"They don't know how to aim them," Justiniani said. "With that weight of shot they ought to aim very high. I suppose they'll work that out in a day or two, but no need to worry, Sire, until they do. Oafs! Idiots!" he yelled, at the incompetent enemy, invisible once more in drifts of black smoke.

"We must see what is happening elsewhere," said the Emperor, urgently riding on.

In the Lycus valley, where the regiments of the heathen were massed thickest and the Sultan's own tent stood behind the lines, the enemy were still working on their guns, building platforms of felled trees, with great boulders to break the recoil, and making a neat stockpile of stone balls of monstrous size. They did not seem ready to fire yet. Varangian John was keeping a hawk-like watch on them. The Varangians were ranged on the wide terrace between the inner and outer walls, and a Cretan bowman was with them, waiting to pick off Urban the gunsmith, who was down there in view, if he was fool enough to step within range.

Farther south Theophilus Palaeologos and Contarini the Venetian were at their posts, watching the vast horde of the Sultan's irregular troops, the bashi-bazouks, and with nothing more to report than the enemy approaching the moat and yelling. Demetrios Cantacuzenos beyond the Golden Gate said the Turks were patrolling the whole Marmara shore with a group of ships. "Let me know at once if they attack," said the Emperor. "You'd need reinforcements, fast." From this southernmost stretch of land wall the whole City could be seen in prospect. It was still lovely, and still loud with bells. The Emperor reined in his horse, and said to Cantacuzenos, "Send messengers to bid them stop ringing; we shall need the bells for worse moments than this."

Slowly, as they rode back to Blachernae between the two great walls, the bells died down, first the near, then slowly, one by one, the distant ones, and, last of all, the great sonorous voice of the Church of the Holy Wisdom.

Once the bells were silent, the remorseless irregular thudding of the guns at the Charisian Gate could be clearly heard all over the City.

•

ALL DAY THE GUNS CONTINUED, AND ALL NIGHT. THE EMPEROR
rode next morning to hear the Liturgy in the Church of the
Holy Wisdom. The streets were full of agitated citizens,
women and old men going to the churches; but the Great
Church was nearly deserted as it had been every day since the
Latin Mass was said in it by Cardinal Isadore. The Emperor
said nothing, but on the return ride he turned aside from the
main road, and he and his escort mounted the endless flights
of steps that wound up the steep of one of the City's hills, to
the Pantocrator Monastery at the top. The square in front of
its triple church was full of people, for the churches themselves were packed full. Outside the door folk knelt in the
dust, praying and weeping. On the door that led to the cells
of the monks a paper was pinned up, ragged from the tugging
breeze of the hilltop. The Emperor sent Stephanos to read it.
It said, Woe to those who put their faith in the West rather
than in God and underneath, in newer, less faded writing,
it added, They shall lose both the earthly and the Heavenly
Kingdom.

In silence they turned away, and descended the slopes
again.

"My Lord," said Stephanos, anxiously, "do not let him
perturb you. When help comes from Venice or the Pope, the
people will all flock to your side again."

"Yes," said the Emperor gloomily. "They change. And he
has changed. He signed in favor of it ... Scholarios himself
signed ... but ... if only I were certain he is now wrong!"

"My Lord," said Stephanos, "what you do, you must. You
can no other."

AT THE END OF ANOTHER DAY OF CEASELESS POUNDING, A
section of the outer wall by the Charisian Gate suddenly

collapsed into the fosse in an avalanche of rubble. Behind it, the inner wall was cracked and the battlements tumbled. A cheer went up from the ranks of the janissaries, outside, when they saw the wall collapse—a horrible meaningless whooping and halooing lasting for nearly half an hour, and audible within the walls for half a mile or so. Justiniani, who had been fighting nearby all day, coped with the crisis with great coolness. He went in person to intercept the men leaving the walls for their rest, those who had been relieved by others for the night, and asked them to stay and cart earth. They began bringing earth from the fields tilled by the monks of St. Saviour in Chora just within the walls, and soon a party of monks came out, their robes girded up to the knee and baskets on their backs, to help in the labor. Justiniani praised God for them, and went to drum up a work party to clear the fosse.

When the Emperor rode out after supper to see what was afoot, a great crowd of citizens were toiling away down in the fosse, in the darkness, working without light save for a fire burning up on one of the towers, so that there was a faint light to make work possible but not enough to draw attention to what was happening. Men and donkeys were carrying away the debris of the fallen walls so that it would not make a slope and foothold out of the fosse for Turks to scramble up. Meanwhile a pile of loose masonry was being built, block by block, across the breach in the wall, and beams and timbers were being built into a palisade, with barrels of earth set upon it for battlements, behind which the defenders could fight in shelter as before. The work went on all night.

The moment he woke next morning, the Emperor sent Stephanos out to bring news of the repair work, and to bid Justiniani come and breakfast with him. Stephanos returned saying the repairs were completed and looked robust enough, but Justiniani would not come till he had had the pleasure of seeing the Turkish captains ride up and see how little yesterday's work had gained them. The Emperor smiled his stiff slow smile at that, and sent out a jug of hot wine and fresh bread to his gallant commander. Vrethiki would have loved that errand, but Manuel was sent.

At noon the Emperor held a council of war. It was not like his other councils. Nobody kissed his feet; nobody remained standing. The Emperor did not put on purple for it, but came in his armor. So also did his captains come, wearing their bronze or oiled steel. A map was on the table, and chairs set round it. Stephanos and Manuel had orders to bring food and wine, and offer it quietly. "A man can neither fight nor think well when he's hungry," said the Emperor.

"Along the whole length of the wall they are trying to fill in the fosse," said Theophilus Palaeologos. "We have to keep up a shower of stones and arrows to stop them. They keep trying."

"They must not succeed," said Justiniani.

"What more can we do to prevent them?" asked Contarini. "We could sally out, perhaps."

"That would have to be in massive strength," said Theophilus, "to be sure of not getting cut off. Once we are fighting in the open they have every advantage."

"Too dangerous," said the Emperor. "It would certainly cost lives. Outnumbered as we are, every life we lose is a major victory to them."

"What we need is a sally port," said Justiniani. "If only we could rush them from their flank, when they're actually in the fosse …"

At that an old servant, attending Lukas Notaras, came forward on a stick, stammering and bowing. "Forgive me, my

Emperor, my lords ... forgive my presumption ..."

The Emperor turned to look at him.

"What have you to say, then, old father?" he asked.

"He has a special tone for speaking to his commoners," Vrethiki noticed. "A special gentleness."

"My lords, there is a sally port," said the old man. "A little door that gives into the moat, right down below ground level. I remember seeing my father ride out through it when I was a boy, when the old Sultan was outside. It has been bricked up these many years."

"Where is it?" demanded Justiniani, eyes glittering with excitement, thrusting the map forward at the old man.

The old man screwed up his eyes, and stared at the map. His finger trembled as he tried to follow the lines, to pinpoint. Then he shook his gray head. "I can't see as I used to, my lords, but you know where the wall takes a sudden turn, where it juts out around this palace area? Well, the new wall crosses the old fosse there, and in the lee of one of the new towers—it's very well hidden, right low down—there is a little door. Kerkoporta, that's what it was called. Kerkoporta; that's right."

"We could break out through it, and sweep them out of the fosse," said Justiniani. "We can take them by surprise. It won't need nearly so much force as a full-scale sortie through one of the main gates ... it's a godsend!"

"Open it up, then," said the Emperor. "And set a guard on it, night and day."

"Why was it bricked up, I wonder," said Theophilus.

"There was a prophecy ..." the old man said, "that through it the City would one day ..."

"Oh, tush!" said Justiniani. "If prophecies were soldiers you Greeks would be in little need of help!"

"We are Romans, sir," said Notaras. "Ronzaioi. Romans."

"Yes, yes," said Justiniani. "So is the Pope. How soon can we open up that door?"

"The Bocciardo brothers are in charge there," said Notaras. "Perhaps they can open it tonight."

THE NEXT MORNING THE ALARM CAME FROM THE OTHER END of the City. Watchers on the Acropolis had seen at dawn the Turkish fleet sweeping down the Bosporus, and were waving flares, and sounding trumpets to alert the sleepy sailors along the boom. The Turkish ships seemed to be trying to maneuver themselves into a row, side by side, facing the boom, but smooth though those lovely waters seem, deep fierce currents tug through them; a gusty wind added to their difficulties. Soon the Turkish galleys were fouling each other's banks of oars, with a sound of splintering wood that could be heard on the shore. The Christian vessels were safely tied up to the boom; and being Western-style ships, with poop and forecastle, they stood high out of the water, towering above the decks of their enemies, and the sailors aboard them poured down arrows and shot upon the infidels like rain. A galley bristling with armed men like a hedgehog struggled to draw near the boom. She had a great blade fastened to her bow, in hopes, it seemed, of cutting her way through and setting the boom adrift; but the boom was made of steel chain, not of rope; and in any case the galley got nowhere near it. As soon as the defenders brought up their most powerful weapon—the terrible flame thrower known as Greek fire—the Turkish fleet turned tail and fled. They had been routed in only half an hour. By nightfall a ship chandler from Pera who had been selling ropes and gear to the Turks came over with the news that the admiral had decided to wait for more ships—those yet more ships that were on their way from the Black Sea coast, from Sinope and Samsun.

The Genoese at Pera were adept at both of the ship chandler's skills—trading with the Turks, and letting news slip through. Nobody doubted they carried news the other way, into the Turkish camp. Safe behind their own walls, and not themselves under attack, they were well hated in the City. For the most part they were on the side of their fellow Christians, and many had crossed the Golden Horn to fight on the walls; but because of the careful neutrality of their Podestà, because of others, who had not come, because of whispers and news and rumors of double-dealing, all the Genoese, even those who were fighting gallantly for the Emperor, were under ceaseless suspicion—all except Justiniani. Because he had nothing to do with Pera, but still more because of his vigor and skill, his manly openness of manner, there was not a man in the City who would not trust and honor him. To Vrethiki he seemed so incomparably nobler than his countrymen, he wondered how it was possible he should spring from the same stock.

In the meantime, in the evenings, when the little oyster catchers flew—flocks of shadowy flickering birds, flitting swiftly, skimming the surface of the molten sea—when, among the birds, hundreds of little boats put out on the shining water to catch the silver fishes, the enemy galleys prowling in the sea of Marmara chased them all back into harbor again, and put up the price of fish in all the markets.

APART FROM THE BRIEF SALLY AGAINST THE BOOM, THINGS HAD seemed somewhat quiet that day. But the next morning—it was the morning of the tenth of April, and it dawned into a sweet clear golden day of sunshine and mild breezes—there was a hideous spectacle from the walls. The Turks had stormed and taken, it seemed, two small strongholds outside the City: a little castle at Therapia on the Bosporus beyond the Sultan's new castle, and an even smaller walled enclosure at the village of Studios. Now the survivors of those two hopeless garrisons were being impaled, one by one, and stuck up in a row upon the earthwork in front of the Turkish lines, in full view of the defenders on the walls. The screams of their terrible agony were wafted on the morning breeze to sicken the citizens. Women climbed up to stare and weep, and call down curses.

At dawn when the impalement began, Justiniani was sleeping. He seemed to need far less rest than other men, but after patrolling and overseeing repairs for half the night, he was resting at dawn. The news from the walls brought him and the Emperor arriving on the scene together. The first sight that met their eyes was a party of priests, with incense and prayer books, stretching out their hands in blessing, and intoning the Mass for the Dying. Grim-faced, they took in the spectacle below. Then Justiniani sent messages to summon the crack bowmen the Emperor had recruited from Crete.

For some reason the arrival of the bowmen infuriated the Turks. They fired their smoky cannon at random toward the walls; they brought up archers of their own who tried to strike the archers on the battlements. Nevertheless, slowly, one by one, the Cretans picked off the transfixed sufferers, taking careful merciful aim. The screams and groans were silenced, little by little, leaving at last the tranquil afternoon to birdsong, and the endless small chinks and noises of armed men moving, on the walls, and on the plain.

Vrethiki saw nothing of this because before they mounted the wall Stephanos had murmured a word or two to the Emperor, and the Emperor had sent Vrethiki home on the excuse that he needed a check made on the number of usable weapons in his personal armory. Vrethiki, therefore, spent the day heaving bundles of tarnished blades and spears around in a deep cellar, sorting out the fairly straight ones from the dented and the bent, and making a careful tally.

"You think tenderly of that child," said the Emperor to Stephanos when they had seen an end made of that day's work.

"He has been in the hands of the Turks, Sire," said Stephanos. "Sometimes he dreams, and in his sleep I hear him talking."

"God save us all!" said the Emperor, fiercely.

THAT EVENING, MANUEL KNELT AT THE EMPEROR'S FEET, AND asked to be allowed to go. "Let me join the Varangians, Lord Emperor," he said. "Give me a man's part to play."

At that Stephanos flinched, and turned away, pretending to occupy himself with the supper dishes, and Vrethiki saw, and his attention was caught. "Who will clean my cup, and bring me wine?" asked the Emperor, gently. He sounded sad and amused at once, and Vrethiki heard the ambivalent tone in his grave voice, and strained to understand. "Shall I parch with thirst, endlessly riding the walls in the heat of the sun, the dust on the wind?" the Emperor was saying. Vrethiki knew "thirst" and "ride" and "walls."

"There is Vrethiki," said Manuel. "He could do it."

"So he could," said the Emperor, sadly. "Very well. Go, my son. Take care; sell your life as dear as you can. Stephanos, have Vrethiki bring here the best weapons he found today."

Vrethiki chose a good sword. He chose a chain-mail corselet, a small one that he thought would fit Manuel's slender frame. And, especially pleased with it, he found a shiny breastplate, and, staggering under the weight of it, he clambered up the stairs back to the Emperor's room.

"He can't have that one, Vrethiki," said Stephanos, looking at the breastplate. "It was made for an Emperor. Look, it has the two-headed eagle upon it."

"Made for an Emperor, and worn by an Emperor's man," said the Lord Constantine, lifting the bronze himself, and holding it against his cupbearer, to examine the fit. "It will do very well," he said. Together, he and Stephanos did up the leather straps. "Well, then, man, be off with you, and see if Varangian John will have you."

Manuel hesitated a moment, as though he would have said something, then bowed low, and clattered away down the staircase. And Vrethiki had to find his way to the cellars, and asked the aged keeper of casks down there which tap to turn to bring wine for the Emperor's supper.

THE NEXT MORNING VRETHIKI WAS ALMOST BLASTED OUT OF his bed by a vast clap of raw sound like preternatural thunder. For a moment this sound brought a vibrant silence with it, a sort of singing numbness in his ears; then a detritus of ragged noises came behind it: glass rattled in the windows, tiles slipped, dislodged, and scraped down the roof, there was a wild cawing of frightened birds, a howling of dogs, people screaming, running feet all over the palace, cries of alarm, and then the clang clang of a silly cracked high-pitched church bell, to be taken up in chorus by a hundred others. Through the bells came the repeated thudding of other explosions. The Turks had opened up their guns on the walls in the Lycus valley, beginning with a blast from the great gun Basilica that Urban had cast for them. It was two hours before they got it ready to fire again, but the smaller guns were fired without cease all day long; a continuous thunderous noise could be heard all over the City.

The people brought mattresses and bales of wool and sheets of leather to hang over the walls, to deaden the earthquake impact of the huge stone balls. Still the walls cracked and crumbled. The balls shivered into a thousand fragments when they struck solid masonry, flying in all directions and showering the defenders with sharp-edged splinters. And the Turks were learning fast to point their guns upward. Remorselessly, as the day wore on, they continued to batter at the same section of the wall. Behind the wall, in the streets leading to Blachernae, to the Studion Monastery, and through the fields and gardens to the gates in the wall, little processions of people wound along, carrying not icons, but stones and rubble, earth and timber, for the repairs that would be done under cover of night. Women carried heavy burdens beside their menfolk; even the children could bring pebbles or earth by the handful, and the mules and donkeys of the poor were ruthlessly overladen and worked half to death.

THE SHIPS FROM THE BLACK SEA, THOSE THE TURKS HAD BEEN waiting for, arrived at the Turkish admirals' station, on the Bosporus, a little beyond Pera, the same day the great gun was first fired. Bad though the state of the walls was, it was the defense of the boom that seemed most urgent. The moment the new ships were sighted—for the enemy station could be clearly seen from the tip of the City—Lukas Notaras had come to the Emperor, asking permission to move his reserve contingents to help the sailors at the boom.

The naval attack was formidable when it came. Vrethiki, standing in the Emperor's party, watching from the battlements, found himself shivering in the warm sunlight. The Turks had brought up larger ships than before, with decks loaded with cuirassiers and archers. The moment these drew within bowshot, they let fly arrows tipped with burning cotton. The arrows beat down on the Christian decks like burning rain. Barrels of pitch and torches blazed ready on the Turkish decks to set fire to anything within reach. In the bows of their galleys heavily armed men stood with huge axes, ready to cut hawsers, or hack at the boom itself. They even had light cannon mounted on their vessels that threw stone shot at the Christian ships, and added to the confusion and fear of the onlookers by wreathing the whole scene in veils of dispersing smoke. Straining their eyes, the watchers on the walls saw grappling irons hanging ready amidships on the gunwales of the Turkish ships, and thickly packed soldiers ready on the middle decks to board at the first chance.

The Emperor watched this terrible massed attack approach his people, churning the blue Bosporus to white foam with beating oars. He stood calmly, seeming unmoved and immovable, watching from the battlements of the walls, and only Vrethiki beside him could have seen his thumb constantly rubbing and twisting the great Imperial ring on the first finger of his clenched hand.

There were terrible moments when the Turkish ships were still standing a little way off. Their cannon balls were striking the Christian ships, and the horrible juddering of the wooden hulls as they were struck could be seen as well as heard from the shore. Fires were burning in the rigging and on the decks, everywhere, and sailors running frantically to and fro. But when the Turks pressed nearer, suddenly the impression changed. For the tall galleys of Genoa and Venice, and the Imperial fleet, were higher than even these largest Turkish ships, and so gave the advantage to their bowmen and javelin throwers. Lukas Notaras had set up an incredible living chain of men, passing barrels of water from hand to hand all along the line of the boom, from rafts to ships; the deck fires were swiftly quenched. And when the Turkish captains forced their way alongside, trying to grapple and board, they were met with a simple and devastating answer. Slung from the crossyards of the Christian vessels, high up the masts, were huge cannon balls hanging in nets. The moment the yard of a Christian vessel stretched over a Turkish ship, a man in the rigging cut the rope with a yell, and the ball hurtled downward. It crashed through deck and bottom, leaving a splintered ragged hole, and a rapidly sinking ship. Vrethiki, astonished, threw back his head and laughed—it reminded him of the walnut shells he had floated down the stream at home, and sunk by tossing tiny pebbles.

Suddenly a gap opened in the boom. For a horrified moment Vrethiki thought it had been breached by the enemy, but then a great Genoese galley moved through the gap, followed at once by another, and another, and they maneuvered as though they would encircle the tangled group of enemy ships. At that the cries of Allah, Allah! died away; trumpets sounded, and those Turkish ships that could still move began to back water, and slip away. "Hurrah, hurrah!" shouted Vrethiki, dancing like a madman on the wall, and throwing his cap in the air, and all the solemn foreigners around him, as pleased as he, laughed and smiled at him.

Gleefully they watched the battered enemy struggling back up to their distant anchorages. And before they left their viewpoint, Lukas Notaras, clad in long robes of silk, immaculate and unruffled, came to salute the Emperor, and bow impassively as his smiling master told him he had done well.

"THERE WILL BE AN ATTACK ON THE WALL SOON," SAID JUSTINIANI. "Their guns have done a lot of damage; they're bound to try to get through."

In just over a week the Sultan's ceaselessly pounding guns had brought down a hundred yards of the outer wall into the moat, and broken two great towers on the inner wall behind the breach. An earth and wood palisade, repaired every night, stretched across the damaged section, but the fosse was filled right up with rubble, and offered no obstacle at all to an onrushing enemy. For five days running they expected trouble, bracing themselves at dawn, lined up behind the rickety palisade, staring tensely at the enemy lines so short a distance away.

They could see every detail of their assailants' garb and gear. The janissaries, the Sultan's crack troops, lined up behind their tall standards on plumed poles, wore wide helmets that strapped on over their turbans and came so low on their brows that they had two half-circles cut out of the lower rim for eyes, with brazen flanges for eyebrows. The helmets were chased and fluted, and rose to a point on top, from which great plumes curled and fluttered. These helmets gave them, to the enemy view, heads of monstrous size, and ferocious metal frowns. They wore no cast and polished body armor, as the Romans did, let alone heavy hinged steel casings like Western armor; but coats of chain mail, strengthened round the midriff with rings of steel like the hoops of a barrel. Their legs and arms were clad in cloth or leather, and Justiniani had pointed this out to his men, and expounded the value of flesh wounds for weakening the force of an attack. By contrast, their swords were horrific: very long, with double-edged serpentine blades, or nasty-looking scythe-shaped curves.

Peering from behind their battlements, or between their earth-filled barrels atop the palisade, the defenders watched for any sign of the janissaries' standards being carried forward. But for five days the dawn showed them still in place. Pear-shaped plates of gold or bronze, each pierced and fretted with the shape of some word from the Koran, they stood on tall poles before blocks of tents, groups of campfires, with horsetails flying from their necks. Five times a day the camp rang with the coarse raucous howling of the call to heathen prayer. In response the Turks spread the ground with little rugs and handkerchiefs, and, kneeling toward the land walls, they beat their brows on the ground, and remained so for some time, with their heads down, and their arses in the air. At first this performance provoked gales of crude laughter from the Christians, and a shower of lewd remarks, dirty songs and rotting rubbish cascaded from the walls among the prostrate heathen. But as the days passed, and each day, five times a day, the prayers were faithfully said, the jeering died away. It is an awesome sight to see a hundred thousand men at prayer; and looking at a spectacle of such barbaric majesty, the Christians uneasily remembered the ferocity of Islam, and how for the hordes outside the City this was jihad—a holy war. And it was disconcerting to have them facing so, toward the City—as though their great hostile God reigned already within the wall, in the heart of the City, instead of at Mecca, far away.

Five times a day the enemy prayed, and seven times a day they fired their monstrous gun, and all day, every day, the citizens manned the walls, and stood in sun and rain, waiting and afraid. The defenders at Blachernae, Vrethiki noticed—riding with the Emperor on his daily round of the walls—and those at the Golden Gate, could see at least a prospect of the City behind them. At the Golden Gate the whole peninsular of domes and roofs and columns could be seen; at the northern end the defenders had behind them the courts and gardens of the Imperial palace; but all the way in between, the rise of the land behind the wall cut off the view.

Even in the Lycus valley, where the men atop the wall could see farther, there was nothing in sight but gardens and open fields, and one or two churches. It was as though they were defending some lonely and remote frontier, winding through desolate country, rather than the circuit of a City. And all day, every day, the smell of the enemy reeked across the wall. There was a stench of human sweat and excrement, of the sweat and excrement of horses, of camp-fire smoke, of the rotting detritus of meals, the sulfurous reek of guns. When the wind blew west or north, it suffocated the defenders, and they prayed for the clean cool air that flowed from the Marmara shore.

WHEN THE LONG-AWAITED ATTACK CAME, IT CAME NOT AT dawn but two hours after nightfall, when the defenders were fewer, and tired from a long day's watch. Opposite the broken stretch of wall the enemy encampment was abruptly lit up by thousands of flaring torches; in the lurid pool of sudden light there were fiery men marching in a racket of cymbals and drums, and a great rhythmic howling of Allallallallallaaa! They rushed screeching at the stockade, leaping light-footed over the loose rubble that filled the moat; they brought torches to fire the stockade, and hooks to pull down the earth barrels, and spears and arrows to thin the ranks of the Romans. For a few moments there was chaos among the sleepy defenders; then Justiniani was there, shouting encouragement, mustering men and cheering them. By the light of the Turkish flares they saw scaling ladders being brought up, and little groups crouched ready for them, waiting till the ladder was loaded with climbing men, then stepping from hiding, and pushing it off with a pole, and watching it topple, men and all.

The Emperor and his escort were at prayer in the Church

of the Holy Apostles when the messengers came for him. But seeing the scale of the attack, and seeing Justiniani already there, he went at once to rouse and warn his captains all along the wall, riding from post to post with the news that he feared a general attack was beginning. But everywhere except the Lycus valley was quiet: the campfires burned as usual in the enemy camps; there was no sound or sign of unusual movement among them. The Emperor made quite sure, riding all the way to the Golden Gate and back, with Vrethiki riding a pace or two behind him, trembling with cold or excitement so that the fittings on his pony's bridle jingled like little bells.

They returned to the Lycus valley to find that the palisade had been torn down. It had been broken, not burned. But instead of letting the enemy in, it had allowed the Genoese and the Varangians to surge out, and drive the Turks back across the fosse, killing a good number before they were put to flight. As the Emperor returned, the Turkish trumpets were sounding the recall, and the attack was over. The enemy retreated and the light went too as they carried their torches away with them. Wearily in the darkness the Christians began to repair their stockade.

At dawn Justiniani reported two hundred enemy dead lying in the fosse. No Christian dead; some wounded. The stockade repaired again.

"How is this possible?" said the Emperor. "God must indeed be with us!"

"God, and some other things," said Justiniani. "They had only a hundred yards of broken wall and filled-in fosse to attack over. They couldn't make use of their numbers. And man to man they are not so heavily armed as we are. Besides, it's only a Sultan they fight for; your people fight for you, and for wives and children too. They fight like lions, Sire."

"Sit and eat with me, Prince of Lions," said the Emperor, smiling, "and then we will ride out among them, and praise them."

So, by and by, they went out into a cool clear rain-washed morning, side by side, with Vrethiki and Stephanos, and Justiniani's two dapper swaggering page boys just behind them. On the wall, and in the gardens, and all over the dusty ruins on the stony wastes of the City, flowers crept and bloomed. In hopeless cracks and crevices they had taken root, and in the mild April weather fanned or trumpeted or starred their delicate petals. And between those two brave men riding, between Stephanos and Vrethiki following, taking root on as unpromising a ground, a wild hope grew: an improbable, fragile hope, unspoken, but bravely flaunted in smiling eyes. The Emperor was almost gay that morning. He dismounted, and moved among his dusty soldiers, their garments grimed with smoke, and gray dust from falling masonry, from crumbled mortar. He gave his hand to be kissed; he talked to them, and thanked them; he visited the wounded who lay in one of the great vaulted chambers in the thickness of the walls, and told them that their blood had purchased victory, and then gave the doctor gold to buy eggs and wine and bandages.

That evening he called all his captains and councilors to dine with him in his palace, and made them all sit down around the board. "This is a soldier's table as much as an Emperor's now," he said. And indeed all the talk was of devices of war, chiefly how to clear the fosse again. With Manuel gone, it was Vrethiki who poured the wine, and that gave him plenty of chances to gaze adoringly at Justiniani, as he hovered behind the great man's chair, making sure his cup was not for a moment dry.

Chapter 12

Next morning the same sweet south wind blew. Neither the Emperor nor his servants had slept well, for the Turks had brought up guns to batter the walls round the Blachernae Palace. The rooms that had belonged to the Empress Helena had been devastated by a cannon ball dropping through the roof, and everywhere tiles had slipped and windows cracked. Phrantzes was with the Emperor early, telling him that in common prudence he must move his personal quarters to a place of better safety. But as they talked a messenger arrived. The Emperor's face lit up as he heard the news; even Phrantzes, who always had a harassed brow, looked hopeful, and rising at once they went down to the courtyard, calling for horses.

"What is it, Stephanos?" asked Vrethiki, as they followed.

"Ships sighted," said Stephanos, "on a south wind, coming here."

There were four ships, big galleys with poop and forecastle, all with full sail set, beating up the wind off the Marmara. The streets of the City were full of people hastening to see them, for the news had traveled fast. The Emperor went to the southeastern end of the sea walls. His party strained their eyes into the luminous seascape to make out the nationality of the newcomers, but it was an hour or more before they were sure. Looking up at the slopes and terraces behind him, Vrethiki saw a great mass of people like a swarm on a tree, clustering on the arches and walls of the Hippodrome, crowding the ruins of the old palace sloping up behind the walls, thronging the slopes and heights of the citadel. Every viewpoint and high spot was occupied by a clinging anxious watcher.

After an hour they could make out the banners and insignia of the approaching ships. One of them flew the Imperial purple—that, Stephanos said, was a galley of the Emperor's own, commanded by Phlatanelas, that had gone to fetch supplies of corn from Sicily. The other three were flying Papal colors—at last, at last, the long-awaited and dearly bought help from the West!

Anxiously the watchers scanned the horizon for more ships, for the great fleet that was to come and rescue them. But no more could be seen. Meantime an agitated message arrived from Cardinal Isadore, who was in command on the walls below the Acropolis as far as the boom: he could see signs of activity at the Turkish naval station and ships putting out and marshaling there. The Turks too had seen the newcomers.

The Sultan's ships swept down the Bosporus, sounding horns, and beating drums, the oars of their galleys creaking and frothing. They came without sails, for the wind was blowing briskly against them, but they came on steadily under oars. They had lashed shields and bucklers round the decks of their boats to make a defensive breastwork against arrows and spears. They had some of the Sultan's best men of arms on their decks, and small cannon and culverins too. They bore down on the Christian vessels under the eyes of the onlookers on the walls, shouting gleefully, triumphantly—a hundred and forty ships against four.

It was about noon, just under the lighthouse on the walls, that the Turkish armada came up with the four ships. The Emperor rode along the catwalk on the walls, moving as the ships moved, to keep up with them. They could hear the Turkish admiral shouting to Phlatanelas to lower sail; with the wind behind them the Christian ships swept on. Swiftly the four were among the enemy vessels, and surrounded. A hail of arrows and spears cascaded round them, but, as it had done before, the greater height of the Christian ships gave them the advantage. Frantically the Turks tried to board, scrambling up the tall sides of the Western ships—axes and boathooks awaited them when they reached the gunwales. And all the time—while the whole stretch of water was seething with struggling shipping, the oarsmen contending with current which flowed strongly one way while the wind blew strongly the other—all the time the great galleys were still under way, dragging their assailants with them, moving inexorably toward the Golden Horn. And all the vast crowd that watched them from the shore hardly murmured. Only now and then when they could see some new attack they gasped, or groaned, and then fell silent again, tensely watching.

Vrethiki was reminded of a hunt—the ships like four great stags, with the running pack bobbing round them, tearing at their flanks ... And now the struggling ships had all but rounded the point of the City. They were not a stone's throw offshore, under the slopes of the Citadel, when suddenly the wind dropped. The great sails sagged and flapped, the bravely fluttering banners sank, and dangled limply from the mastheads. The vessels lay helplessly becalmed in the midst of their enemies.

Groaning and wringing their hands, the people of Byzantium called out to the sailors, so near, and yet so far from help. Vrethiki looked instinctively at the Emperor's hand, and saw him twisting his ring ... "I'm thirsty," he said. Vrethiki opened the wine flask that hung with the chained cup on his belt, and offered his master a drink. His own throat was dry, but it was not thirst that made it so.

The Turkish admiral was marshaling his vessels. They stood off a little way, jostling and maneuvering till they had entirely surrounded the galleys, and then began to fire off their guns, and let fly a storm of fire arrows and spears. But for all the shudders of horror that this sent through the watching crowd, it did very little harm. The guns were discharged at the level, and most of the balls fell short, and dropped into the sea. There seemed to be plenty of water barrels and hands ready to put out fires on deck.

Then with a blast of trumpets the Turkish galleys moved in. The galley bearing the enemy admiral rammed the prow of the Imperial galley, and hung on to her, while, all around, ships pressed up with grappling irons, or hooked themselves onto anchor chains or anything they could find to grip by, in frantic attempts to climb up and board. And all the while the ships were drifting, slowly drifting, away from the City, and toward Pera or beyond, where the Sultan could be seen, watching with his courtiers on the shore. At first the citizens could see the Genoese sailors on the Papal galley chopping hands and heads as they fought the boarders, and on the decks of the Imperial galley could distinguish the person of Phlatanelas, swinging his sword, and fighting bravely. But as the ships drifted farther off it became impossible to see what was happening, except in outline.

They could see the Imperial galley using clay pots of Greek fire. They could see Turkish ships falling back from her, mauled and broken, though nothing dislodged the admiral's ship. And however many Turkish vessels withdrew, there were always fresh ones pressing up to replace them, to confront the Christian fighters with gang after gang of eager unwearied men. In a while the Imperial galley seemed to be in trouble, and hard-pressed though they were themselves, the other three came to her aid, and managed to maneuver up beside her. The four ships lashed themselves together, and stood out above the swarming enemy like a four-towered fortress. Flotsam and jetsam and discharged weapons and broken spars and oars so clogged the curdled sea now that the oars could not be properly worked; and so smashed were some of the attacking vessels, so laden with bleeding and dying men, that they could not retire and make room for others.

The afternoon wore on, and the light softened. Bodies floated in the heaving wreckage on the water. On the walls of the City the voices of the citizens were raised in prayer. "Kyrie eleison, Christe eleison," they muttered to heaven. The setting sun was gilding the water, and the Turks were marshaling yet another wave of vessels for the attack.

And then suddenly the wind returned. A great gust filled the idle sails, and the galleys began to move again. They crashed through their tangled opponents, clearing a path for themselves. They put about, and sailed toward the boom, and took refuge beneath the friendly walls of the City. Darkness was falling fast.

After darkness, blowing trumpets enough for three times as many vessels, and making as much noise as they could, to seem like many, four ships put out through the boom, and escorted the newcomers safely in. The Emperor would not go home till he had himself welcomed his new captains; so they lingered in streets full of excited talk and laughter, with men coming and going carrying torches to gossip gleefully with neighbors. Good news came with their supper baskets to the cold cramped men who had kept the land walls all day. They sang round their little fire baskets, clapped each other on the back, and spoke of more help coming from the West, and how the Turks could not stop it getting through. The Emperor's council looked gladly over bills of lading showing cargoes of corn, arrows, spears, gunpowder, shot, salt, meat, saltpeter—everything the Pope had thought might be welcome to them. And Phlatanelas, both arms bandaged, laughed as he told them how he had drifted so near the enemy shore he had actually seen the Sultan. "He had urged his horse into the water so far his cloak was draggled in the waves; and there he sat, up to his knees, on his saddle, waving his arms and shouting, and crying curses like a madman ... and his officers trying to lead him ashore again."

"What does he look like?" asked the Emperor.

"He was too far off, Sire, to make out his features clearly ... But he looks hooked, and cruel, like a bird ... like an eagle, and his lips are full and red."

Late though it was, the Emperor and his council went from the shore to the Church of the Holy Wisdom, to give thanks. And there was a throng of citizens there, and candles burning ... some would accept the Union, this night at least.

So at last, riding homeward under a brilliant moon, hearing the sound of voices far and near, the contented murmur of the City wreathing the tall columns faintly like the starlight; hearing from a window, and farther on, from a camp of soldiers, the sound of a brave old song, wearily as he rode, Vrethiki thought, "This is what this place was meant for, made for—for triumph and for joy!"

AT DAYBREAK THE NEXT MORNING—IT WAS THE MORNING OF the twenty-first of April, and Vrethiki noticed it because it was his birthday—mind, and he was thinking of that, and of his cousins Alys and Tom, who would have put on their best, and come and dined with him had he been safe at home. And the primroses would have been thick in the wood. That morning Vrethiki and Stephanos and the other servants of the Emperor did not go riding with him to see and oversee the battle along the walls, but were busied instead in moving the Emperor's lodging from Blachernae to the Monastery of Chora, which was near enough the walls, yet out of reach of the pounding guns. The monks of this place had found three small cells together for the Emperor's bedroom, and sleeping room for his attendants, and beside the church was a funerary chapel, finely painted and adorned, where the Imperial throne could be placed, and the Emperor's councils held. Around the cluster of domes and buildings was a garden, on the slope, that mounted to the wall, and the wall itself was very near.

To carry the Emperor's bedding, his clothes and books, his robes of state, and food and wine enough from the palace stores, Stephanos went out with Vrethiki, looking for porters. But the streets had changed these last weeks. No one was loitering in the markets, looking for work. Only women were buying; few were selling anything. Fish and lettuces and rounds of bread were on sale in the Forum of the Bull; but on carts half empty, and at prices that astonished Stephanos. He began to ask where he might find porters.

"Haven't you heard, master?" said a bent old crone who was peddling raisins—last year's, dried up hard and small. "The great Bactanian Tower fell down this morning, and the Italians have been rounding up everyone and driving them off like mules to help carry rock and earth for repairs. You are too late, master."

"Come, woman," said Stephanos. "Not everyone can be on the walls. Where will I find folk in need of money?" And he added to Vrethiki, "If bread and fish are three times up in price, there must be folk who need to work."

"You could try down by the Marmara harbors," said the crone. "The fisherfolk cannot put out there."

So they went down a steep street, with steps here and there, toward the blue and silver expanse of the open sea, to a little harbor closed now with a boom where it broke the run of the sea wall. But the men who could no longer fish, they were told, had gone to defend the walls.

"Nothing else for it then," muttered Stephanos. "Have you got that precious dagger the Italian gave you, boy? Well, keep your hand upon the hilt of it, and stand close, by my side." So saying, he turned his back on the harbor, and they plunged into the back streets.

Vrethiki found himself in a part of the City like none he had seen before. It was not grand, and it was not ruined—merely squalid and tumbledown. Rickety wooden houses clustered along narrow evil-smelling lanes. Their upper stories projected over the muddy tracks between them, shutting out the light. Rubbish lay rotting in piles, with flies crawling on it. The people were in rags, and standing in the doorways were women who were not veiled, not decently covered even, but whose grimy breasts, like unbaked dough, hung out of their bodices in the shadows where they stood. They tittered and laughed when they saw Stephanos and his boy. A nearly naked child was sitting on the body of a mule upon a rubbish heap, singing to itself among the flies. Vrethiki heard footsteps behind him, and swung round to find the lane blocked by a crowd of urchins, creeping along behind them, staring sullenly. They fell back only a pace when he turned on them.

Then one of them began to whine, holding out his hands. In a few more minutes they came to an open space. It was unpaved, and steeply sloping. Looking up, Vrethiki saw the houses mounting the hill, so closely packed they seemed to be climbing on each other's shoulders, and above and to the right he could see the great arches of the Hippodrome against the sky. In this place Stephanos halted. He took his great bunch of keys from his pocket, and struck them with his knife, jangling them like cracked bells. "Work, work!" he shouted. "One day's work, paid this evening!"

And from side alleys, and muddy lanes, and houses men crept out. Hideous, ragged men. Men with their noses slit, their ears cut off, their hands lopped off at the wrist. Vrethiki stared and trembled. It seemed as though his nightmares walked in daylight.

Stephanos chose out twelve of these pitiful figures. He turned away a man with only one foot, he took four with chopped and deformed faces, but all their limbs intact, four with no tongues, and four with one hand missing. And with these they trudged back across the City. Up the slummy lanes to the Hippodrome, and in under one of its arches, across the great cursus lying grassy and flowering among its tumbled terraces, and empty, save for two boys who were riding on horseback, and playing some strange game Vrethiki had never seen before, hitting a ball with a long-handled mallet that they could wield from the saddle. Along the spine of the huge oval space they were crossing stood columns and obelisks, and one tall twisted column made of snakes entwined, finishing with their three heads. Stephanos led his limping followers past it, and out of the great enclosure, and so to the road back to the palace at Blachernae.

He made sure everything was locked and roped before he

let them touch it. Those with hands helped to heave burdens onto the backs of those without. Stephanos drummed up from somewhere two sleepy Varangians to guard the procession as it went, and in his own hands he carried the box in which the crown was kept. So at last they got the baggage carried the mile or so to the monastery. At once Stephanos set his workers to bring firewood, and light a little brazen stove to warm the cells, which were bleak, and chill with the thickness of their stone walls. It was afternoon before the workers were paid off. Stephanos opened his leather purse, and called the ghastly crew before him. But the first man refused the money, and in a whining and pleading tone, cringing while he spoke, wheedled Stephanos. Stephanos listened, impassively, and then nodded. He sent Vrethiki to the piles of stores that they had brought, and opening a sack of grain, he doled out a measure of wheat to each man in turn. They made aprons out of their rags to take it in, or held out their caps, and one man took it in his shoe.

Then at last, to Vrethiki's great relief, they were rid of them. At first he had to tend the fire, but when it was burning brightly he could talk to Stephanos, who was unpacking, making up a bed, checking over the things he had brought. The monks had brought a plain wooden chest they could use to keep the Emperor's linen.

"Stephanos," said Vrethiki while the two of them worked, "those men—what had happened to them?"

"What? Oh, they are criminals, bearing their punishments."

"Punishments? Mutilations?" asked Vrethiki, sickly.

"Yes, yes. Those who have lost a hand are thieves, those with no tongues perjurers, those with slit ears ..."

"Ugh! Stop!" said Vrethiki.

"Why then," said Stephanos, faintly amused, "what do they do with thieves where you come from, may I ask?"

"Hang them, of course!" said Vrethiki. "And that's a doubtful mercy, I suppose," he thought to himself. "But at least they do not linger in the gutters, creeping reminders of their sins ..."

At last, when the cell was made comfortable, they went to the monastery kitchen to make broth and roast a fowl for the Emperor's supper. Stephanos tasted the bread that was baked there for the monks, found it coarse but good enough, and gave the wheat he had brought to the cooks there, in exchange for a future supply of bread.

It was late when the Emperor came from the wall. He was tired. Kneeling before him, Vrethiki pulled off his boots, and brought a cushion for his feet. Stephanos brought a bowl of water for his master to wash his hands, and Vrethiki ladled broth into a pewter bowl.

The Emperor seemed pleased by his cell. He seemed better at ease there than he ever had in his palaces. He sat sprawled in his chair, with his feet stretched out to the warmth of the stove, and sipped his broth.

"How has it gone today, Sire?" Stephanos asked him, and Vrethiki took note of that, for when men of rank were near, Stephanos never addressed his master, but just stood silently by.

"Their guns have brought down the Bactanian Tower, by St. Romanus Gate," said the Emperor. "As it fell, it took down with it a length of the outer wall. Very bad. Had they attacked in force, God knows we could not have held them; they would have been through. But they did not attack. They're so thick on the ground there you cannot see a blade of grass, only white plumes on the janissaries and red fezzes on the rest;

white and red as far as the eye can see. But they didn't attack. There's a wall of earth and rubble across the gap already, and it will grow higher and firmer all night." He handed his empty bowl to Vrethiki, and Stephanos brought bread and meat. "I wonder why they held back," he remarked, giving the Emperor his knife and fork. "The Sultan was not there himself. I suppose in his absence none liked to make the decision. They say," he added, smiling suddenly, "he had gone to deal with his admiral, about yesterday. That could be. There's a lot of cannon fire aimed at the boom today, and the whole of Pera is wreathed in smoke. This is a good supper, Stephanos. Is there enough for you and the boy?"

"Plenty, I thank you, Sire," said Stephanos.

"I'm going to pray, then, before I sleep," said the Emperor. "No, no, man; no need to come. Take your supper.

Stephanos and Vrethiki sat and ate. Stephanos' face was extraordinarily peaceful, suffused with joy.

"He's like a dog," thought the boy. "Like a fawning dog who lives for the moment when his master pats him, or speaks to him." Then another thought came to him. "It is true that as far as he is concerned I am just something his master has need of, like, it might be, a cushion, or a sword … but then, as far as he is concerned, that is all he is himself." And by contrast, in his mind, he was thinking of Justiniani, who even at that moment, not half a mile away, was laboring on the ruined wall, leading men like a hero.

IN THE DARKNESS OF THE NIGHT, VRETHIKI WOKE, SCREAMING. Stephanos was holding him, saying over and over, "Wake up, boy, it's nothing! Wake up, boy!" and as the web of nightmare receded, Stephanos left him sitting on his pallet and trembling, and went to light a lamp. The flap of sandals along the stone flags of the yard could be heard, and a knocking on the door. As the flame took hold on the wick and a dancing leaf-shaped light leaped up, casting vast hovering shadows on the walls of the little cell, Stephanos opened the door. A monk was outside, asking what was amiss.

"The boy has bad dreams," said Stephanos.

"Ah," said the monk, entering the cell. He wore a tall hat, that cast a giant's shadow to the top of the wall and folded over the ceiling. He had a long bushy beard, and spiky eyebrows. But he looked kindly enough. He made the sign of the cross over Vrethiki's crouching form, and said words to cast out evil spirits. "Tell me what devil possessed you," he said. Vrethiki shook his head, uncomprehending. Stephanos translated.

Vrethiki began in a terrified high voice to tell of a great crowd of mutilated faces that had thronged round him with their hideous gaping red nostrils, their loathsome red stumps, all pointing, pointing at him ... "Thief! Thief!" they had cried after him, and then had come his uncle's face, at its remotest, and sternest, and he was wearing the Emperor's robe. "What hast thou done with the goods that were given thee to trade with? Where is the profit therefrom?" Uncle Norton's voice had asked. "Thief, wastrel, crusader, stretch forth thy hands ..." And there was an ax ...

Stephanos, softly, in a deploring voice, murmured after him in Greek. The monk shook his head, and answered at length before he left.

"What did he say?" asked Vrethiki, after a little.

Stephanos had raked up the ashes in the stove, and had set a pan of milk to warm on it. "He bid you remember the text that it is better to enter into life with one eye, rather than having two eyes to be cast into the fire. And he said you should wake a little before you slept again, and that he is keeping a vigil all this night, and is even now praying for you."

Vrethiki nodded. "His text is harsh, but he is kindly," added Stephanos. He stirred a spoonful of honey into the warm milk. "Here, child, drink this. My mother used to give this to me when I could not sleep. It's long ago now, but as I remember it worked well enough."

"Thank you," said Vrethiki, taking the cup, and sipping it gingerly, for it was too hot to gulp down. When at length he had finished it he did indeed feel calmer, though wide awake. Stephanos lay down, and pulled his blanket over himself, but he did not extinguish the lamp. Vrethiki watched him lying there, drowsy, with the lamplight gilding his smooth beardless cheeks, his expression of unseasonable youth. He wondered ...

At last, "Stephanos?" he said. "What did you do?"

"I? Do?" murmured Stephanos sleepily. "What do you mean?"

"Well," said Vrethiki, flushing with embarrassment, "if all those wounds were punishments ... and you ... what were you punished for?"

"Mother of Christ!" said Stephanos, sitting bolt upright. He stared at Vrethiki, not for the first time, in disbelief. Then he seemed to resign himself to explaining. "Eunuchs are different," he said. "They are not made for a punishment. Do I seem like a criminal?"

"No, no, of course not," said Vrethiki, shamefacedly.

"What was done to me, was done by my own father," said Stephanos.

Vrethiki jerked upright on the bed, his flesh creeping. "Why?" he cried.

"When I showed signs of cleverness as a boy. It was for my good. When it was done and healed he took me to a scholar who agreed to teach me, for a share in my price later on. Then when I read and wrote both Latin and Greek, I was sold into the Emperor's household, there to advance myself. I have done well. I have no regrets. I should be like my brother, otherwise, who toils to scratch a living out of a bare plot of land, laboring like a beast, year in year out."

"But why did he have to do that?" asked Vrethiki.

"Eunuchs can do what nobody else can do. Because they can never be Emperors, Emperors can trust them. They can be trusted in the women's quarters; because they can have no ambitions of their own they make good servants ... that's why."

"But Stephanos, don't you mind?" cried the boy, with tears in his eyes.

"No," said Stephanos, leaning back on his pillow, gazing at the ceiling. "I told you, I have few regrets. I have lived long enough to judge what I have missed—to see what other men have. I don't mind when I see young men and girls ... still less when I see men with their wives ... Serving my master compensates well for all that. Only sometimes, when I see a man with his son, I mind ... We will hear the great gun soon, I think. They have taken to firing it at night once, as well as all the day. We will listen for it, and then we will go to sleep."

The sound when it came was always louder than one remembered it. It shook the building, and left their ears numb. In the humming silence that followed, Stephanos leaned over and snuffed the lamp. But then in the darkness he spoke again. "Listen, boy. There's no telling what may happen to anyone if the Turks get in. But if ... if it should ever matter to you, remember there are worse fates by far than mine."

Chapter 13

Next morning the emperor went early to look at what repairs had been contrived for the gaping hole in the walls made yesterday. The earth wall looked makeshift enough, but it provided cover for the defenders, and an obstacle to hold back any onrush of the enemy. Justiniani had gathered some extra men and placed them on the rubble of the fallen section of the inner wall, so making up for the weaker masonry with a stronger line. But he was worried about the insidious, continuous filling up of the fosse. And the night was not long enough to clear away the day's avalanche of destruction and rubble.

That day was Sunday, and the Emperor went to hear the Liturgy in the Church of the Holy Apostles. And there, at the very door, messengers came running, distraught, crying aloud in dismay, and the words they spoke to the Emperor caused uproar among the people gathered round, so that not only did the Emperor remount at once, and ride away, with Theophilus and Demetrios Cantacuzenos, who were with him, but half the congregation left the church and ran helter-skelter in the same direction, shouting as they went.

Stephanos was not with the Emperor that day, having still much to arrange to keep the Emperor's apartment supplied in a new place, and so Vrethiki had no one to tell him what was happening, and in all the cries around him he could pick out only the words for "Turk," and "ship." And he was puzzled by the direction in which everyone was rushing, for they were going northward, toward the only safe stretch of wall—the shore of the Golden Horn behind the boom—and if a disaster had overtaken them, surely it would be at the land walls.

Puzzled and tense, Vrethiki rode behind his master, and they came in a short while to the length of wall that Lukas Notaras patrolled with his reservists. Lukas was there, white-faced, and talking fast. He led the Emperor up to the roof of a tower on the wall, and they looked across the Golden Horn.

Already three Turkish ships were afloat there, the crescent of Islam flying from their mastheads. And behind them the impossible explanation for this impossibility could be seen by the horrified Christians. The Turkish ships had not forced the boom. They had been dragged overland. Winding over the hill behind the walls of Pera, and down the slopes to the little bay called the Valley of the Springs, was a slipway of logs, laid end to end, and side by side, that had been built, at least where it was visible from the City, under cover of darkness in a single night. And proceeding down it, with teams of oxen roped fore and aft of each one, a great line of ships was slowly coming, a fantastic cavalcade down the hill, and into the sheltered water. Each ship was being dragged upon a sledge-shaped cradle, but they came with sails unfurled, and all their crews sitting in them, the banks of oars beating steadily in the air like wings; trumpets and drumbeats could be heard faintly in the distance, and the triumphant dancing of a great crowd of heathen, escorting the vessels on their incredible road, could clearly be seen. The Emperor stood watching. The count of vessels slithering into view from behind the folds of the opposite hills rose every moment: forty ... fifty ... Vrethiki saw that his master was trembling, and he was afraid.

Suddenly Justiniani was there, and with him Minotto, the Venetian Bailey. They talked in low rapid voices, looking grim. The Emperor nodded, and there was a bustle of messengers being hastily briefed, and sent running. The Emperor turned. He descended, and confronted a nearly hysterical crowd in the streets below. Vrethiki had to push and shove, and shout to clear a way for him. He mounted, and then said something to the crowd. A sort of hushed groan answered him. Then they rode away.

Justiniani lingered awhile, staring across the blue water. "The saints preserve us!" he said to no one in particular. "But, you know, that's magnificent!"

IT WAS TO THE LITTLE CHURCH OF ST. MARY THAT THEY WENT. it stood just within the sea walls, in the quarter of the City that had been granted to the Venetians. Minotto had called a meeting there. All the Venetian captains were assembled, and some of their officers, and most of the important Venetians in the City. Justiniani, the Emperor and the boy were the only non-Venetians present. Without Stephanos to whisper to him, Vrethiki strained to follow the course of the colloquy, but the words were difficult and spoken rapidly, with urgency and passion.

"We must ask the Genoese at Pera to bring their twelve galleys and help us attack," said Minotto. "With them we are a match for seventy Turks."

"They won't do that," said Trevisano. "They won't risk their precious neutrality—in case we lose anyway, and their necks depend on it. Besides, what is known in Pera, the

Sultan knows within the hour. I'd sooner fight alone at any odds, than allied with that nest of traitors!"

"Perhaps we could do damage enough ourselves, if we could first knock out the guns they have mounted by the Valley of the Springs," said Contarini. "Suppose we put a raiding party across to the other shore to spike those guns; and then attack in full force, with every ship we have ..."

"I think that too dangerous," said the Emperor. "It would cost lives. And we have none to spare. We are in a desperate state already. Now that we must defend the Golden Horn walls as well, I do not know how we are to find men. We cannot risk lives."

Thus the talk weaved to and fro. Vrethiki could see that everything suggested was being turned down. Suddenly, a large burly redheaded man, whom he did not know, spoke up.

"We must burn them," he said. "By night. Tonight."

A clamor of talk broke out, questions, comments. The Emperor said, "How would that be possible, Coco, my friend?"

"I'll do it," said Coco, bluntly. "If you give me, say, two big transports, two galleys, and two little fustae. And plenty of Greek fire."

"Who goes with you?" said the Emperor.

"Let's keep it among ourselves," said Minotto at once. "We have ships enough without asking round. And it ought to be kept secret. Let's keep the Genoese well out of it. Forgive me, Justiniani, but we all know you're different."

"Tonight then," said Coco.

"Hold on, hold on," said Trevisano. "Whose ships are we using, exactly? Can all be ready by tonight?"

It seemed not. Watching Coco with interest, Vrethiki saw

him getting more and more disgruntled. He seemed very surly, and short-spoken, while the others babbled on. At last it was agreed to put off the attempt till two nights hence, by which time all could be made ready. The meeting broke up, and the Emperor, deeply anxious, returned to the wall at Blachernae, to look despairingly at the fleet of seventy Turkish vessels, riding peacefully at anchor in the Golden Horn. Already the Sultan's numberless army were busying themselves making a floating bridge across the water, above the line of the land walls, which would cut short the long trail round the marshy headwaters of the Horn, and quicken his messengers between army and fleet on the Bosporus. The bridge was floated on barrels lashed together, and covered with planks to make a wide flat roadway.

By the second day they had finished their bridge. By the third, the morning of Coco's expedition, they had mounted guns on it, and were firing at the weakest part of the wall, where it encompassed the Palace of Blachernae.

THE EMPEROR WAS VISITING BLACHERNAE WHEN THE GUNS opened up from the new bridge. He was meeting with Phrantzes and others, and Vrethiki found himself free to go looking for Varangian John, and his old friends, seeking the pleasure of speaking English for a little while. He was welcomed warmly enough. The soldiers were weary from a night spent on the wall, and there was work in earnest to be done, cleaning armor, not just to make it shine on parade, but to remove the grime, the mud and dust of the walls. Vrethiki sat down and set to work with a rag and a pot of oil, and listened to the talk.

"Think they're sitting pretty out there," observed Martin, jerking his head toward the racket over the wall. "Wait till tonight, eh?" And he winked at nobody in particular.

"Have you seen Coco's ship? Or Trevisano's?" said another. "They've padded them with bales of cotton like a fat woman bulging through her corsets!" Pricking up his ears, Vrethiki soon learned very fully what the meeting in St. Mary's had been about. "Don't talk about it, please!" he said to Varangian John. "It's supposed to be secret, I'm sure it is!"

"It's all over the City," said Varangian John, "secret or not." He pulled a breastplate off the pile that was waiting to be cleaned, and Vrethiki saw the one beneath. It was striped with lines of dark clotted blood dried onto it, but there was no mistaking the two-headed eagle. It was—it had been— Manuel's.

"Dead," said Varangian John, when he saw the boy staring at it. "Kaput. Now, don't take on, boy. He died bravely; and just between you and me, there's none of us likely to come better out of all this than that."

VRETHIKI COULD NOT TELL STEPHANOS AT ONCE, BECAUSE when he found him he was standing behind the Emperor's chair, in the middle of some kind of audience.

The men with the Emperor were all Genoese. Cattaneo was there, and the two Langasco brothers, and the Bocciardo brothers, all three. Their voices were raised, barely respectful.

"We came to fight for you, Sire, not to prowl your walls like nightwatchmen!"

"How can the City be defended, except by watching the walls?" said the Emperor. "Do we not share that burden all alike?"

"And when a chance for glory comes, you shut us out of it!" Cattaneo continued.

"But you must see that it had to be secret. It was not to deprive anyone of glory, merely that tactically it seemed best that few should know ..."

"If you think us not good enough for you ... not worthy to be trusted ..." said the elder Langasco, between his teeth.

"If you think you can't trust us, we'll go," Cattaneo said. "We'll take ourselves over to Pera, and there's an end of it!"

"You are well trusted," said the Emperor wearily. "Why should I not trust you? As you say, you could go off to Pera at any moment, and save yourselves. It is of your good will, of your honesty, that you are here instead. I know that. I trust you well."

"Then let us, too, go on this adventure," said Langasco. "Some of us go too. Right?"

"Fetch Coco to me," said the Emperor to Stephanos. And while he went Vrethiki poured out wine for the angry Genoese, and the Emperor talked to them in a careful, soothing voice. When Coco came, the Emperor talked to him first, in the doorway, telling him what was afoot in a rapid undertone. Coco looked distraught. At last he came forward, and confronted the others.

"Very well," he said, "I'll take one Genoese vessel. You'll have to be ready tonight. You'll have to take orders from me.

"Why certainly, brother Coco," said Cattaneo. "You are the commander. We are no rabble. We'll take orders. But as for tonight, we're not ready, can't be ready so soon. You'll have to wait for us."

"Wait?" cried Coco. He turned to the Emperor. "Sire we've been too long about this already. It needs surprise, or it cannot work!"

"What he says is true," said the Emperor, turning to Cattaneo with a gesture of appeal.

"Whose fault is it we are unprepared?" demanded Cattaneo. "If you had told us about it in the first place we would not have been the last to be ready!"

"Very well," said the Emperor. "It has delayed two days already, I suppose another day makes little difference."

"Two days hence," said Langasco firmly. "The night of the twenty-eighth. We'll be ready then. Don't beetle your brows at me, friend Coco; see how we'll fight. There never was a Venetian armada that wouldn't have been better for a few Genoese!"

IT WAS TWO NIGHTS LATER, THEREFORE, THAT THE ATTEMPT was made. The monks woke Stephanos at the third hour, and he woke the Emperor, wrapped him in a thick cloak, and went with him to a tower on the sea wall. The moon had set, and the darkness was thick as velvet, but the Emperor had said that there would be light enough to see something by if Coco was as good as his word, and he was determined to see it. Vrethiki hurried after them with a flask of warm wine wrapped in a cloth to keep the heat in, and a basket of little loaves and cheese. Stephanos was beginning to fret a little over his master; and it was true that the Emperor was thinner than ever, and often looked deadly tired.

Once on the tower they had chosen, the Emperor had them put out the torches they had come by, for standing in a pool of light made them blind to all but blackness beyond. Even without the torches it was so dark that Vrethiki could not make out anything at all beyond the battlements. Footsteps climbed up behind them, and Phrantzes joined them, and Theophilus, and Notaras, to watch with them. Deprived of sight they stood silent, straining to hear. The water slopped and slapped round a little boat anchored below them. The creak of a straining hawser came intermittently from the nearest of the Turkish vessels, as it pulled and slackened its anchor rope. They heard a dog howling on the farther shore, faint and far.

The thin and widely spaced line of men keeping the walls, stretching on either side of them, brought nearer noises in the dark. On the right somewhere a man stamped his cold feet, yawned, put down his quiver with a rattle of loose shafts.

"What's that?" said Theophilus, suddenly. Over to the right, across the water, a sudden light blazed out, and then was gone.

"Someone has signaled from Pera," said Phrantzes. "We are betrayed."

"It may not be that," said Theophilus, always hopeful. "A watchman's lamp, perhaps?"

"It vanished as suddenly as it came," said Notaras grimly. He called to a sentry and consulted with him. "He says he has not seen any lamps over yonder, on any of the past six nights he has watched here," he reported, more grimly still.

In agony of mind they strained to listen. Vrethiki thought he heard a splash once; but so stealthily did Coco come that his ships had moved right beneath the tower they stood on, and farther yet, and the anxious listeners had heard nothing before the guns opened up. They saw the lurid flash of cannon from the Valley of the Springs and outlined on the suddenly scarlet water were the black outlines of their own ships. They heard, even through the thunderous crash of cannon fire, the sickening splintering noise of the impact of ball on wood. There were splashes and screams, and clearly audible across the water, shrieks of laughter from the Turks. A choking smell of smoke drifted out of the dark. Then flares were lighted in the Turkish ships, and one by one they moved forward to the fight.

"They knew. They were warned," said the Emperor dully. Screams still reached them out of the night. They could see small areas of the Turkish vessels, lit by their flares, floating to and fro like patches of light on a wall. They could not make out what was happening. The cannon fire continued from the farther shore and from enemy ships, and all this confusion of moving lights and fires was doubled, mirrored in the glossy black water. For an hour and a half they stood in anguish, watching this strange and terrible spectacle. Then dawn began to break, and a dim gray light showed the two large galleys surrounded by enemy ships on the dark water, and all around things floating, broken spars, broken men. Of the other ships that had gone with Coco there was no sign. The Emperor covered his face, and bowed his head.

In the lightening day the galleys began to move, and seeing, at last, the distress of their fellows, other Christian ships began belatedly to move up from the boom to bring aid. The Turkish vessels retired hastily.

"Bring me the reckoning when it is known," said the Emperor, departing.

Phrantzes came with it later in the day. Coco's ship lost, with all hands. Trevisano's also, though he and some others swam ashore. Ninety men dead, shot or drowned; and only one Turkish ship destroyed. The Emperor heard him out, white-lipped, taut in every muscle, silent.

But just behind Phrantzes came Trevisano, he who had stayed, he said, for the honor of Christendom, and he was in a pitiable state. Tears were running down his face, and his eyes were reddened and swollen. A gash gaped in his forehead, and his clothes were tattered and damp.

"Lord Emperor!" he cried. "Lord Emperor!" And he fell on his knees at the Emperor's feet. "They have taken prisoners

... all who swam the wrong way in the dark ... to the opposite shore, my friends, my country-men ..." The Emperor reached out his hands, and took I Trevisano's. "They have impaled them all along the shore, and they are out of bowshot ... we can do nothing to help them ... nothing ..." He was shaken with sobs.

Vrethiki stiffened to see the dark flash in the Emperor's eyes.

"Have we any prisoners?" he asked Phrantzes.

"Two hundred and sixty in all, my Lord."

"Take them every one down to the sea wall, and hang them from the battlements there," said the Emperor.

And Varangian John marched forth to do his bidding.

Chapter 14

After that there was a long respite from serious attack. The guns hammered on, remorselessly, without cease. Men coming from duty on the wall were deaf for an hour or two, from the numbness left by the noise. And yet already used to it, and finding no danger in it for themselves, the birds no longer flew up from the trees at the gunclaps, but sang peacefully on in gardens and bushes only a mile within the walls. Nearly every day the Turkish vessels sallied out and made as if to attack the boom, or brought scaling ladders, and made feint attacks on the walls at their weakest and lowest, along the Golden Horn. But the walls were patched and botched up every night; the attacks were only shadow play and came to nothing.

Had the Christians only known as much! As it was, they were continuously sounding the alarm, springing to their posts, hurriedly transferring men from one point of the wall to another, so that men were less and less willing to go. Tempers ran short. Only the Emperor remained calm. Day by day, Vrethiki watched him. The problems, and quarrels, and difficulties were brought to him to be dealt with. He worked long hours in council; he soothed people; he tried to find them guns or shot, or extra working hands; he thanked them and flattered them. He rode round the walls every day, to see for himself, to listen to problems, to praise, to cheer his people. He prayed every day, in public in the churches, and, with a kind of despairing abandon, stretched out before his icon at night. He ate and slept very little.

Sometimes Vrethiki remembered the night he had the terrible dream. The dream itself he had forgotten, except that he remembered he had seen Uncle Norton, wearing the Emperor's robe. He wondered why. It seemed absurd to him now. "Uncle Norton made more fuss and bossiness out of a ship and a ware-house," the boy thought, "than the Lord Constantine does of an Empire." And Uncle Norton, he couldn't help thinking, had never been the man to ask his servant if there was food enough for his supper. Then when the boy watched Justiniani talking to the Emperor, he saw how the great captain deferred to his master. He was not ceremoniously polite, not at all—rather, brisk and inclined to make wry jests. But anyone could see he was serving a man he respected. "What did I hate about the Emperor?" the boy found himself wondering. "Only that he brought me here. And that was only because I was, I am afraid. And yet others have come freely into the same danger, out of greatness of heart." He glanced again at Justiniani, his dark head with its white streak bent intently over a map they were discussing. "I should be ashamed of myself," Vrethiki thought ruefully. And his hand traveled to the hilt of the dagger that had been given him that he might play his part.

The day came when the Emperor, riding on one of his ceaselessly repeated patrols, found a section of the wall without defenders. Just beyond the empty stretch they came upon a quarrel, so loud and violent that the group of men involved did not see or hear the Emperor and his party till they were right upon them.

"What is happening here?" asked the Emperor sternly.

"This man will not keep his post," said the captain, who was barring the top of the steps down to the City, and holding a man back at sword point.

"What have you to say for yourself?" said the Emperor, and Vrethiki saw again that dark flash of anger in his eyes.

"Forgive your servant," said the man, collapsing to his knees, "but my wife ... my child is sick ... they have nothing to eat. I only wanted to find some food, I would have returned at once, at once ..."

"Yesterday I let three men from my watch go to find food, and they did not return for five hours," said the captain.

"And what if the attack comes while you are gone?" said the Emperor. "Cannot your wife buy food for your children?" But at that a murmur, an angry murmur, came from all the listening men.

"Things are difficult, Lord Emperor," said the captain. "There's next to nothing to be had, whole districts of the City where nothing can be bought. We tramp round for hours, looking for something, anything, and when we find it the price is often too high. Those Genoese rats from Pera charge the last obol they can squeeze from the hungry ... the fishermen cannot put out, nothing grows much at this season, only lettuces, and those have been taken before they were ripe. As you know, Lord Emperor, there are not many cattle or sheep within the walls, and there is barely any bread ..."

"Enough, my son. I understand," said the Emperor. "I will do what I can. But you must stay at your post," he added, looking down at the kneeling man.

"THIS IS LUDICROUS," SAID THE EMPEROR TO HIS COUNCIL. "We have made a soldier out of every citizen, man, woman and child. We must provide food for them."

"I don't see how we can ..." said Notaras.

"We must. We must buy all the food in the City, all of it; beasts on the hoof, salad in the fields, everything; then we must issue a daily share to everyone."

"My Lord," said Phrantzes, "for that there is not money enough in your treasury, though you spent it to the last coin."

"The prices have so risen, with scarcity ..."

"We should have thought of this sooner," said the Emperor. "But there is money enough in the City. We shall have to levy contributions from wealthy citizens, and from churches. They can spare us their candlesticks, their surplus plate ..."

"This will cause anger, Sire," said Phrantzes.

"That can't be helped. Will it be better if the Turks get it all? Get the demarchs of each district to work with you, Theophilus; I am giving this job to you. Make very sure that money is taken from the churches of those who support the Union, and those who do not, with perfect fairness; and when you buy, do not pay absurd prices, take the food, and give what is reasonable. And when shares are distributed, make sure the poor get as much as the rich, and nobody, whoever he is, gets more. Wait ... yes, an extra measure for those who fight on the walls."

"May I suggest, Sire," said Theophilus, "that extra measure should be given also to those who work repairing the wall at night?"

"Yes, that would be only right."

"Furthermore, Sire," said Phrantzes, "perhaps we should promise reparations to the churches, should we succeed in repulsing the Turks."

"Promise it fourfold," said the Emperor.

·

NEXT TIME VRETHIKI RAN INTO VARANGIAN JOHN, HE HAD A wide grin on his face. "Guess what happened, boy," he said, "to that swine of a gunsmith!"

"Can't guess," said the boy. "You tell me."

"Kaput!" said John. "Blown into nasty oozy little pieces. And guess what did it?"

"Oh, do tell me!"

"Well, listen. What do you hear?"

"Guns, as usual."

"When did you last hear the big one—you know, that monstrous one that shakes the houses end to end of the City, and rocks the ships in the harbor? When did you last hear that one?"

"Oh," said Vrethiki. "Now you mention it, I haven't heard that one today."

"It blew up yesterday," said John with great satisfaction. "And it blew its bloody maker with it!"

"How do you know?" said the boy doubtfully.

"Ways and means," said Varangian John.

"Just what are your ways and means, John?" asked Vrethiki.

"Look here," said John, and he pulled from his pocket a little scrap of paper, rolled tightly into a tube. He flattened it out, and showed Vrethiki writing on it. "Someone out there thinks we ought to know this and that," he said. "He feathers his arrows with this pretty scrap of plumage, and shoots it over."

"So the Turks have traitors, too!"

"Traitor is a strong word for it. There are Christians out there, too, you know. The Despot of Serbia, for example. He's the Sultan's vassal, so he's had to send some troops to help him. Perhaps some of them aren't quite as keen as they might be to help Christian against Turk."

That evening, as the boy rode beside Stephanos, a few paces behind the Emperor, making the evening inspection of the walls, he said to Stephanos, "Can it be true that there are Christians in the Sultan's army?"

"There are some," said Stephanos. He was keeping a solicitous eye on the figure of the Emperor in front, riding as always with Phrantzes on one hand, and Don Francisco on the other.

"How can they?" demanded the boy.

"Well," said Stephanos, "on our side there is Prince Orhan, and the men of his court, who are Turks, and Mohammedans. Should they not fight for us?"

"Oh," said Vrethiki, his swelling indignation suddenly pricked.

"Still wanting everything simple?" said Stephanos with a half smile. The Emperor had halted to talk with a Genoese captain. "You're all the same, you Westerners! Hungry for simplicity, like Crusaders! Did you know the Crusader Lords were scandalized that the Emperor had dealings with the infidels; but the Emperors have had a frontier with Islam for nearly eight hundred years! Nothing is simple here; time complicates." He was talking quietly, almost as though to himself. "The Emperors are Christ on earth, the chosen of God, like Solomon, like David. Yet they have been usurpers, image-breakers, adulterers, torturers, tricksters. An Empress once put out her own son's eyes that her lover might reign unthreatened. Time weaves complexities. And this place, this City, the seat of majesty, the throne of Christ on earth, it was once a palpable glory, and is now a ruin, a memory—a memory clad in a web of dream. Look around you, Vrethiki, and see this amazing thing. Here are good men ready to fight and die for it—for a ruin, a memory, and a dream. And over there"—he pointed to the Turkish camp below them and beyond—"more brave men, and what are they fighting for? It is a dream of their own that brings them here; a promise their prophet made them, a blessing on the army, on the prince, that should conquer us. Why us? Why did the heathen prophet set his men on us? Because this place was crowned with a dream of Christendom, with the ideal of Christ's kingdom upon earth. It is because of what we dream this place to be, because of what it never in truth has been, that they, too, lust and long for it, and come marching against us to wrest it from us. If all men saw the world for what it is, Vrethiki, this City would be left to molder peacefully in its powerless old age, and the Sultan would stay at home and build his palaces and gardens, and not a drop of blood would be shed!"

"You know, Stephanos," said the boy. "I think you're wrong!" But at that moment the Emperor finished talking to the captain, and rode on, and although Stephanos looked at the boy with an amused inquiry on his face, there was time for no more talk just then.

THE EMPEROR CALLED A MEETING OF THE CHIEF VENETIANS in the City. Since Minotto had sent urgently to Venice for help, nothing more had been heard. "Would it be possible," inquired the Emperor, "to sneak a ship past the Turks, and go in search of the fleet that is on its way to help us? They may not realize how desperate is the need for haste."

"I should think it could be done," said Minotto. "A small, fast ship—a brigantine, or such like. It's taking a chance on the Dardanelles being unguarded, but I expect they've left it open by bringing every ship they have up here."

"God knows, we could do with good news," said the Emperor. "If we could tell the people help was coming ..."

"We will make a ship ready," said Minotto.

THAT EVENING WHEN STEPHANOS AND VRETHIKI WERE SERVING the Emperor his supper, and the three of them were alone in the cells of the Chora, the Emperor said to Stephanos, "Tell the boy about the ship that is going. I am putting on board her, safely concealed in the hold, one or two elderly ladies who served my mother, or my late wife. I have a duty to save them from suffering if I can. And I have it in mind that I have injured the boy, too, in bringing him into peril whether he would or no. Tell him he may go to safety with them."

Vrethiki saw Stephanos glance at him, with an expression full of pain. Then Stephanos translated the Emperor's words.

"But what about the prophecy?" cried Vrethiki, wildly. "He needs me because of that! I've got to stay!"

Stephanos made this answer to the Emperor, who was sitting slumped with weariness in his chair, gazing at the flames of the fire in the little stove and turning his ring of state round and round on his delicate long finger. The Emperor looked up at Vrethiki with a trace of surprise, and spoke with sudden passion.

"He says," said Stephanos, "do you think he is a fool? Do you think he cares for prophecies? He says he brought you here to please Plethon, and he thinks even if the citizens here all knew about it, they have forgotten by now. He says why should he take thought for the prophecies, since whatever he does, and whatever happens, the people will hold him to blame? Do you think he doesn't know how they blame him even for his name, saying it has been prophesied that

Constantine, son of Helena, shall be the last Emperor, as also was the first? Do you think he hasn't heard them say that the Turks will break in, and get as far as the Column of the Cross in the Forum of Constantine, and then will come an angel with a fiery sword and give it to a simple poor man, who happens to be standing by, and he will turn back the Turks, and lead the Romans to victory? If that simple poor man who can do so much better than my Lord would only present himself now, how gladly would the Emperor lay down his burden! What use is it to seek to avoid blame by a people such as that? The Emperor says he wishes to die with a clear conscience, with no one having a cause of complaint against him, and he thought you longed to go home."

But Vrethiki was shattered and confused. The solid ground was cut from beneath him and he floundered in a conflict of feeling like a man in a quagmire. At last, "It's true, I did want to go home," he said miserably. "But to leave now! And the Emperor, and Justiniani, and you, Stephanos, all stay here still, and I am to go, and have no share in what is to happen! Let me stay!"

"There's nothing to stay for," said Stephanos quietly. "Nothing for you here, and those who stay will die."

"What is he saying?" asked the Emperor, watching them.

"He says he will die for the Empire," said Stephanos. But Vrethiki had been hearing Greek for a long time now, and the sentence was simple, made up of familiar words. He understood it.

"No," he said. "To die for the Empire is the Emperor's privilege—but lesser folk may dare for lesser things. And you, Stephanos, you with your 'nothing here,' your 'ruin and memory and dream,' you are quite wrong; the people here are real, and so their courage is, and while the Lord

Constantine is alive, and fighting for it, ruin, memory and dream are all alike real for me!"

"So, he would stay," said the Emperor gently, when Stephanos translated that. "Tell him to take care what he wishes, in case it is given to him. Tell him that when I was a young man I wanted above all to be Emperor, to inherit my brother's place. I plotted and maneuvered, and quarreled with my other brothers, all to further my ambition. God punished me by granting my desire. I have got what I wished for, and it is a heavy and a long ordeal, that I am hard put to to bear with dignity. A little while ago the boy wanted release; and now it is given to him he draws back and says he wants another thing instead. So tell him he shall have what he asks for; tell him to be sure of what he asks."

"Let me stay!" said Vrethiki, stubbornly, near to tears.

"Let him stay, then," said the Emperor to Stephanos. "And out of all possible lesser things, what is it, I wonder, that keeps him?"

As though for an answer, the boy fell on his knees, and with a swift clumsy gesture took the Emperor's right hand, and managing at last to get his tongue round two words of Greek, he said, "A ff endi mou!—My true Lord."

"If I had a son, you know, Stephanos … " said the Emperor.

"Yes, Sire, I know," said Stephanos.

THE VENETIANS MADE READY THEIR BRIGANTINE. IT HAD A crew of twelve volunteers, who blackened their faces with charcoal, and wore turbans and Turkish trousers and jackets. She slipped through the boom on the night of the third of May, flying the red crescent from her masthead, and she got safely away, though Vrethiki was not on board her.

Chapter 15

Days passed. Twice a day the Emperor rode along the walls. He spent less time than he used to in churches, though he visited one church or another nearly every day; he spent much more time conferring with his council, with his captains. The ambit of his days had shrunk down to almost nothing but the walls and the few churches near the walls, for he had no time to ride through the middle of the City. Thus it was that neither Stephanos nor Vrethiki, and perhaps not the Emperor himself, had realized the change in the feeling of the people—what the wear and tear of hunger and fear, and the leprous creeping growth of despair had done to the mood of the citizens.

But when one morning the Emperor visited the Church of the Holy Wisdom, the people turned their faces from him in the street. They hissed and spat as he passed, and screamed curses after him, crying that it was because he had united the churches that the curse of God had fallen upon the City. The Emperor took not the least notice of this; but Stephanos and Vrethiki, knowing their master, flinched on his behalf, and hated his accusers.

Rumors began to reach them of quarrels and brawling between the Venetians and the Genoese; at first just rumors, and then complaints. At last several of the demarchs came to the Emperor, and told him that they could not keep the peace in the streets of their districts, so widespread and bitter had disorder and fighting become; the foreigners fought each other, or threatened and insulted each other, and the demarchs could not control them because they would pay no heed to orders given by Romans. The Emperor called the leaders of the Venetians and the Genoese before him, and asked what was the cause of the trouble between them. There was a sullen silence at first. The two nations had ranged themselves on either side of the hall like antagonists before a battle. They glowered at each other, and so sulfurous was the atmosphere in the room, thought Vrethiki, that had anyone put a match to it, it would have exploded like a charge of powder. "Come, gentlemen," said the Emperor sternly. He had robed himself in purple, and put on his crown for this audience. He sat on the Gospel-book side of his throne, and held in his right hand his orb of state, in his left his silken bag of dust. "What have you to say for yourselves?" he demanded, frowning at his turbulent allies.

"They provoke us," said one of the Langascos, the Genoese, at last. "They say it was our fault the attempt to burn the Turkish fleet failed. They taunt us with it …"

"It was your fault!" cried Minotto. "Because of you there was delay, and delay brought failure. Can you deny that? You said you wanted it put off so that you could join in, and that gave you time to get a message to your precious accomplices in Pera, and they gave the game away, like the stinking traitors they are!"

"It's a fine thing to be called a traitor by you!" cried Cattaneo, his hand on the hilt of his sword, "when you Venetian rats have been sneaking ships out to safety whenever you get the chance!"

"Our ships," snarled Minotto, "have their rudders unshipped, and their sails and gear folded and stored within the City, so that all men can see we mean to stay. And yours? They are all ready to run at a moment's notice!"

"We certainly have no intention of making our vessels unseaworthy when they may be needed at any time to fight. We aren't cowards!" retorted Langasco.

"You are all in league with the men of Pera, and they are hand in glove with the Sultan!" said Minotto, ostentatiously turning his back.

The Emperor sat listening to them with his lips tight and a curious gray tinge on his sallow cheeks. Vrethiki, looking anxiously at him, thought he might be going to faint. But his voice was steady enough as he suddenly cried out to them, "For the pity of God, gentlemen, is not the enemy without enough for you, that you must start a war between yourselves?"

There was a silence. The nobles and captains looked ashamed. There were bowed heads, flushed cheeks. "Indeed we must strive and work together," said the Emperor. "God knows we will die together if we fail. Come now, there are no traitors here, but only brave and honorable Christians. Let me see you friends again before you leave my presence."

Very slowly, very slowly and reluctantly, the two groups drew near each other. The movement was started by Justiniani, who had been standing quietly among the Genoese. He walked over and saluted Minotto gravely, and then took his hand. Then one by one the others followed suit.

But when they had trooped out, leaving Phrantzes, and Theophilus, and Notaras, and one or two other Romans standing round the throne, the Emperor said, despairingly, "We get weaker and less united by the day."

Phrantzes said, "My Lord, I think we should negotiate."

"Is it possible we will get any good of that?" said the Emperor doubtfully.

"I think there is a faint chance, my Lord," said Phrantzes. "There is a peace party in the Sultan's camp. He must be disappointed at finding us so tough a nut to crack; he has failed on both sea and land. It is true we are weary; but then he has to keep his vast army in the field, and well fed, and in good heart. Time wears heavily on him too, we may be sure."

"I will not deal openly with him," said the Emperor. "But if it can be done secretly .

"We can do it through the men of Pera," said Notaras. "We can find out what his terms would be."

"Very well, find out," said the Emperor wearily, rising to go to his prayers.

There seemed to be difficulty in getting an answer. A sealed letter was delivered to the Emperor two days later. The Sultan would give his word as a Moslem, that if the City were surrendered without conditions, the people and their property would be safe. The Emperor might go to the Morea if he wished, with his courtiers and his property. If the City were not surrendered it would be stormed.

"No," said the Emperor to that. And not a man of his council advised saying yes. But Notaras spoke up, declaring he was speaking for many of them, and urged the Emperor to leave the City. "If you fall, my Lord, perhaps to some stray arrow, the City and the Empire both are lost forever; if you are in safety, the loss of the City itself will not be the end. Surely your presence in their midst will rouse the Westerners as nothing else can? Perhaps the Hungarians will support you, perhaps the Serbs. Your presence in his rear may make the Sultan lift the siege at once."

"No," said the Emperor.

"My Lord, this advice is the advice of us all," said Phrantzes.

"Theophilus?" said the Emperor, looking round for him. "What do you say, dear cousin?"

"The same as all the rest," said Theophilus, quietly, fixing his unsmiling eyes on the Emperor.

"Justiniani?" said the Emperor, as though he would appeal to him.

"I will make ready one of my ships to take you safely hence, Lord Emperor," said Justiniani.

The Emperor bowed his head. Then he said, "No. Do not ask it of me. Ask me rather to remain with you. I am ready to die with you."

"My Lord, prudence bids you ..." Theophilus began.

"Prudence?" said the Emperor, looking up at him. "Prudence? You tell me to leave the City, the churches, the people, the monks and nuns, the holy icons ... I can see that what you advise would be for my safety, but what would the world say of me? Prudence? I would rather follow the example of the Good Shepherd, who laid down His life for His sheep."

Then Phrantzes and Theophilus were weeping openly, and Notaras looked at his master with a fleeting softness on his proud face.

"My Lord, if you will not go," said Justiniani in a while, "will you not at least remove your lodgings to a better place? You are too close within the walls here, too near the battered part. If they break through ..."

"I must be near the walls," said the Emperor. "I am already wearied out with riding, and I cannot give myself yet more miles to cover."

"Nearby you must indeed be," said Justiniani. "But need

you be just where they might break through? Suppose they got in at night? You are so near they would be upon you before there was time for warning, and if they found you sleeping, they would take you alive ... I pray you, for your servants' peace of mind, take your rest farther off."

"Very well," said the Emperor. "I will return to Blachernae. But I will have a tent pitched just within the St. Romanus Gate. If I am as near as that there will be time for warning."

SO THE NEXT DAY VRETHIKI AND STEPHANOS WERE BUSY again. a small contingent of Justiniani's men was dispatched to help them pitch the tent, and carry things, so the hard work was swiftly accomplished with laughter and Italian voices, chatting and chaffing in their tantalizing babel, that Vrethiki with his now well practiced Latin could nearly—so it seemed to him— but not quite understand. It was a tall wide tent of purple linen they had found. Outside, it had fringes and banners, all scarlet and gold. It seemed made for ceremonies, for a king going to a tournament in a green field, rather than for the dry verge of a roadway just within the wall of a doomed, dusty City. Stephanos curtained off a portion of it for the Emperor's bed, and he found a screen behind which to unroll his bedding and Vrethiki's, out of sight of the grand men who would doubtless be coming in and out. They kept only what was needed for the barest comfort; everything else went back to Blachernae.

It was while they were still disposing things neatly in the tent that there came suddenly a thunderclap of sound. Vrethiki saw the tent walls bulge inward, like sails catching the wind, felt a moment later the blast like a gust of wind, pressing on him, hurting his ears. He and Stephanos both rushed out of the tent. They could hear cries a little distance off, toward the Lycus valley. They scrambled hastily up the long flight of steps that climbed the back of the inner wall to the catwalk, and having reached the battlements looked anxiously down the slope to the valley bottom. A great pinkish cloud of dust hung over the wall. Through veils of thinning smoke they could see the great gun with a dribble of smoke still floating from its muzzle. It stood with its back embedded in timber balks and mud to hold its tremendous recoil. A Turkish soldier poured water on it that went up in a hiss of white steam, rolling off the hot metal.

"So they've mended it," said Stephanos gloomily. A cannonade of balls from the smaller cannon that were drawn up in endless rows rumbled toward them. They could see the shot arching toward the walls, and hear the crack of their impact. "Come on," said Stephanos. "Who wants to watch this dismal sight? We have work to do."

That day the bombardment was particularly heavy. The blasts of noise rolled ceaselessly over them like the waves beating one after another on the shore. The newly recast gun was fired five times. And the fleet in the Golden Horn was maneuvering too. Little skiffs bustled round it bringing supplies; it seemed they were making ready for battle. In the afternoon the Emperor was summoned by Lukas Notaras to see what was happening at the boom; there, too, a cannonade was being fired. The Turks had set up guns behind the walls of Pera, and were firing very high into the air right over the colony, so that the balls plummeted downward onto the ships at the boom. They were not, of course, accurately aimed, but they had sunk one vessel that day, and they were enough to threaten and alarm the sailors.

"An assault is coming," said the Emperor. "We must do all we can to be ready for it."

On the land walls the bombardment did not cease even with darkness. The enemy fired blindly all night, hoping no doubt to prevent Justiniani's repair gangs from making the damage good. But Justiniani made a stockade farther back, across the line of the smashed and fallen inner wall, instead of at the outer wall, and he mustered troops on the terrace between the walls on either side of the gap to take the attackers in the flank. When dawn came, therefore, there was no way open into the City but the same obstacle course as before— the partly filled-up fosse, full of loose rubble, treacherous footing, then earth walls, and the stockade, grimly defended. The Turks kept up the bombardment for another day. Then, in the middle of the night, the attack came.

Thirty thousand of them rushed the breach in the walls in the Lycus valley. The Emperor, who was sleeping in his tent, was woken at once by the noise, and Vrethiki and Stephanos helped him on with his armor by lamplight. Chain corselet, great golden breastplate—Vrethiki fumbling with the straps, all fingers and thumbs in his haste—then the purple surcoat, with the double eagle woven on it, and last the sword. Hastily they prepared him, and he went out into the night.

He was gone for some three hours, and Vrethiki, who had been left behind—Stephanos would not let him go after the Emperor in the dark, but took up the cup and flask and went himself—sat trembling alone in the tent, listening to the fearful din of battle, expecting every moment to see Turks bursting into the tent. He remembered that if he were not at the Emperor's side, the City might fall, and he felt that might even be true, and he ought to disobey Stephanos and go and find the Emperor. But the blackness of the night and the noise defeated him, and he stayed where he was. Never had three hours seemed longer!

At last the Emperor returned, escorted by a handful of his Varangians, and Vrethiki jumped up, and came to help him off with his burdensome armor. The noise in the distance was gradually dying away, receding through rise and fall like an ebbing tide. But the Emperor was weeping. Silent tears ran down the hollows in his ravaged face, and he said not a word. Vrethiki brought him warm wine from a pan upon the stove, but he would not have it, and went, still weeping, straight to his bed.

"What has happened?" said Vrethiki fearfully. He almost thought the City might have been taken, and that, after all, the Turks would come rushing in and slaughter them all.

"Rhangabe has been killed," whispered Stephanos, "an old friend of the Emperor's, who fought with him often, and saved his life, they say, at the battle of the Hexamilion. He cut the Sultan's standard-bearer in two, but then they surrounded him and killed him. The Emperor is grieved for him."

"Did they get through the wall?" Vrethiki asked hoarsely.

"No, they were driven back. God knows how. Sleep now; we must wake him at dawn."

It seemed to Vrethiki he had been sleeping only a moment or two when Stephanos shook him awake, and asked him to light a lamp and warm some wine. He could not keep his eyes open or raise his head from the pillow till Stephanos came again and pulled the covers off him to let the chill air of morning do the job.

"No dreams and waking last night, then?" said Stephanos, who was laying out clean linen for the Emperor.

"No," said Vrethiki. "It's strange. I haven't had any bad dreams for quite a while. Not since the Emperor let me go, and I chose to stay. And yet in a way I'm more afraid than ever."

"Real Turks are bad enough, you mean, but better than

nightmare ones?" said Stephanos, with his quizzical smile.

"They were real before—those pirate Turks," said Vrethiki. "I can remember now all about it, though I'd rather not—I try to turn my mind away from it."

"I was glad when you chose to stay," said Stephanos, without a flicker of emotion on his impassive face. "Selfish perhaps, but mostly I was glad for your sake. What you run away from is always just behind you."

"I had to stay," said Vrethiki. "And I expect you're right. Though I'm not sure what good can come of turning to face things when you can't hope to conquer."

"We can conquer ourselves," said Stephanos, lifting the curtain and going to wake the Emperor.

The Emperor rose and dressed. He sipped a little mulled wine and ate a round of bread while Stephanos and Vrethiki strapped on his armor. At the tent door Don Francisco and Theophilus awaited him, and his groom with his horse. Stephanos and Vrethiki were still eating their bread when they mounted to go with him.

They went first to the sea wall along the Golden Horn. But in spite of all the maneuvering there had been no attack. However, the cannon fire from beyond Pera had driven the ships from the boom; they had taken shelter in the lee of the Genoese walls, and in the little harbor below the Acropolis. Things were getting very difficult. The Emperor turned back, and rode round the Blachernae walls, looking at the increasing number of guns mounted on the Turkish pontoon bridge with a grim stare. Then up the slope, toward St. Romanus, and along the land walls. The battle of the night before had left the fosse thickly strewn with corpses. In the still, gray air of dawn a smell of blood tainted the air breathed by the defenders. Behind the stockade men sat or leaned in attitudes of the utmost weariness; beyond it, creeping cautiously among the dead, Turkish soldiers were recovering their fellows for burial, and dragging them away. One of the bodies shrieked as it was pulled, and the Emperor looked up. "Should we allow that?" he asked the nearest captain. The captain seemed to make an effort to answer. "They're unhealthy when they rot, Sire," he said. "They stink bad." The Emperor nodded. "I am watching them, to make sure what they're up to, Sire," said the captain. His voice was sluggish and low-pitched with fatigue.

The Emperor rode on. And along that middle stretch of wall he found half the sentries sleeping at their posts. Some of them were literally asleep on their feet, leaning forward through the battlements, or slumped on their cannon, where cannon there was, on the towers of the outer wall.

"Shall I dismount, and wake them, Sire?" asked Don Francisco, when they found the first few sleeping men.

The Emperor looked at his soldiers with a certain weary tenderness in his eyes. It happened that the sentry they were standing over had a gash in his cheek, and blood crusted his hand, where it lay flung out beside him, fingers lightly curled round the grasp of his bow. "They sleep the sleep that will not be denied," said the Emperor. "If you woke him, he would sleep again before we had ridden as far as the next tower. Leave him be."

And, indeed, a slowness and weariness seemed to hang over the tents of the enemy also; there was no stir or bustle over there, only, in a little while, the melancholy howling of the call to morning prayer.

THAT WHOLE DAY WAS QUIET. THE VENETIANS CAME TO THE Emperor, saying they thought it was no longer safe to keep powder and arms in their ships on the Golden Horn. For some reason the Turks had not yet attacked the boom from the Bosporus and at the same time from the Golden Horn, but if they did ... It would be better to shift the Venetian armaments to the Emperor's arsenal at Blachernae, and their ships into the harbor called Neorion; they would bring the crews to help the defense of the walls. The Emperor thanked them. Every man was needed. He asked them to go to the section of wall that was being pounded by the guns on the pontoon bridge.

Days passed. The Venetian captains had trouble persuading their men to move—they were used to sea fighting, and preferred to remain afloat. Besides, hardly a day went by without some sort of demonstration from the great fleet in the Bosporus. The infidel ships would sail out bravely toward the boom, trumpets and drums sounding; the weary Christian sailors would muster, at the alert, and then without so much as a shot fired, the Turks would withdraw. This ludicrous performance was yet enough to fray men's nerves, especially since everyone was hungry—however fairly shared out, the rations were small—and tired, and suffering from a special kind of irritability and weariness. Vrethiki, who felt it himself, understood it well enough. It came from being always tensed up to meet a crisis—to face disaster—and then finding that the crisis had passed, and the same readiness must be kept up another day, another night, another day. It made everyone heartsick. It was like watching at his father's sickbed, and coming slowly, and guiltily, almost to wish for what one feared—the end.

The Emperor drove himself ceaselessly. He hardly ate, he scarcely slept. He kept up his endless touring the walls. He encouraged his soldiers, he gave them his thanks, he remained practical and cheerful with his captains, shrewd and diplomatic in his council. But when the long day was over, and he sat toying with his supper, too tired by far to eat, or when he slept at last, then his two quiet slaves could see the truth on his face. The hollows of his cheeks had so deepened that the lower edge of his cheekbones stood out clearly. The rims of his eye-sockets circled his hollow eyes. One night Stephanos found him already asleep, leaning against the bed, having slept while he still prayed. He fetched Vrethiki to help him lift the Emperor onto the bed and cover him up. Then the two of them stood looking down at the ravaged face of the sleeping man. He had not woken even when they lifted him. "Oh, if only what must happen would be soon—would come tomorrow!" said Vrethiki.

"It won't come tomorrow," said Stephanos somberly. "The moon is still waxing. And this is the City of the Moon, they say, and will fall when the moon is on the wane."

"I can't make you out," said Vrethiki, when they had withdrawn from the Emperor's bedside, the boy having seized the bread the Emperor had not eaten, for he was ravenous. "One day you scorn all this prophecy; the next day you don't."

"When prophecies speak for the future," said Stephanos, who was sunk in gloom, "what use are they? But what is left for us now, except all those threatened fulfillments?"

"There's the one that says all will be well while I am close by the Emperor," said Vrethiki. "There's that one."

"They are all uncertain," said Stephanos, refusing to smile.

"I'll make you a prophecy certain of fulfillment," said Vrethiki, "Tomorrow will be a horrible day!" And washing down his bread with a gulp of wine, and wishing it were good English ale for once, he took himself to bed.

•

YET IT WAS A FINE DAY, AS FAR AS WEATHER WENT. BUT WITH noise, and dust, and hours and hours on horseback, and little time to rest or eat, and continuous agitated talking in foreign tongues, it was, as far as Vrethiki was concerned, as horrible as any other. At sunset the Emperor took a few hours' rest before going to the night service in the Church of the Holy Wisdom, where those priests who would accept the Union were keeping almost as remorseless a vigil as the fighters on the walls. So the Emperor's party put on state robes again, and set out by torchlight through the dark streets, under a sky thickly encrusted with stars, and a bright moon, nearly at full.

In shades of gray and silver the configurations of the City, its soaring columns, and swelling domes, passed by them as they rode, the arches brimming with shadows like silver cups with wine. Ahead, the enormous bulking mass of the Church of the Holy Wisdom, flooded with moonlight on the arc of its mighty dome, rose up before them, like a ghost of itself. Within, all was golden: warm lamplight, faithful and hopeful candlelight, the floating odor of incense, and the sonorous mournful music weaving structures in the formless air. And, "How huge it is, and beautiful!" thought Vrethiki, entering. "I always think I have remembered it, and yet always find that I have shrunk and diminished it in memory."

The service was long, and after a while the Emperor withdrew to the gallery to rest a little.

The Emperor's gallery was richly adorned with mosaic. All round were portraits of earlier, happy Emperors and their consorts, gleaming. On one wall, in a wide bay of the gallery, head and shoulders against a ground of gold, a huge figure stared down at Vrethiki. In one hand it clasped a jeweled book. The bearded face was hollow-cheeked, saturnine, like the Emperor's; the forehead was grooved. An expression of ineffable sternness, muted ferocity, suffused this visage, and its large dark eyes were fixed on Vrethiki. Wherever he moved in the space of the wide gallery, still the eyes fixedly stared straight at him.

"Who's that?" whispered Vrethiki to Stephanos in an interval when the choir's song was hushed.

"It is Christ," said Stephanos. "Who else could it be? Do they not picture Christ in your miserable churches?"

"Not like that!" murmured Vrethiki. He shrank from that stark fierce image. "We would show Him crucified, or with His disciples, or in the manger ..."

"This image does not mean that Christ was once in Galilee," Stephanos answered. "It means that He is here, now."

Shuddering at the thought, Vrethiki raised his eyes again, timidly, to that fearful picture; and saw that the expression seemed, now, to be not fierce, but pitiful, not remote and stern, but melting into compassion for something terrible that it looked upon.

"Oh, what will happen to us," cried Vrethiki in his heart, "that it looks on us like Christ looking on Jerusalem?"

ALMOST IN ANSWER TO THIS THOUGHT CAME THE SOUND OF running footsteps along the gallery toward the Emperor's marble doors; an agitated messenger brought news of an attack, not in the Lycus valley but at Blachernae, where the wall turned. The Emperor sent Vrethiki to fetch Phrantzes and Notaras, who were praying in the nave of the church, and the little group galloped frantically toward the far end of the City.

They reached the walls at the same moment as Justiniani, arriving from his section. The Turks were hurling thousands of men at a breach that had been made just before sunset.

They had crossed the fosse and forced their way over the outer wall; a desperate fight was going on along the line of the fallen inner wall. If the defenders failed to hold them they would be through into the City at a bound.

"The Kerkoporta!" cried Justiniani. "Out and we'll take them in the flank!" Shouting and yelling above the chaos, he collected a few of the reserves and disappeared round the corner of the palace buildings, making his way to the sally port. Spurring his horse, the Emperor rode after him, crying words that were lost in the ear-splitting din. Stephanos rushed after him, and Vrethiki followed Stephanos. But when they reached the descent to the Kerkoporta, through which Justiniani's men had just surged, yelling wildly, they found Varangian John there, holding the Emperor's horse by the bridle, and shouting, "No, Lord Emperor, no!"

"Let go!" cried the Emperor. "Let me go!"

"For the pity of Christ, Sire," said Stephanos, coming up beside him. "Into that turmoil? Unarmed, and wearing the purple? Keep back, my Lord, do!"

And even as they argued with him, the Turkish trumpets outside the wall sounded the retreat. The attack melted away into the darkness, the uproar distanced, and faded.

Justiniani reappeared in a minute or two, grinning widely, saying, "We put a cat after that pigeon then!" His eyes were shining. Vrethiki realized for the first time that Justiniani actually liked fighting; he glowed, he shone with it. Surely there was no braver man in all the world! Soon he had an arm round the shoulders of two Greek captains, and was calling them fine fellows, congratulating them on holding the breach. A repair gang was sent for, and the Emperor rode up and down, talking to soldiers and looking at the gap in the wall with an anxious eye.

"Too narrow," said Justiniani. "They need a really big gap to get advantage of their numbers."

Just as the Emperor was leaving, the repair gang came up: a long line of citizens carting earth and stones. Vrethiki saw by the light of the torches they carried that half of them at least were women, and some children, younger even than himself. Seeing them staggering, bent under their loads of earth and stone, Vrethiki felt ashamed to be tired merely from long hours riding or standing. And when he returned to the Emperor's tent, he insisted on Stephanos sitting down while he made the supper himself, and got the beds ready.

Chapter 16

The next day, the still-reluctant Venetian sailors were finally talked into leaving their ships; they went to help the defense of the Blachernae quarter, and once they were gone the Sultan moved the guns he had placed at the Valley of the Springs and brought them down to the Lycus valley. His ships were still sailing up and down the Bosporus, making shadow-boxer attacks on the boom.

A few days after the failure of the assault on the Blachernae walls Minotto came to the Emperor in the early morning, deeply agitated. He said his sentries had heard noises, strange noises, below the walls at night. They had lit flares to see what was happening, and had seen nothing; not a mouse moving. But the sounds went on. And at dawn, when they reported to him, he had seen, some way behind the Turkish lines, a mound of freshly turned earth that had appeared in the last few days. "I think they are digging mines, Sire," he said. "Tunneling under the walls."

At that moment Justiniani arrived, and the tale was told over to him.

"Tunneling to get in?" asked the Emperor.

"Perhaps," said Minotto. "Or perhaps to place explosives under the walls, and blow them up."

"What can be done about it?" asked the Emperor in alarm.

"I've got an expert sapper in my company," said Justiniani. "Brought along on double wages in case of this sort of thing. He's John Grant. I'll send him to you at once."

"Grant?" said Minotto. "What manner of name is that?"

"He's a Scotsman, I think," said Justiniani.

JOHN GRANT CAME ONLY JUST IN TIME. HE FOUND A TUNNEL that had nearly reached the wall, near the Caligarian Gate. He got men digging a countermine, broke into the Turkish workings, and threw in Greek fire which burnt the roof props, so that the whole tunnel collapsed, and buried the men in it alive. But any pleasure this achievement gave the Emperor's advisers was muted by the thought that if there was one tunnel there might be many, and there could be no certainty of finding them all. John Grant with an interpreter was sent to tour the walls, telling all the sentries what kind of thing to watch for, what to listen for; and tired and tense as they already were, that made them still more jumpy.

IT SEEMED EACH DAY THAT NOT ANOTHER DAY COULD BE borne; yet every day men somehow managed what was needful, somehow lived through it. Then at dawn on the eighteenth of May, excited soldiers arrived to summon the Emperor to the wall. They waved their hands high in the air, urgently describing something. The Emperor, who was at breakfast, put aside the dish, and went with them. "What is it now?" wondered Vrethiki, following. "And I do wish he would eat. He will waste away and die on horseback if this goes on much longer!"

They had only to ride the few yards to the wall to see

what was amiss. A huge siege engine had appeared at the St. Romanus Gate, overnight. It was a scaling tower—a great square wooden scaffold, higher than the outer wall. It was weighed down and steadied with a load of earth and stones, covered with bull hides to protect it from fire, and mounted on wheels, so that it could be trolleyed forward. The platform on top was higher than the battlements, and gave the Turkish bowmen and slingmen who were perched there the advantage over the defenders. And from the top of it hung scaling ladders, ready for use. Certainly Vrethiki needed no interpreter. One had only to look, to see what a terrible difference it made. The stockade made so laboriously, night after night, gave no shelter now to the defenders.

"All the men in the City could not have made such a thing in a month," cried the Emperor, in dismay. "And they have made it in a single night!"

His voice was cut off by the firing of the great gun from across the fosse on their left. The overpowering flash, bang, roar, and cloud of black smoke rolled over them, and hardly had the sound died away when another thunderous roar followed; the ground quaked beneath their feet, and hordes of soldiers rushed frantically toward them, with a great billowing cloud of pinkish dust rising behind. One of the towers of the wall had been brought down into the moat. And this time the defenders could not simply shore it all up again, and shoot down the Turks who tried to fill in the fosse. The tables were turned. The Turks on the scaling tower shot at them when they tried to rig up a stockade, and the defenders could not get near enough to hinder the operations outside. All day, therefore, they watched helplessly as the bustling innumerable hordes labored to fill up the fosse. The fallen tower helped the besiegers and they brought up quantities of earth and rubble, rubbish and brushwood, everything they could find to lay on top of it, and fill up the ditch, and make a level causeway over which they could push their scaling tower right up to the wall. By nightfall they had succeeded. The ditch was bridged, the scaling tower was within a few paces of the outer wall, and Justiniani had been forced to withdraw his men from a wide stretch of the terrace there, and man the inner battlement instead.

He summoned John Grant. The Emperor, who had been on the wall all day, would not leave, but stayed and took a soldier's supper on the battlements among his men, and would have set his hand to carrying rubble for repairs if Stephanos and Phrantzes had not stopped him. He was like Justiniani, Vrethiki observed, in that danger excited him. An almost feverish light burned in his dark eyes.

Grant surveyed the filling of the moat. Then he asked for gunpowder, and a handful of picked men. He scrambled down into the darkness with them and disappeared. All the while the defenders were at work on the fallen tower on the wall. The left-hand angle of the stonework was still standing to half its original height, and building onto this, using blocks of stone whenever they could recover them from the moat, the frantic workers produced a stoutly built, roughly finished strong point where the tower had been.

At two in the morning Grant clambered back onto the terrace and said he was ready; everyone was to take shelter, heads down. Because the roadway across the moat had been partly laid on brushwood he had managed to set charges underneath it. There was a dull, rumbling bang, and then fire. The scaling tower caught light easily enough; the beams of it blazed above their heads, and they heard it crash downward when it fell. An hour later, when the flames had died to a pile of glowing ashes, work parties climbed down into the moat, and began the task of clearing the fosse again.

So at dawn there was no scaling tower, no way across the moat, and no yawning gap in the wall. "We too can work miracles in the space of a single night," said the Emperor.

But the soldiers were desperately tired. Four more scaling towers had appeared along the line of the walls at other places, though as yet no attempt was made to fill the fosse in front of them, and there was perilously little gunpowder left in the Emperor's arsenal.

JOHN GRANT FOUND A MINE ON EACH OF THE NEXT FOUR days. They were all under the wall round the Blachernae quarter, where the wall was single instead of double, and mostly where the wall jutted outward and for a short distance there was no moat. Grant flooded one mine, smoked out another, and blew up two. Then one evening he came to the Emperor at the evening council, bringing with him a Turkish officer in chains. Justiniani explained he had dug a countermine which had cut off a number of Turks in the end of their tunnel, and he had captured them alive. "This man is an officer, Sire," he finished off. "But we cannot persuade him to talk. If there are other mines, Sire, he knows where."

The Emperor asked nobody's advice. His soldiers stood waiting, looking at him expectantly, anxiously. An expression of distress and distaste showed on Phrantzes' face. Theophilus had turned away. Notaras looked resolved, but tense. The Emperor sat staring at the Turkish officer, who stood defiantly, his swarthy face set, his head held high. He was sweating visibly, and a muscle in his cheek twitched. "He is afraid," thought Vrethiki curiously. It had not struck him till then that one of them might be as afraid as he.

"Why is he here?" whispered Vrethiki to Stephanos, but he got no answer. The Emperor looked grieved. He rested his forehead in his hands, and then looked up again at the prisoner.

Then, "God forgive me, but he must be persuaded," he said. Vrethiki saw the relief on Grant's face, the flicker of faint surprise but approval on Justiniani's. They dragged the Turk away. Only Theophilus challenged the decision with his eyes.

Next morning Grant came to report that all the mines were found, blocked and destroyed.

IN THE AFTERNOON THE EMPEROR WAS CALLED TO CARDINAL Isadore's position. The men on the sea walls had sighted a ship, a small ship, coming alone. She was flying Turkish colors, but keeping well off the Asian shore, and setting a course as if for the Golden Horn. Horses were brought, and the Imperial party made ready to go and see what was happening. But though he was briefly tempted by the thought of the open dewy air blowing off the sea, Vrethiki was so chafed and fretted by this life of continuously riding, continuously walking, like a captive in chains, just behind the Emperor, that he pretended to be having trouble with his stirrup, and as the others moved off he dismounted and fiddled with the strap. Then, remounting, he followed some distance behind. As soon as they started down the Mese, he turned off down a side street, and a feeling of freedom and joy swept over him straight away, to be just once on his own, deciding where he would go, what he would do.

Almost at once he found himself in a street of wooden houses. A little way along was a small church made of the palest possible rose-pink brick, its walls all patterned and embossed and its little domes nestling together above. A trailing plant festooned with purple flowers hung over a garden wall beyond it. The noise of the guns was distant; Vrethiki could hear the bees in the blossoms at his side. The street was empty, though behind the lattice shutters of upper windows Vrethiki discerned one or two shadowy movements. And these houses were not tumbledown at all, but rather neat and pretty; just the kind of thing, Vrethiki thought, that his own family might live in, a house of the middle sort, neither grand nor miserable. And this wasn't what he was looking for at all. He needed somewhere scruffy, somewhere a trifle villainous; for, it had come to him all at once, what he wanted was food. Of course, all the food in the City was rationed, but Vrethiki knew enough of life to know that even so there was bound to be somewhere where things could be had. He slipped his hand inside his shirt, where he had sewn the little red bundle with the coronation bounty in it, and the coin he had been given for nursing the Emperor—how long ago!—on the voyage from the Morea. He grinned to himself a little, thinking how eagerly he had hoarded it, and how it had been donkey rides and ships' passages all the way home to England, and how now, if he could get a fish for it, or a chicken ... And all the while he was riding on.

He passed a water-seller, leading a donkey with great clay jars slung on its either flank, and then the road wound down-hill, descending gently to the Marmara shore. It seemed as if good luck had brought the boy to the sort of place he was looking for: the streets opened out here, there was a lettuce plot, and a man with a flock of four or five skinny sheep. Beyond was a house with a goat tethered at the door. Vrethiki looked into the courtyard of this house, and saw three hens pecking in the dust. His mouth watered. He had found the quarter where farming folk lived, and none of them looked peaked or starving, he remarked. So he dismounted, and leading his horse by the bridle, walked over to an old woman, sitting in her doorway, and with his halting Greek, and an elaborate mime of eating and paying, asked if she had food to sell.

She jumped up, shaking her head, and waving her arms, and let loose a great stream of Greek of which he understood not a word. It was very clear though that she was saying no. But why was she advancing on him shaking her fist? He backed away, and turning to a man in the little crowd that had gathered, he began to make the request again, only to meet the same infuriated outburst. This time they made it plain by gestures that he had better be off, and when he mounted his pony, and rode smartly away toward the Marmara, glittering in the distance, he was followed by catcalls, and handfuls of pebbles thrown after him.

Still determined, he rode on, till he reached the sea wall, and turning, followed a road that led along it. This soon came out on one of the harbors in the southern wall where he found an old man sitting, splicing rope, and two small children throwing pebbles in the water. The boy asked again for food, this time showing his money. The old man shook his head. He waved an arm toward the arches that led out to sea, and said, "Turki!" Vrethiki said, "Basileus"—the Greek for "Emperor" at least he did know. Then he put his hands on his stomach, and grimaced sadly; then he pressed his fingers into his cheeks to make hollows in them.

The old man looked shrewdly at him from under bushy brows; then he simply got up and walked away. Vrethiki gloomily stayed looking at the water, baffled, but unwilling to give up. Presently he saw the old man returning, accompanied by an equally elderly monk, who walked on two sticks, and whose legs seemed to bend at every step. The two came slowly toward him, and the newcomer asked in a quavering voice, in Latin, "You want food?"

"Yes," said Vrethiki. "I can pay."

"Did the Emperor send you?"

"No, no," said Vrethiki. "He doesn't know where I am, and neither does anyone else. But he looks so tired and thin … I would like to find him some supper."

"You have not come to spy on us?"

"No, I swear it," cried Vrethiki, light dawning. That was what the fuss had been about; everybody knew he was the Emperor's page, and they thought he was tricking them, to catch them out in shady dealing.

The monk stared at him for a long time. Then, "We will catch a fish for you," he said, "but you must swear not to say where you got it."

The old man stared anxiously up at the wall, where one or two soldiers stood. "Give us the money now," the monk said to Vrethiki. He offered his hoard. They took the bronze coins and one of the silver. Then the monk led Vrethiki to a tiny boat tied up in the harbor while the other climbed up the sea wall, and talked to the guard there, and, Vrethiki guessed, bribed him. Then the three of them, with Vrethiki and the fisherman paddling, put out to sea through a narrow low archway in the fortified quay, for the main entrance to the harbor had been blocked with balks of timber and scuttled ships.

They put out only a little way. Behind them, the gray mass of the sea wall with its bands of red loomed up out of its own wavy reflection. The fisherman cast his nets, and the monk kept a watch out for Turkish galleys. They landed a large fish almost at once, but the monk said they could not go in till they had got three—"One for you, one for us, one for the sentry." And there were not so many fish to be got like that, hugging the foot of the wall where the water was shallow. While they waited, trailing the net, the little boat edged along, drifting toward the tip of the City. "Paddle harder," said the monk to Vrethiki. "We mustn't be far from that arch if a Turkish galley comes."

"The current is strong here," said Vrethiki.

"Not as strong as over there, where the Bosporus flows out," said the monk, bending over the net so low that his beard was almost in the water. "This current along the wall is only an eddy, my brother tells me, made by the suck of the stronger one. Out there it goes so fast on the surface that an orange thrown overboard will catch up with the ship, and knock against it."

"The current would speed the ship also," said Vrethiki, grinning. "Tell your brother that's a real fisherman's tale!"

"Deeper down there are cross currents. A big ship, riding deep, is pulled several ways at once."

"That sounds like perilous water," said Vrethiki, looking at the serene surface of the sea.

"You have seen the little birds on the water at even-fall?" said the monk. "Souls of dead sailors. Souls of the drowned."

At that moment the net tugged a little. They drew it in with three more fish tangled in it, and then paddled for safety, not before time, because the venal sentry on the walls above them began just then to call out that an enemy vessel was coming.

Thus it was that Vrethiki set out to ride back with a fine fresh halibut in his saddlebag. But he thought better of going home again the way he had come, past all those angry folk, especially with a visible bulge in his bag, so he rode along the wall as far as the Studion Monastery, which lay serenely in its gardens on its lovely windswept slope, facing the sea and the prospect of islands, and then he cut toward the wall, and rode back by way of the wide paved road that ran along at the foot of the inner wall. So he came to be riding past Justiniani's quarters, which were great arched rooms in the thickness of the wall, facing the City, and there he saw standing a cart piled with rubbish, a patient donkey between the shafts. A body was thrown on the tailboard of the cart, among the refuse and the mutton bones. Flies crawled over it. A cannon boomed, and they buzzed a few inches into the festering air, and then settled again. The body was hideous with injury. The hands tied together had no fingernails, the naked feet neither nails nor toes. The ribs were striped and flayed with blows and burns, and even though the head was hanging upside down over the edge of the cart, Vrethiki knew who it was, or had been. It was the Turkish officer they had captured the day before. Vrethiki's stomach lurched. He turned his eyes away and rode past.

"WHERE HAVE YOU BEEN?" DEMANDED STEPHANOS, AS HE entered the Emperor's tent. "Come on at once. The Emperor is going to Blachernae. That ship was the brigantine that left here twenty days ago, in search of news, the one you might have been on. Her captain is on his way to report to the Emperor."

The Emperor sat in the great golden throne room of the palace, and the captain and his crew trooped in, and bowed low. In a subdued voice, the captain told the Emperor they had sailed the Aegean for days and days, and found neither a fleet coming to aid the City, nor in any harbor any news of one. "When we thought it useless to search longer, Lord Emperor," he said, and his voice shook as he spoke, "we debated all together what we should do. And one man said it was useless to return to a City doubtless already fallen and laid waste; but all the rest of us said that whether it was to life or death, it was our duty to return to you, and tell you."

The Emperor sank his head in his hands and wept. He rose from his throne, and going to the captain embraced him like a brother. He thanked him for his loyalty, and still weeping silent tears, and still holding the captain's hand, he said, "No earthly aid, then, will be given us. We must put our faith in Christ, and in His Holy Mother, and in St. Constantine, the founder and helper of our City."

That night the Emperor prayed for hours, on his knees before the icon of the Virgin that hung in his rooms at Blachernae. It was late before they rode back in the soft moonlight, to sleep in the tent by the walls.

"I feel ill," said the Emperor to Stephanos, as Stephanos drew off his boots.

"You should eat more, my Lord," said Stephanos.

"To cure despair?" said the Emperor, with a trace of a bitter smile.

"To give you strength to bear it," said Stephanos almost sternly.

"I can't eat more bread than I do," said the Emperor. "It lies on my stomach like a stone."

And just at that moment Vrethiki brought his saddlebag in, and proudly showed Stephanos his fish.

"But I promised not to say where I got it," he added.

So the Emperor had a piece of fish, grilled on the fire in his tent, to fortify him against despair. And when he was in bed and sleeping, Vrethiki and Stephanos ate up the rest.

Chapter 17

There was a quarrel the next day. The Venetians had made wooden mantles, covered with skins and padding, behind which to fight where the walls had lost their battlements. They asked some citizens to carry them to the walls, and the Romans refused unless they were paid. Why should they take orders from foreigners, and followers of the heathenish Latin rite? The Venetians fought a whole day without their protective cover, and their resentment knew no bounds. The Emperor patched it up, talked them into making peace with each other, but only with difficulty. The sullen citizens told him they must have time or money, to find food for their families. That was why they would not work unpaid.

"How will your families fare if the defense of the City fails?" he asked them.

"What is it to us, if the City stands, and our families starve?" they muttered.

That night was the night of the full moon. The Emperor was coming away from the night Liturgy in the Church of the Holy Apostles, the streets were full of people dispersing from the churches, and suddenly a great crying and wailing and groaning was set up; everyone was pointing and looking skyward, with voices full of dismay. The silver moon of Byzantium, shining in her gossamer sky among the stars, was being slowly blacked out, eclipsed. A black shadow crept across half her face; the rest was suffused with a blood-red stain. The Emperor and his party rode home in thickening darkness with random cries of anguish ringing in their ears. At the tent door, Vrethiki paused and looked up. The superstition of the Romans no longer filled him with derision, but with a kind of heaviness of heart. He tried to imagine what he would feel if he really thought the moon was the symbol of his City, and he saw, where the moon should be, a circle of coppery red, glowing somberly like the ashes of a dying fire. He stood looking up for some time, and then as he watched, the darkness began to pass off the moon. A bright silver sliver of clear moon appeared, but between the darkness and the brightness was a wide band of blood-red light.

EARLY NEXT MORNING THE EMPEROR SUMMONED HIS COUNCIL, and all the priests of importance in the City—those who would come when he summoned. "We must do something to steady the people," he said. "They will become a terrified rabble if we cannot calm and encourage them. We must carry the sacred icon of the Virgin round the City, and to the Church of the Holy Wisdom. The people all together can pray for a blessing. Can this be done?"

"It shall be done," the priests promised him.

"At this time, above all we should be united," said the Emperor. "Fathers, will you ask Scholarios to walk with you?" But at this there was an outburst of indignation from Archbishop Leonard, one of those who had come with Cardinal Isadore.

"We can take no part in a ceremony in which that enemy

of the Union partakes—that turncoat, that arch heretic!"

The Emperor sighed. Notaras spoke. "Good Father," he said to Leonard, "we are all in one peril. Cannot we all pray together, and forget our differences?"

"There can be no differences!" cried the Latin bishop. "The Union of our Churches was agreed, agreed and signed to. Those who will not accept it now are damned heretics! We should spurn them, punish them till they are of a better mind. As for your procession: I will not walk with Scholarios—I would as soon go in procession with the devil himself!"

Cardinal Isadore put a hand on his bishop's arm, as though to restrain him, but Notaras cried, "For my part I would sooner see the Turkish turban in the Church of the Holy Wisdom than the Latin miter!"

And at that a silence fell, and men looked at each other warily. "Oh, Lukas, Lukas," said the Emperor. "And that wish too likely to be granted!"

"Make your procession, Lord Emperor," said Cardinal Isadore quietly. "I and my clergy will take part, and look neither to right nor to left to see who else is with us."

Yet the outburst cast a shadow on the procession; and it was wasted too, for Scholarios would not come, but sent prophetic damnations from his tightly locked cell. And hardly had they got the great icon on its wooden platform, resting on the shoulders of four priests, than someone stumbled, and it slipped, and fell in the mire, face down. A horrified gasp ran round the crowded faithful. The icon had to be blessed before it was lifted, and then it seemed very heavy, like lead, and it took six men to raise it up again. It was a picture so covered and cased in silver and crusted over with jewels that only the Virgin's face was visible, and that was a little brown oval, in which her features could be dimly descried through a coating of hundreds of years of candle smoke and incense. But it was immensely holy, Stephanos told Vrethiki, because it had been painted from the life, by St. Luke.

After that the procession did start to move, intoning Kyrie Eleison. They had hardly gone a step when the sun went in, and, looking up, Vrethiki saw the sort of thick melted dark-gray cloud that he hardly remembered seeing since he left England, and a large raindrop splashed his cheek. At first, so used had they all become to the sound of bombardment all day, they did not realize it was thunder that rolled overhead, but soon it growled and boomed louder than the guns of the Sultan. Rain pattered down. The icon itself was being carried under a silken canopy, and when the rain suddenly hardened, and changed from gentle drops to a solid down-pour, the procession only wavered, and continued onward. The rain daggers churned up the road to puddles and mud in moments, and soaked the worshippers to the skin. Children clung to their parents, pulling folds of their mothers' clothes round their heads. Vrethiki, bare-headed, could feel the rain tapping on his scalp through his hair, and a rivulet ran chilly down his spine. The head of the procession reached a forum, where roads came up from the Marmara, and from the Horn.

Here an icy-cold gust of wind suddenly reached them, and with it came hailstones, huge hailstones as large as eggs, which stung and bruised, and battered the cringing people. The canopy over the icon was ripped to ribbons, the banners the people were carrying were beaten down into the mud, their lamps extinguished. Vrethiki put his hands over his head, trying to ward off the stinging impact of the cascade of ice bullets. For a moment more the great thronging mass of people swayed and bowed under the wrath of heaven; then everyone began to run for shelter, helter-skelter, each for himself.

Vrethiki turned down a side street, and pressed into the first doorway arch he came to, whimpering from pain and cold. As he stood there, under the columned doorway arch of the house, with the rain and hail lashing down an inch from his nose, a cistern somewhere must have flooded or burst, for suddenly a great torrent of water cascaded past him down the street, and a little girl, washed off her feet, was being dragged slithering in the foul muddy cataract down the hill. Vrethiki leaped after her, and struggling on the slippery roadway, with the fierce pull of the water tugging at his ankles, he dragged her to safety with him. A few moments later a distraught woman came struggling after her. Then, as suddenly as it had started, the hailstorm ceased. Vrethiki emerged from shelter into what now seemed the gentle downfall of rain, and went to look for the Emperor's retinue, leaving the mother comforting her terrified child.

There was nothing left of the procession that was to have calmed and comforted the people. Banners and flowers lay draggled and trampled in the mud. Forlorn little groups of drenched and dripping people stood in doorways, or fled homeward. And a cold wind still blew from Thrace, driving the storm before it. It blew all the rest of the day, tormenting the men on the wall, exposed to its cruel fingering in their cold armor, and their clammy rain-soaked clothes.

THE NEXT MORNING VRETHIKI, WAKING, WONDERED FOR a moment where he was. He looked uncomprehending at the stretch of purple cloth gently sagging overhead. He had thought to see the little casement of the dormer window of his attic at home; and what had come to him so strongly was the thought of the ripe fruit in the apple orchard. He got up, puzzled. No one else was yet stirring, so he poked up the ashes in the fire, and put fuel on. He went to the door of the tent. Outside the ground was dewy, and the air was thick. White drifting mist veiled everything. He could see only a yard or two, and the noise of the guns—still spasmodic, for the day's work was only beginning—came curiously muffled, yet clear, for all lesser noises had been snuffed out. Fog; the faint smell of it tingled in his memory, like autumn mornings in England.

The moment the others woke up, he gathered that it was an unheard-of thing in the City, in spring. They would have been cast into deep gloom by it, were it not that after yesterday no deeper gloom was possible. The explanation seemed clear to everyone—the Divine Presence was veiling its departure from the City. All day, a still and windless day, the fog lingered. It dissolved the substance of the walls and buildings, which seemed to hover palely, to come and go, to quaver on each movement of the swirling air, like dreams or ghosts. And men loomed up at each other along the walls, all out of scale and context, like ghosts on the march. The enemy could not be seen at all, though they could be heard; apart from gunfire the sound of their voices, of the racket of comings and goings, drifted eerily out of the white emptiness beyond the wall.

At nightfall a wind sprang up and rolled the fog away. Outside the walls the myriad campfires of the enemy sprang into view. And in the sky above, the stars.

YET THE ORDEAL WAS NOT YET OVER. IN THE CLEAR NIGHT that followed the misty day, suddenly the citizens were horrified to see a strange red flickering light that played upon the dome of the Church of the Holy Wisdom. The Emperor stood at the window of his throne room in Blachernae, and saw it from far off. It seemed as though the base of the dome were circled with a bright fiery band of light, that mounted the dome, flowing upward, and converging on the great cross at the apex. "What does this mean?" murmured the Emperor. "What does this mean? I am afraid that Heaven itself has turned against us."

He was still staring out of his high window when a group of his courtiers came to him. Phrantzes, his gray grave secretary, and Theophilus, and Don Francisco, the Spaniard who called himself the Emperor's cousin. Lukas Notaras was there, and Minotto the Venetian, and Justiniani, and Cardinal Isadore.

"Have you seen that?" the Emperor asked them. "What can it mean?"

"Whatever it may mean, there is no hope for us now," said Phrantzes. "We have come to beg you, to implore you"—and at these words they all knelt down suddenly as if in church—"to go to a place of safety while there is time."

"My dear Lord," said Theophilus, "think how it has happened before that the Emperor was driven from the City, and yet the Empire continued, and the City was won back again. Go to the Morea; your brothers will come to you, and perhaps Hunyadi, and the Pope ..."

Vrethiki, watching the Emperor, saw the color ebb from his cheeks. Beneath his golden sallow skin the pallor gave him a deathly greenish tinge. His lips were white and bloodless. Suddenly the whites of his eyes flashed; his pupils rolled. He bent at the knees, and fell forward with a soft thud on the floor, while Theophilus was still speaking.

They ran to lift him, to lay him on his couch. He was breathing through parted lips; a light froth of spittle bubbled on his mouth.

"Bring water!" cried Phrantzes, wringing his hands in distress. Stephanos came with an alabaster bottle in his hands. He thrust his way through the clustered noblemen crowded round the couch. "He has only fainted, I think," he said, bending over his master. "Oh, why must you press him so?" And, unstoppering the bottle, he dashed the contents in the Emperor's face. It was rose water. A faint scent of embalmed flowers rose from the pillow. The Emperor's dark lashes flickered, and then his eyes swam open. It took him some moments, staring vacantly round at the circle of anxious faces, to recollect himself. Then he said, "No. If it be the will of God, whither could I fly? It was said long ago this City, this Empire, would make a splendid winding sheet. It shall be mine."

"Yet, Lord Emperor, hear what we have to say ..." began Notaras, urgently.

"I have said I will not abandon you," said the Emperor. His voice was weak. "Have pity on me—do not urge it further."

Stephanos was kneeling by the pillow, wiping his master's forehead with a cloth wrung out in rose water. Vrethiki, watching the courtiers, saw them give up, saw the heads bowed, and shoulders drooped. Phrantzes was in tears. And the boy would have liked to take his hand, to embrace these lordly men, each one. They loved their master, and they had tried to save him. Vrethiki knew.

IT SEEMED TO VRETHIKI, TOSSING AND TURNING ON HIS mattress in the tent, watching the canvas shift on the flowing night air, that the guns were worse than ever. So ceaseless was the banging and rumbling that the noise was almost the element he lived in, like air. But usually they were less rowdy in the night, and that night they were at full force. Hearing him restlessly tossing, Stephanos reached out a hand to him in the dark. The boy held it till he fell asleep.

THE NEXT DAY WAS SUNDAY; THE EMPEROR AND HIS ENTOURAGE went to hear the Liturgy before going to the walls. It was halfway through the morning, in bright clear weather, as though the storms and portents had never been, when they rode down to the wall in the Lycus valley. A great spectacle stretched out before them in the Turkish camp. Line upon line, the mind-numbing hundreds of their hordes were drawn up across the plain, plumed headdresses rippling like ripe wheat in the wind, the kaleidoscope colors of their dress like gaudy flowers. Banners and spears and standards bristled over their heads; their helms and weapons gleamed and glinted in the sun. And along the lines they could see the Sultan riding, on a horse draped all over with embroidered silks. Trumpeters rode before him and behind, blasting discordantly. Every so often the Sultan stopped and addressed his gathered ranks. And a vast cheer answered him, a cheer that came from so many distended throats it seemed not human, but like the shrieking of stormwinds over mountaintops, or the sense-less roar of the sea. AllallaaIlaallalaaa! rang toward the silent listeners on the walls.

The Emperor's party halted beside Justiniani, halfway along the stockade. "Whatever pleases them so hugely bodes little good for us," said Justiniani grimly.

They were all looking intently at what was happening far off. Nearby, Urban's great gun, leveled at the stockade, and loaded, was being fused and fired. They heard the bang, and the whistle of the flying ball. Then there was chaos, earth and splinters flying everywhere, the horses whinnying, rearing and bolting. Stephanos had leaped forward, arms extended. Something hit Vrethiki's cheek, like a punch in the face, and his eyes were full of dust and grit. Something wet and sticky was on his collar. He tugged at it, and then rubbed his eyes, blinking. When he could see again, he saw a terrible sight. A stretch of the palisade was down, and the ground was thick with the writhing and groaning bodies of the men who had been lined up behind it. Already their companions were bending over them, and voices were raised, urgently or in distress. A few dazed men were staggering around in a state of shock. A splinter had struck Justiniani's arm, and he was bleeding slightly through his chain mail. The Emperor was standing stock still, covered thickly in dust and grime from head to foot, but unharmed. At his feet, on the ground, lay a body pierced in twenty places by jagged fragments of the shattered ball that had been flying toward the Emperor.

Vrethiki stared at the dead man. A great strip of his face had been torn away. "Why is he wearing Stephanos' clothes?" thought Vrethiki dully. He looked round for Stephanos. "Why is he wearing your clothes?" he wanted to ask him. He was not there. "Stephanos?" said the boy, shakily. "Stephanos, Stephanos!" And he began to scream in his piercing high-pitched boy's voice. Justiniani grabbed him, carried him bodily across the terrace, and put him in a corner by the angle of the inner wall. "No panic here!" he was saying. "Noli hic clamare!" with a hand over Vrethiki's mouth. The boy fell quiet, and nodded, dumbly. For indeed there was panic enough: cries and wails, and shouted questions, and men running everywhere. Then two of Justiniani's men took the Emperor up on their shoulders, and carried him up and down the line.

"For God's sake, Sire, take cover!" cried Theophilus'

voice, from the inner wall behind them. "The Turks can see you too!" The Emperor was put on his feet again. The dead were being dragged across the terrace, to be laid out along the foot of the inner wall. The wounded were being carried through one of the doors to the City. The Emperor came over to Vrethiki. A crowd of men were with him, and the sight of Vrethiki seemed to fill them with dismay. The Emperor was shaking. He looked at Vrethiki with concern, and his and other voices were asking, asking …

"Oh, oh, what are you saying?" wept the boy. "Oh, Stephanos, get up and tell me what they're saying!" A dull ache throbbed in his cheek. What were they fussing about? So dazed was he that he did not realize yet that his cheek was cut; it was blood that had run down between his collar and his neck—he had coated his hands with it, and then rubbed his smarting eyes. He had plastered his face with blood, and they thought he was badly hurt.

One of Varangian John's men picked him up and carried him, back through a door in the inner wall, along the road behind, and to the Emperor's tent. He found a cloth, and washed Vrethiki's face; then he grinned, patted Vrethiki's cheek, said something to him in a cheering sort of voice, and left. Vrethiki lay on his back for a moment or two, and then slid swiftly into a deep exhausted sleep, as though he had been knocked unconscious. On the wall the Emperor's horse was led back to him, and he mounted, and rode off to visit other positions. Justiniani went to have his cut cleaned and bound up. Theophilus directed a repair gang for the damaged stockade. And a work party buried Stephanos with fifteen others in a shallow grave at the foot of the inner wall. A priest made one blessing, one prayer, do for them all.

Chapter 18

It was dusk when vrethiki awoke. He awoke clearheaded in the empty tent. The cut in his cheek hurt. He sat up and looked around. While part of him wanted to think, to sit and weep over Stephanos, he could see there was no fire lit, no lamps burning, neither wine nor food for supper; and so, getting up, he set to work at once, doing what Stephanos would have done, to make some comfort ready for the Emperor. And when everything he could think of was prepared, and before he had time to sit and think, the Emperor returned. Vrethiki knelt, and pulled off his boots; brought clean water for him to wash in, and fresh clothes, for the grit of the ruined walls still clung to him. Hesitantly, feeling suddenly awkward at such familiarity, he picked up the Emperor's ivory comb, and creeping up behind him, began gently to comb out the dusty tangles in his hair. They were silent, having so few words in common. The Emperor made the boy sit down with him, and eat a share of what there was, though Vrethiki had not been able to find much, and the meal was only bread and broth. Vrethiki remembered longingly all those gluttonous banquets he had seen, and then felt cruelly ashamed of himself for feeling hungry when another man was dead.

After supper the Emperor put on his cloak, and with Vrethiki at his side went to pray in the Church of the Chora, because it was nearby. It was three hours after nightfall when they left the church, and yet it was not dark outside. A misty orange sky was visible above them, and the rooftops and domes of the City were all luridly lit up. The Emperor rode at once to the nearest tower of the inner wall, and he and the boy mounted it, and looked out. All over the enemy camp outside the City, huge fires were burning, and bloodcurdling cries could be heard from the blazing camp. The light flooded earth and sky, it lit up the Golden Horn like molten iron, it showed the distant towers of Galata, and the ships lying as far off as Scutari.

"Their camp is on fire!" thought Vrethiki, with a wild spiraling lift of the heart. He followed the Emperor running down the stairs of the tower, and out onto the terrace. And there the defenders were helplessly watching a huge swarm of enemy workers, with flares and fires to give them light, laboring to fill the fosse. They worked feverishly, like men possessed, and the discharge of the defenders' cannon, arrows and slingshot, though they reaped swathes of men, did not for one moment cow or stop the rest, but the work went on without pause. And just beyond the fosse, great rings of Turks were dancing and leaping to the crazy skirling of pipes and drums and trumpets, the firelight burning on their crazed faces; some of them whirled on one spot like tops, and others ran up and down, and turned somersaults like tumblers. Vrethiki saw that the fearful noise they were making was not cries of alarm at the conflagration, but howls of frenzied joy. And the glow from the lights and torches showed Vrethiki also the battered walls, and the lines of men on them; many of them kneeling at their posts, in terrified prayer.

By this time it was midnight. A bell sounded from the midst of that bedlam of bonfires; and suddenly the workers in the fosse retreated. A silence fell, as sudden and stunning as the racket had been. And almost at once the fires and torches were put out. Darkness and silence swept over the plain, leaving the Christians on the wall staring blindly into the night.

VRETHIKI WOKE IN THE NIGHT, LURCHING OUT OF NIGHTMARE, and crying out. From the darkness a hand came, and held his firmly. "Stephanos?" murmured the boy, sleepily. He was drowsing again almost at once. Only, as he slipped away into sleep, he noticed fuzzily that the hand he held had thin long fingers, and a great chunky ring ... In the morning Vrethiki reckoned it part of his dream.

THE MORNING DAWNED STRANGE AND SILENT. THERE WERE no guns. No shouting, but a quiet brightening of the light. Vrethiki woke early and went out. He walked a little way in the open, through the wilderness that was now the Lycus valley, through a cluster of ruined houses. The silence made all the world seem made new. The sound of the stream came as sweetly as music to the boy's ears, battered into deafness by all those weeks of gunfire. He stood for a while beside a rambling clump of wild rosebush, its arched sprays breaking out in fragile papery pink petals, and listened enchanted while far and near the air was full of the melodious exotic chanting of all the tribes of birds. He did not think of yesterday, or of today, but simply drank in the morning moment all around him. It was a short moment; he had to return to his duties.

He had to poke up the fire, and warm a pan of milk. Then run across to the Chora Monastery, and bring bread and olives for the Emperor's breakfast. There hadn't been much else to eat this long while past, and now even this was a luxury. When that was done Vrethiki opened the huge wooden chest that held the Emperor's clothes. He chose a clean linen under-coat, to go next to his master's skin, picking out the one he liked best, that had a border of fruits and flowers woven in black on white. He laid that out ready, smoothing the creases away. Then he fetched the corselet of gilded chain, and the golden breastplate, and all the polished war gear. Then a pair of undershoes: a sort of slipper and legging in one that went under the greaves; there was only one clean pair of these left, and they were of purple silk, woven with golden eagles. Then he found the Emperor's boots, of purple hide with bands of pearls sewn on the seams, and, last, the great purple surcoat the Emperor wore, that came to his knees over his armor, and was blazoned all over with golden embroidery. Then he woke his sleeping master, brought him his breakfast to eat sitting in his nightshirt, and then helped him dress.

That day made strange by silence began, like so many other days, with a quarrel, brought before the Emperor to settle, voices raised, the sour atmosphere of anger and suspicion. This time it was Justiniani and Notaras, who came to the Emperor's tent, and, almost snarling at each other, appealed to the Emperor, each asking him to rebuke the other.

The boy, offering them wine, and being angrily brushed aside, tried to make out what was happening. He was lost without Stephanos, and his helplessness frightened him. But he could make out roughly, from manner and gesture, that Justiniani wanted something that Notaras refused him. "Helepolis"—it would seem to be guns. The Emperor thought Justiniani should have them. With a cry of dismay Notaras began to talk about the Golden Horn, the wall there. The Emperor mentioned the Lycus valley. "It's about the placing of guns," thought Vrethiki.. And he was glad the Emperor took Justiniani's part, for he was sure that Justiniani was always right.

The Emperor insisted. Notaras was white-lipped with anger, and would not come with the Emperor to the walls. On the land walls the terrible endless treadmill labor of repairs was continuing. But beyond—outside in the camps of the enemy—there was still awesome silence. No noise; no movement; not a man visible round the tents. The sentries on the walls said the Turks had lit no fires, cooked no breakfasts, neither drilled nor ridden horses, nor prepared their guns. Instead there was that unearthly hush.

"They are preparing to go, perhaps," said one sentry.

"No," said Justiniani. "They are fasting. They are placating their God."

"A day of prayer," said John Dalmata. "And then? Look at this, my Lord," and he held out to the Emperor one of those little rolls of paper that came on arrow shafts over the wall. It bore one word: "Tomorrow."

The Emperor said, "So. Well, we, too, have a God. Let us pray to Him, and all His saints."

It was at noon the bells began to ring. In a great gathering metallic clamor, they filled the terrifying hush left by the guns with insistent harmonious noise. The citizens flocked into the streets—old men, women, children, monks and nuns, and whoever could be spared from the walls. Images, icons, relics were carried out of the churches, and a great procession escorted them toward the walls. Incense was swung, smoking, in silver vessels; the people took lighted candles in their hands. They Sang; they repeated endlessly, Kyrie eleison, Christe eleison, Kyrie eleison.

When the procession had gathered strength, the Emperor joined it, bareheaded, with Vrethiki at his side. Someone gave them each a candle. The great throng of people wound along the walls. At each battered and broken place they stopped. The priests in the procession gave Communion and a blessing to the soldiers there; the icons were placed on each battered parapet or rough stockade in turn, that their ineffable holiness might avert the danger. The solemn intoning music of the hymns was swelled by the pleading voices of thousands. Vrethiki, too, found himself praying. "O God, put forth your strength!" he said to himself, over and over. Ahead of him, under its canopy, moved the queen of icons, the image painted by St. Luke, that this time allowed itself to be carried through the streets.

It was four o'clock before the procession was over, and the icon of St. Luke was returned to Blachernae.

At Blachernae the Emperor went to his throne room. He sat on his wide golden throne, with the Gospels open beside him, and he wore his crown. Flocking into the tall marbled room, under the golden roof, came all his nobles and the demarchs of the City. "Another great meeting," thought Vrethiki, "of which I shall understand so little." And his heart lurched at the thought of Stephanos, who would have explained. But it was not a conference; it was a speech, the Emperor's last words to his people, before the crisis came. And one of Isadore's priests translated it, passage by passage, into Latin for the benefit of those who knew little Greek, and so Vrethiki did understand it.

"Noble princes," said the Emperor. "Councilors, and famous soldiers, our most generous fellows in arms, and all faithful and honorable citizens—the crisis has come. The enemy will now exert his utmost force by land and sea against us, and, if he can, like a lion he will devour us. Therefore I pray you, and exhort you, to resist the enemy of our faith, with steadfast and magnanimous courage, as you have always done till now. I give into your keeping, I commend to you, this most famous and illustrious citadel, our motherland, Queen of cities. You know, my brothers, that there are four things for which any of us ought to be ready to die—for our faith, for our motherland, for our Emperor, God's anointed servant, and for our family and friends. And if we are bound in duty to defend any one of these with our lives, how much more, now that all four are at risk, should we face death, unflinching! But if, because of my sins, God gives victory to the infidel, still let us face our ordeal in the true faith, bought with the blood of Christ. Yet this is the fifty-seventh day on which that vile and contemptible Sultan has besieged us, and with every possible device, and all his strength, day and night he has not ceased to fight us. And yet till now, by the grace of God, we have repelled him from the walls. For he puts his faith in engines of war, and force of numbers; but ours is in God, our Lord and Saviour."

The Emperor spoke quietly, in a firm level voice. They listened still as stones, with their eyes fixed on his face. When he paused for his words to be said over in Latin, nobody moved, but heard them out intently.

"Be of good courage, therefore," he continued. "Wield your swords stoutly. You have good serviceable armor to protect you, which most of them have not; you fight within the walls, they in the open. Remember how long ago a great number of Roman horses were put to flight by the mere sight and sound of a few Carthaginian elephants. And if brute beasts could accomplish that, how much more easily we, who are the thinking masters of animals, can do the same, especially as those who fight against us are like animals, more brutal even than brute beasts! Think of yourselves as hunting a herd of swine, whom you know to be blasphemers, and fight, not like such beasts as they are, but like their lords and masters, the proud posterity of Greece and Rome. For you know, brothers, how the vile Sultan has without any just cause or provocation broken the peace with us, and besieged us, to wrest from us this City, which the great and thrice-blessed Emperor Constantine founded and gave to the Virgin Mary, that she might be its patroness, and its protectress, and that it might be the refuge of Christians. Shall this City, which is the hope and joy of all the Hellenes, the glory of the Eastern Empire, this splendid City, that flourished once like the rose of the field and was mistress of almost all peoples under the sun—shall it now be trampled on by blasphemers, and yoked in slavery? Shall our holy churches, where we have worshipped the Trinity, and sung the Liturgy, and celebrated the mystery of the Word made Flesh, be made shrines for the blasphemy of their driveling prophet Mohammed, stables for their horses and camels? Think of this, when you fight for our liberty."

The Emperor turned then to the Venetians, who were grouped at his right. "My dearly beloved Venetian brothers in Christ," he said to them. "Famous and stalwart fighters, I charge you today to defend this City heart and soul. And it shall always be your country; a second mother and father to you."

And then he turned to the Genoese. "My noble and courageous brothers," he said. "You know this unhappy City is not only mine, but yours also. We have needed your help before, now we need it again." And then he spread out his arms, and said to everyone, "If we all fight bravely, I hope

God will grant us our liberty on earth. And an imperishable crown awaits us in heaven, and an immortal memory."

A stone-struck solemnity enwrapped them all. He finished, but they did not move. "Hope against hope," thought Vrethiki, aching inwardly at the Emperor's words. "Hope that is nothing but a kind of courage in the face of despair."

The Emperor had risen from his throne. He had gone down among the throng. He moved slowly from one man to another, saying to each man in turn, "If ever I have wronged you, I pray you now, forgive me." Notaras, that stiff man, suddenly burst into tears when the Emperor spoke that to him. He rushed across the room to Justiniani, and the two of them were clasped in embrace like brothers; all round the room men turned to each other with the Emperor's words, "If ever I have wronged you …" on their lips. They took their leave of one another in tears, like men who expect to die.

It was already dusk when this great gathering dispersed. The Emperor made his way to the Great Church. Don Francisco, Theophilus, and John Dalmata rode with him. The streets of the City were quiet, scarcely anyone was abroad. As they rode, they passed a group of women with roses in their hands, going to decorate the Church of St. Theodosia, whose feast was on the morrow. One of these women spoke a blessing on the Emperor; he stopped and thanked her, and called her sister. So they came to the portals of the Holy Wisdom. Her deep-throated bells tolled endlessly overhead. The Emperor paused in the narthex and put off his crown.

And once more Vrethiki thought he remembered; thought he knew the great expanse of marble floor, the vast sculptured empty spaces of the shining church—only again he had not remembered how large, how beautiful, and this time it was full of people. A throng of citizens packed the vast nave; they filled the aisles and galleries. The immense airy arcs and domes were vibrant with their voices; a myriad lamps and candles danced, and struck dark gleaming echoes from the myriad facets of the golden roof. At the altar, Cardinal Isadore wearing Greek vestments was surrounded by priests who had denounced the Union, who would never accept his creed. And in the aisles long lines of people stood, waiting their turn for confession, no matter whether Greek priest or Latin priest absolved them. At the altar thirty priests prepared to concelebrate the Holy Liturgy. Only yesterday this church was shunned as a den of iniquity by half the citizens, and now who was absent, save those who manned the walls?

The Emperor stood a moment on the threshold as he took this in. "They have come to my requiem," he murmured. Then he went to make his confession. There was a lectern, with a Bible and a cross upon it. The Emperor stood before it, with a priest at his side, and named his sins, in a low voice. "And now, Lord God," said the priest loudly, "forgive your servant Constantine..." The Emperor returned to his place, and other men moved up the waiting line, and the voices of the priests went on and on, "Forgive your servant Theophilus ... your servant Lukas ... your servant Justiniani ... Now, O Lord, forgive your servants ..."

Vrethiki gazed, dazzled, at the shining silken robes of all those priests; slowly they moved in their appointed order as in a ponderous dance. And at the people flocking to take Communion, the little fragment of bread soaked in wine, offered them on a sacred silver spoon. Once more the church echoed to the murmurous repetition of thousands of names: "Who are you, who ask for the body and blood of the Lord?"

"Constantine," said the Emperor simply, on his knees.

Constantine, John, George, Theophilus ... Basil ... Lukas
... Michael ... the great roll of names went on. At last the
solemnities drew to a close. The great swelling mass of voices
rose and filled the church with the people's hymn, and Vrethiki
felt his heart lift with it, to swell and soar, and fill so vast a
place ... to be one of God's people, in the light of God's Holy
Wisdom ... "I have loved, O Lord, the beauty of Thy house
..." sang voices all around him. "Lord, hear my voice ..."

Then the priests all blessed the people, saying, "Go in
peace."

A CERTAIN GRAVE TRANQUILLITY LINGERED ABOUT THE DISPERSING
people. The Emperor rode in a great crowd of captains and
commanders, returning to the wall. They hardly spoke to
one another, but carried the silence with them, like a blessing.
At the road to Blachernae they parted company, the Emperor
going with only a few to the palace. The palace servants
awaited him there: his household, his domestic slaves. Many
wore armor, having been fighting on the walls these many
weeks past, and having come now only at his bidding. Going
round them all, the Emperor embraced each one, and said, "If
ever I have wronged you, I pray you now forgive me." Soon
everyone in the room was in tears.

The Emperor left quickly. He rode with Phrantzes the
whole length of the land walls and back, under the brilliant
and unfeeling stars, speaking briefly to each captain in turn,
checking everything. On the return ride he dismounted
at the Caligarian Gate, and he and Phrantzes and Vrethiki
climbed a tower. It was the outermost tower of the newer
jutting wall around Blachernae; from it they could look out
across the enemy lines, and down to the Golden Horn.

Below them in the darkness there were noises—the jumbled sounds of men at work, things being dragged and moved. And on the dark waters of the Horn, lights were moving, doubled in the glossy water. "This has gone on since sunset," the watchman told them. The Emperor stood at the window of the tower room, looking out. There was a kind of peace, a serenity in the room. And yet it was not peaceful to Vrethiki—he wanted to cry out against it. The Emperor had done his duty. He had done all he could, and made his peace with God and man. And now he was neither hopeful, nor despairing, nor afraid, only ready.

But the boy, in his heart, was still crying "No!" to Fate.

Chapter 19

It was perhaps an hour they lingered there in the dark tower, watching and listening. Then the Emperor sent Phrantzes away. There was an argument, and Phrantzes shed tears. But the Emperor insisted. He wanted Phrantzes to go and check the reserves of weapons in some other part of the City; his old friend wanted to stay. "Of course," thought Vrethiki, looking at Phrantzes' gray head. "The Emperor is saving his life, and he would rather lose it." But in spite of this flash of understanding, the boy thought there had been quite enough weeping this night, and wished Phrantzes had been made of sterner stuff. Yet when Phrantzes had gone, and the Emperor turned to Vrethiki, and said softly, in hesitant Latin, "My brave Vrethiki, for bringing you to this, and for any unkindness I may have shown you, I pray you now forgive me ..." the boy found he could only answer, "A ffendi mou!" half choking on the words, while the tears ran down his face. The Emperor took his hand, and they climbed down the tower.

They rode to the Lycus valley, where the Varangians stood in ranks, waiting for their Imperial captain. All along the land walls the defenders had locked the doors in the inner wall behind them, and the captains brought the keys, and gave them to the Emperor.

It was nearly two in the morning when the uncertain light of the waning moon, and the flares that the citizens kept burning on their watchtowers, showed movement in the enemy camp; men were gathering in the shadows. The sentries banged their clappers to give the alarm; the Church of St. George, and the Chora nearby, just within the walls, began to ring their bells, and the ringing spread like wild-fire from church to church the length and breadth of the City. Swiftly the sound was answered from without. Screaming and raving, with a patter of drumbeats and wild tuneless wailing of their mountain pipes, a vast herd of Turks flung themselves at the walls. They came in no order, even elbowing each other aside as they jostled for a likely-looking place on the walls. They brought fire, and hundreds of scaling ladders; they were cut down as they mounted them. They were cut down in swathes, in hordes, but, pouring out of the shadows beyond the fosse, more and more of them came on. For the first time the defenders felt the weight of the vast numbers massed against them; so much of the fosse was now filled in that the attack could be mounted on a wide front, and no reinforcements could be brought to the aid of the Christians, because the whole length of the walls was under attack, even the sea walls, along which ships with scaling ladders at the ready were prowling under the stars. The long-expected general assault had come at last.

"This is not the worst of it yet," said Theophilus to the Emperor. "These are only irregulars—without armor." And indeed the arrows of the defense seemed each to kill a man; the stones they hurled into the packed throng below bowled over many of the attackers. The Emperor rode up and down a little way, but from the messages brought to him, and what he could see, it was clear that the main weight of the attack was in the Lycus valley, and he settled there, watching Justiniani, his incomparable captain, fighting behind the stockade. The Turks even stood on each other's shoulders to reach over the bulwark of rubble and stones; they only brought themselves within range of the Romans' swords. And all the time the noise continued, the shouting, and clashing of arms and beat of drums.

It was an unequal encounter. The Turks were killed in hundreds, fighting with their strange mixture of light weapons and unarmed bodies against the stubborn courage and good armor of the defense. And yet it was two hours before their fear of the Christians grew greater than their fear of the Sultan, and they were driven back. The sight of their backs as they fled away into the darkness brought a great cheer from the men along the walls. The captains began to re-form their disordered ranks; a party of women, among them, Vrethiki saw, nuns and young girls, brought pitchers of water along the lines. Vrethiki filled the Emperor's wine flask. And then, within minutes of the retreat, there was a blast of martial music, and the Turks were upon them again.

This time it was the Anatolian divisions. Better drilled and better armed, they came up in good order, and one man covered another as they tried to secure their ladders. A length of wall in the middle of their line was left free from attack; suddenly on this length of wall the full force of the cannon was let rip. The defenders were deafened and blinded by smoke; out of the smoke an onrush of troops came dashing against the stockade. The Emperor moved his station a little, and went to the head of his Varangians. He became very excited, and pressing forward to the stockade, himself unsheathed his sword, and hacked at the hands and heads of the enemy as they scrambled up. He shouted to his men, and they answered him with a roar: "Basileus!" And every man was straining muscle and bone in the struggle, laboring like a hero.

This second attack persisted almost as long as the first. The moon had set, and all was wrapped in the darkness before dawn. Then another shattering blast from the great gun struck them. The ball hit the stockade squarely in the middle, and brought down a long stretch of it. There was a shower of flying fragments of wood and earth; dust and smoke fouled the dark air, and in a moment the enemy charged howling through the gap. With a great cry, the Emperor spurred his horse toward them. His men rushed with him, and the Turks who had broken through found themselves brought up short, facing the great inner wall, fired on and pelted by bowmen and slingmen on top of it, and under savage attack from either flank, as the men on the terrace charged and hacked at them. Some few of them retreated the way they had come; several hundred of them were cut down, and their bodies were rolled forward into the missing line of the stockade. With that the whole attack faltered; for a moment the enemy line swayed, poised between advance and retreat; then they had gone.

The stars were fading in the slowly lightening sky. Behind the walls a faint rose-flush of dawn haloed the domed horizon. The Emperor's troops slumped wearily to the ground, or leaned against the walls. Their heads lolled with fatigue, their fingers slackened on their swords. Dragging away the dead—the many dead—they moved slowly, leaden-limbed. Sweat and dust disfigured them all. A heavy smell of blood hung round them; someone lying by the inner wall groaned ceaselessly, and a little way off in the fosse a Turk dying in agony screamed. It was still barely light enough to see. Vrethiki wondered why the force of the flares and torches should be sapped by daylight too dim to see by.

He was slightly dazed by the noise and confusion of the long night, and was afraid of losing the Emperor in the press of men. He stood back out of the way when the fighting was fierce, but the moment the battle waned a little, he stepped forward again to his master's side, and offered him water.

That is what he was doing when there came the wild skirling of pipes; a shower of iron balls and flights of arrows pelted down on them like rain, a gunfire of drums was struck up once more, and the Sultan's best troops, his famous janissaries, came marching forward, line upon line, solid with arms and armor, gleaming in the shadowy dawn, bearing down on the exhausted defenders. With cries of alarm the Christians scrambled to regain their places. Vrethiki saw Varangian John standing in the front line, yelling to his men, swaying on his feet. In magnificent order the janissaries came on. The discharge of Christian cannon, bows and slingshot tore holes in their lines; the gaps were closed at once, the advance continued unfaltering. And there was so little stockade left to stand behind that in many places the Christians had to hold the line of the crumbled defenses by fighting hand to hand. Wave upon wave the enemy came, fresh, and courageous and well armed. They tore and hacked at the stockade, and clambered up, and fixed ladders ... "It's all over now," thought Vrethiki, crouched down by the inner wall with a wounded man on either side of him. "I must draw my dagger, choose a Turk, die fighting ..." And overhead a bright new day was dawning.

Yet still the line of defenders held. They were stubborn, desperate. To give way was to lose wife, and son, and daughter; to lose was to have nowhere to run to. And at last it seemed the attack was losing force a little, wavering here and there. The janissaries came now, not triumphing, but with a certain caution, like men who think it possible they may fall. Battle, City, Empire, all seemed to hang in the balance, as the Turkish line came to a standstill on the wall.

The Emperor turned round and looked for Vrethiki. The boy came running. He took his water flask, wet his lips, and handed the bottle to Theophilus, and to John Dalmata, and Don Francisco, who had been at his side since the battle began. And at that moment a Genoese came to him, a tired soldier, scarcely able to carry the weight of his elaborate Western armor.

"Lord Emperor, my captain is wounded," the man said. "He asks for the key to the door through the inner wall, that he may be carried away to get help."

It was one of Justiniani's men. The Emperor stood frozen for a moment, the water flask halfway to his lips.

"Give me the key, my Lord," the man insisted. "He suffers. His wound must be dressed."

The Emperor and his three companions and Vrethiki went at once. They rode in single file, easing their way through the mass of soldiers on the terrace, making their way northward to Justiniani's position on the right of the Emperor's. Vrethiki felt sick. He feared to find Justiniani lying torn, unrecognizable, as Stephanos had been. But the great captain was on his feet, leaning heavily against the wall. His breastplate had been pierced, and he was clutching his transfixed shoulder, the blood welling between the fingers of his clawing hand. He was ash-white; beads of sweat stood on his forehead like dew, and ran down his cheeks. The clamor of the battle raged round them, as the janissaries struggled with the swaying ranks of his men.

"My brother, not now," the Emperor said, gently, taking Justiniani's limply hanging right hand. "All would lose heart without you. I beg you, do not leave the field. Stay where you are to hearten us."

Justiniani seemed not to hear him. His breathing was very fast and shallow, as though it hurt him, and he was trembling violently. But he shook his head.

"The force of the Turks' onslaught is spent," said the Emperor. "If you will endure just for another hour ..."

The captain at his side said, "My Lord, he must go. He can return when his wound is dressed."

"My brother!" cried the Emperor in anguish, "I love you dearly, you are flesh and blood to me, it grieves me to the quick to see you hurt, but I beg you, I beseech you, not to desert us now ..."

Justiniani groaned. Then, in a voice that shook and whimpered, he said, "Give me the key!"

Theophilus cried out, "Coward! You! You of all men, unmanned by the sight of your own blood! Shame on you ..."

And Vrethiki, in a frenzy of rage and anger and grief, was scrabbling at the strap that held his scabbard and dagger on his belt.

But the Emperor unhooked a key from his belt, and gave it to Justiniani's man. "Go quickly then, and quickly return," he said.

The boy tore off his dagger and hurled it in the dust at Justiniani's feet. He stamped and spat on it. Justiniani seemed not to see. His eyes were glazed and blank. The Emperor said to John Dalmata and Don Francisco, "Return to my post and see how things are holding there. I will follow in a moment."

They went ahead, returning along the line. The Emperor cast one more long look at Justiniani, who was being laid upon a stretcher, then turned his back, and went after them.

A HELLISH CHAOS WAS RAGING ROUND THE VARANGIANS. THE
battle was so frenzied that it was impossible to see what was
happening; none of the Emperor's three companions was in
sight in the fray. Vrethiki stooped over the body of a man
lying at the foot of the palisade, and helped himself to the
man's dagger. It was a clumsy crude iron thing, but its owner
had had courage unto death. Clutching the weapon to buoy
his own courage, Vrethiki struggled through the press of
men, back to his master's side.

As he reached him, the Emperor looked round, looked
back the way they had come, and saw the terrace on the right
nearly empty. The Genoese had seen their captain carried
away; they had seen the gate to the City open behind them,
and they were streaming away through the gate in full flight,
leaving the Emperor and his Romans alone.

"They must lock it again!" cried the Emperor. "Why did
he not lock it behind him!" He looked frantically round for
messengers, but only Vrethiki was at his side. In the swaying,
screaming mass of fighting men, no one else was within
call.

"Vrethiki!" he said, leaning over the boy. "Take this key.
Go to the Genoese gate. Get the door locked. Lock it yourself, or get anyone to help you; go quickly, quickly!"

Sudden dread flooded over Vrethiki. He was certain, not
in his head but in the very marrow of his bones, he must not
go; he knew he must, must, remain at the Emperor's side. But
the Emperor was saying again, imploring him, "Go, Vrethiki,
tell them to lock the door!"

He could not force his way through the press of men. He
struggled for a moment in the throng, and then shot into the
nearest tower on the inner wall, and hurtled up the stairway

to emerge on the almost deserted upper catwalk. He began to run along it, forcing his tired limbs to speed, slowing up every few moments and looking over at the terrace below on his left to see how far along he had come. The light was dawning now, and a clear and golden morning sky arched over him, the shadows of night had dispersed, and he could see his way. And as he ran, he looked up the rising slope with the wall breasting and mounting it, and saw, just catching the rays of the morning sun, flying bravely from the top of the tower above the Kerkoporta, Turkish flags, Turkish horse-tail banners. Vrethiki came to a sudden stop. The City had fallen.

Chapter 20

He didn't know what to do. the now useless key of the gate was still clutched in his hand. Someone had left the little sally port open, the Kerkoporta. The Turks had got through it. Only a few, surely, through so small a door; it ought to be possible to stop them. Yet even as he thought this he saw Turkish soldiers, far off ahead of him, running along the catwalk toward him, throwing bowmen and slingmen off the parapet. From below him on the terraces rose screams of horror and fear. Turning round, the defenders had seen Turks above and behind them. Watching from his high viewpoint, Vrethiki saw men on the outer wall covering their faces and jumping into the fosse, throwing themselves to instant and ugly death. Most of the defenders were panicking, stampeding along the terraces toward him in a great terrified mob. And as they ran they came to the point just below him, and found the door left open behind the Genoese. It was a narrow gate. Pushing and thrusting to get through it, they fought each other for space. Some lost their footing and fell, but the crowd was borne on, regardless, by the pressure of men coming behind. The strong trampled on the weak, and fell themselves to be trodden down. Behind them, on the deserted outer wall, the Turks fixed ladders unopposed, and flew up them like eagles. But coming to the gate below Vrethiki they could not get in because it was blocked by the dead and dying bodies of their crushed and trampled enemies.

And the Emperor: where was he?

"I must be with him!" cried Vrethiki. "I must be at his side!" He turned and ran back the way he had come. The Turks were running up and down the terrace below him, looking for another way in. He ran, flying up and down the steps where the catwalk passed the towers of the inner wall, half sobbing, half gasping for breath. When he reached the point where, only minutes before, he had climbed up, leaving the Emperor, he hung over the parapet, desperately scanning the crowd. He could see the Emperor nowhere.

A pitiful and frantic struggle was still going on below him. Deserted by the Genoese on their right, the Emperor's Varangians and some of the citizen soldiers had spread out, to try to hold the line. The Turks had gained a foothold on top of the stockade, from which they were now raining death on the Romans below them, and pressed back from the line of the stockade, the Romans had been driven into pits and trenches dug in the terrace floor to give earth and clay for the ceaseless repairs. Losing their footing, and unable to climb out of these slippery pits, they fell on each other, crushed and trampled each other, and were slain. Shuddering, Vrethiki ran on. Cries of despair rose to him on all sides, and he seemed to be the only living creature on top of the inner wall here. Healo he Polis! drifted up to him—the City has fallen! And still he ran, seeking the Emperor.

When he had run right across the Lycus valley, and not seen him, Vrethiki turned again and ran back. "Oh, where is he, where is he, what has happened?" he sobbed to himself. Cramp from running so far and fast stabbed him, and he stopped, doubled up, leaning on the parapet and only slowly able to straighten himself. And then at last he saw the Emperor.

He was not on the terrace between the inner and outer walls, where Vrethiki had been looking, but riding along the roadway behind the inner wall, within the City. He was a little way off, riding with his three companions again by his side. They were coming toward Vrethiki from the direction of the Kerkoporta. The Emperor must have been summoned there, and found nothing there to be done. Now he was returning to his own men.

Vrethiki hastened forward, looking for the nearest stairway down to his master, but just then there was a loud crack and splinter, wood giving way, and through the St. Romanus Gate just below him poured the small battered remnant of the Emperor's guard. They had broken down the door, and were escaping. They rushed through the wall below Vrethiki, and the Turks dashed after them, a torrent of men cascading into the City between Vrethiki and his master. And even then the terrible struggle was not quite over. Within the gate a few brave souls turned and struggled to re-form the line, to hold the onrush of the enemy.

Beyond the struggle the Emperor and his friends dismounted. Theophilus cried out loudly, so that his voice reached to Vrethiki, hanging over the parapet some distance off and far above, "I would now rather die!" and he ran into the midst of the seething throng of the enemy. The Emperor as yet hung back. He was casting off his purple surcoat, and struggling out of his corselet and breastplate. He pulled off, and threw away, his ring. He stooped and cut the straps that held his golden greaves, and kicked them away. He bent a leg, and pulled his boots off, and threw them aside. Vrethiki watched him, horrified. But John Dalmata on his right and

Don Francisco on his left made no move to stop him, but waited calmly. Then, drawing their swords, the three of them ran forward. The last of those who had resisted within the gate had been cut down, but now, for a few moments, the three alone stood, holding the narrow road. Then they fell from sight, and the Turks rushed over them. Vrethiki slipped down behind the high parapet, and crouched there out of sight, in the shadow thrown by the brightly shining morning sun.

FOR SOME WHILE THE RUSH OF TURKS THROUGH THE GATE below him continued. Howling in triumph, the Sultan's regiments crowded in, and then fanned out and dispersed in all directions, looking for plunder. But after a while no more poured through the gate. From the ceasing of the guns, and the distant uproar in the Lycus valley, Vrethiki judged that there was nothing to stop them now from flooding through the breaches in the torn and fallen walls. They would not come through a narrow gate clogged with the dead, when a wide way lay open to them. Telling himself this to keep his courage up, Vrethiki crept along the wall. The staircase was just beyond the gate. Had he only run farther, sooner! He slunk down it, and found himself alone in the street behind the walls. In the distance the sound of tumult rose and fell like the surge of the sea.

Within the gate lay the pile of the slain. They had killed the Emperor, and left him for a common soldier. Vrethiki crept nearer, nearer. He was sick, afraid of what he would see. He stood in the shadow trembling. A wave of outrage swept over him.

"He is the Emperor, the Emperor!" he told himself. "He should not be left like carrion lying in the dust. There should be prayers for him and flowers, seemliness and ceremony!

Oh, God, what had he done to deserve this!" Vrethiki's knees gave way, and he slipped down, and sat, leaning at the foot of the wall. But it came to him at once that the Emperor did deserve it; that was just what he had deserved—what he had wanted—a valiant death, a nameless burial. And that he was likely not to have it, because something had been forgotten. The boy knew; he had seen him forget. The Turks would insult and dishonor him; they would cut off his head, and put it in a bag ...

"But I *can't!*" the boy wailed, answering his innermost heart, and looking where his master's body lay hidden, crushed and pressed in that hideous pile, from which a dark vintage was already seeping across the stones. "I can't!" he thought. But he knew that he must.

He was still moaning, "I can't," to himself when he staggered to his feet, and began to look for his master. He rolled two or three bodies off the pile, before he found him. He saw first the bloodsoaked hem of his undershirt, with its woven fruits and flowers, but he could not move Don Francisco's body off his master's because it was pinned down by several others. He dragged at John Dalmata, until at last the body slipped, and then he could see the Emperor's right side uncovered, his face turned toward him. Try though he might, he could not get the Emperor's body clear; the dead were heavy, and he was not strong enough.

He was trembling violently, as in a fever. To reach the Emperor he had to tread on soft human flesh, and looking down he recognized Theophilus, with his head lolling back, and his throat cut. Vrethiki's gorge rose, and he shrank away. Then he forced himself to take Theophilus by the ankles, and heaved and dragged at him to pull him out of the way. He was heavy. As Vrethiki pulled at him one of his boots came off, and the boy had to take a new grip round the bare anklebone. He was gasping for breath from the effort. At last the body slipped a foot or two on a wet patch of ground, and he could get to the Emperor treading on nothing worse than the slimy flagstones of the road.

But why, he wondered now, had he wanted to? What was he doing here? His head swam. There was something he had to do, something … He laid his fingers on his master's eyelids, and weighed them down to shut them over the dark empty eyes. Something else … He hesitated. Then he remembered. The Emperor had cast off all his purple, had wanted to be unrecognized. But he had forgotten his undershoes, his silken slippers. Vrethiki tried to take a grip on himself, to think clearly, to stop trembling. Then he pulled off the under-shoes. There was something unbearable to him in the sight of the Emperor's naked feet, soft and helpless in the sunlight, projecting from under Don Francisco's shoulders, where he lay across his cousin, face down. Vrethiki looked away, hastily. Then he went and put one of the undershoes on Theophilus. "This is the last thing you must do for him," he told the body. But he couldn't get the second one on. Theophilus' leg seemed to be broken; it wouldn't stay stiff while he pulled the silken legging up it. Vrethiki gave up, feeling sick, and looped the second slipper through his own belt.

Then he went back to the Emperor's body. "You are quite safe, now, affendi," he told him. "No further indignity awaits you." "Nobody will find him, ever again," he thought. "There is no one but me to say goodbye to him. But how ought an Emperor be bidden farewell?"

There came to him a jumbled memory of the ceremonies of the Empire: of the Emperor sitting enthroned with the Gospels beside him, while the great men of many nations pressed forward to kiss his hand and cheek; of the words Stephanos translated from the Empress Helena's requiem ... Kneeling, he kissed the Emperor's right foot, his right hand, his blood-streaked right cheek. Then he stood up and cried out loudly in the silent street, "Depart Emperor; the King of Kings, the Lord of Lords bids thee go forth!"

Chapter 21

After that it seemed to him there was nothing more to be done. He simply stood where he was.

He might have stayed there, dazed and weary, for a long time if another small group of Turks had not clattered through the gate. His hand flew to the slipper looped through his belt, and he fled from them into the shadows, running swiftly, dodging from wall to wall, and then from bush to bush in the open, making for the maze of streets that might offer some cover. If they found him with the purple slipper, they would make him tell where it had come from. He had to hide it; he had to hide. Where could he go? All he knew of the City was palaces and churches; the Turks would go straight to them for plunder. He knew a few ordinary streets, but they would be ransacked for slaves. In the whole of this City nowhere would be safe, nowhere! Then he remembered ... a well shaft with iron footholds going down it ... a well shaft that was dry ... with something bright lying in the bottom. Where was that? Where had he remembered that? Yes—it was the ruined palace, the old Imperial palace by sea.

And though he had to cross the whole City to do it, Vrethiki set himself to get there.

He kept away from noise. When he heard screaming and

clamor he turned aside at once, and took another way. Still he saw horrors. He went down streets in which every house had a little white flag at the door, to show it had been pillaged. The old lay dead on the thresholds, the babies and the sick lay smashed on the roadway, while the shutters of the windows from which they had been thrown swung and creaked on their hinges overhead. In one place a river of blood ran thickly in the gutter. Once he crossed the path of a single puny-looking Turk leading away ten citizens, four of them only girls, so white they could never before have walked out in the sun, but the rest were able-bodied men. They were tied together in their own girdles, and made no resistance. Vrethiki lurked in a doorway till they had passed. He crossed behind a church from which screams of captured women pierced and rent the air, and another from which the sound of singing and prayer still hopelessly seeped. Somehow he had got ahead of the progress of the looting, for just outside the Hippodrome he met a great crowd of citizens, fleeing toward the Great Church. He mingled with them, and then extricated himself, and ran across the floor of the Hippodrome.

The ruins of the old Imperial palace seemed utterly deserted. With a faint unreasonable surprise he saw the poppies growing up through the cracked marble floors, the roses in the overgrown gardens. He had come the other way the day he had found the well, and this place was vast and labyrinthine, but he thought he remembered amore or less unruined church beside the court it was in, and so he found it. He flung himself over the rim, and let himself hastily down the iron ladder. He had been right: it was dry. The bottom was full of dusty rubble and broken things. He lay in the bottom, panting for breath. He felt safe down here, deep down, buried out of sight, and out of seeing. No more blood and suffering to look upon, only a disk of blue sky, far above him, for a lid. Exhausted beyond endurance, he fell asleep there almost at once.

THE SUN WAS HIGHER WHEN HE WOKE; IT WAS FINGERING down the well. The sound of the sack had come nearer. In the world above, perhaps from the nearby church, he could hear running feet, and gleeful shouting, and the sound of smashing and shattering. It went on and on. He lay quite safe and still. "Why am I here?" he wondered. "I should never have left his side. I should have died with him. I wish I were dead."

But after a time it occurred to him to wonder what it was he had seen shining down here, and he shifted around on the rubble floor, looking for it. As soon as he moved, the sun struck it, and flashed daggers of light in his eyes. He reached out his hand.

It was a little bird made of gold. All its feathers were delicately engraved, and it had a round bead of jasper for an eye, and coral claws. It had been crushed, dented and flattened, but it was still charming. "Poor bird," murmured Vrethiki, turning it in his hands. What was that tale Stephanos had told him once? Everything has an object with which its fate is bound up—its stoicheion. The stoicheion of someone or other was a pillar—cut off the top and he fell dead. "And this poor thing might be the stoicheion of the City, so crushed and battered as it is," he thought. "Is it the Turks who broke your wings, my bird? Some Crusader, more likely, sacking and looting here long ago, who took you so roughly from your golden tree he broke you, and then cast you down here."

He fingered the delicate chased feathering. Then, thoughtfully, he placed his fingers along the creases that crushing the bird had made along its back and belly, and squeezing gently he tried to press it back into shape again. Its sides bulged outward as he squeezed. Then, suddenly, the little thing began to tremble and vibrate in his hands. A buzzing and whirring noise came from it, and a golden weight began to descend between his fingers on a golden wire, coming from its belly. He had released some curled-up mechanism, some long-jammed wheels and cogs within it. It ground, and creaked, and buzzed. Its beak flicked open and shut, and its wings juddered as though it should have flapped them, and was struggling in vain to do so. Vrethiki held it, fascinated. He hardly noticed the sounds of the sack receding again above him, dying away into the distance. The bird was slowing down now. Its pulsing energy was running out. And then, above the grinding and whirring, it sang three notes pure and true, on a dying fall.

He shook it, but it sang no more. He tried to find how to wind it, but he could find no cog or key to turn. "Nothing in you but an ending," he said to it at last. "Perhaps you are my stoicheion, for I wish I were dead!"

At that he suddenly heard Stephanos' voice, the Emperor's words: "Let him take care what he wishes in case it is given to him."

"I MUST THINK ABOUT IT," HE TOLD THE BIRD. IT FIXED HIM with its pinpoint beady eye. "You know, stoicheion," he told it, "I'm sure, sure, I want to be dead. I have only to think of my friends, of my dear Lord … but, you know, I always seem to be wrong when I'm sure. I was sure I didn't want to come here … sure Stephanos was unmanly, sure Justiniani was brave, and the Emperor was not … how could I have? But I did, for certain sure." The bird still looked at him.

"My mother would like you, stoicheion," he said to it, remembering her almost childish pleasure in ingenious things, how she loved his father's loadstone, suspended on its little brass astrolabe.

His mother once having come to his mind, he thought how she would be grieving over him, saying nothing, like as not, to anyone, but hugging her loss to herself, day by day. And he knew that he did not belong in the bottom of a well in Byzantium, but must somehow, if he could, save himself. He put the little bird down, to have both hands free. Then he began to climb the iron rungs, hand over hand, hauling himself up into the light.

THE FIRST THING HE NEEDED WAS A HIGH POINT TO SEE FROM. he clambered up onto a ruined wall. To his amazement he saw a company of soldiers on the sea wall below him, still fighting, though they were assailed from within and without. But beside him, on his right, it was all over. He could see a gate standing open, and the blue sea beyond. It was Turkish sailors coming up from there, doubtless, who had sacked the churches in the palace ruins while he had been hiding down the well. He could still hear clamor and shouting, afar off, from somewhere in the hapless City behind him. But Vrethiki fixed his eyes on something else—a flotilla of ships in the Bosporus. They were flying the Imperial flag, or the Genoese, or Venetian colors. They had come through the boom, and were standing off, waiting, perhaps, to see if others would join them. Vrethiki leaped off his wall, and ran down the slope, dodging from one courtyard to another, leaping down ruined stairways, making for that gate that stood open in the sea wall.

The shore was littered with Turkish ships. Their crews had

left them, and gone to join the rape and plunder. That must be how the Christian ships had got through the boom unhindered, and were free now to wait offshore. But the shore was also crowded with a pitiful throng of women, holding out their hands to the ships, beating their breasts, weeping and entreating the sailors to rescue them. Vrethiki wasted no time beating his breast. He took off his boots, scrambled out onto a wave-washed rock, and plunged into the water. He swam steadily toward the nearest ship.

It was farther off than it seemed. He saw as he swam that they had all set sails now, and were beginning to move on the wind. And the current swept him so far out into the Marmara that it was the leading vessel, and not the nearest, that threw a rope to him, and drew him from the water.

"It's the Emperor's English boy," someone said. He looked around, standing on the deck dripping and shivering in the smart north wind that was taking them to safety. They were all Genoese. He had been rescued by Justiniani's ship.

"I hate him," said Vrethiki to them in English. "It is because of his cowardice the Lord Emperor is dead." They did not understand him, but he relished saying it. Behind them the dusky blue outline of the City dimmed and faded as it fell away astern.

The doctor on board the ship spoke Latin. He came and conferred with Vrethiki. "He is dying," he said. "He is raving. He asks and asks what happened to the Emperor. Come and tell him."

Vrethiki's heart had screwed up within him to a tight hard knot of hatred and contempt. But Justiniani lay panting and sweating in his cabin, covered by a bloodstained sheet. His eyes had sunk deep in their sockets, his hair was stuck down to his scalp.

"L'Inglese," he said, when he saw Vrethiki. "Tell me what happened?"

"The Emperor lost everything," said Vrethiki. "He was butchered in the gate."

"He lost nothing," said Justiniani. "I am the one who lost …"

"You see," murmured the doctor. "The pain makes his mind wander." But he made sense enough to Vrethiki.

"There was little enough he had to lose, it's true," he said. "Hardly an Empire, really. Only a ruin, a memory and a dream. But all are lost, now he is dead."

"Nobody conquers a dream," said Justiniani, and his limp hand twitched on the sheet. "He has not lost it. Whenever men think of the City, he will be there; the last … Emperor dying bravely in the gate … but I lost my part in it …"

"OH, IF IT'S DEATH YOU WANTED!" CRIED VRETHIKI, HIS HATRED melting away, "never fear, it is on its way!"

"Ah," said Justiniani. "Thank God."

The boy turned to creep away, for the great captain said no more and had closed his staring eyes. But as he reached the door the painful voice stopped him. "You threw away the dagger I gave you …"

"Yes."

"If I gave you my own, now, would you keep that?"

"Yes," said Vrethiki.

THE GENOESE CAPTAIN GAVE VRETHIKI A WARM MEAL. SOMEONE found him dry clothes. He felt odd wearing doublet and hose again, like a plain Western gentleman. His memory twitched and jerked at the creaking movement of the ship. It struck him that very likely, now, he would get home again. What he would have to tell them! And suddenly, with amazement he knew that his mother would think of the Emperor as a tricky Eastern heretic, and he would have much ado to convince her that he was a truly valiant Christian gentleman. He smiled a little at the thought. And his aunt would be very disapproving. He could almost hear her sharp clipped voice complaining that other than such wild talk he had brought home no merchandise. "Cousin Alys will like to see the purple slipper," he thought, and realized he would have to tell her it was purple once, for the cold salt Bosporus waters had rinsed it a pale rose-pink.

Before he slept, he went up on deck to look at the night. He leaned on the stern rail, watching the curling wake trail out behind the ship. He knew he would never be able to explain to his family at home. How could such a distance be bridged with a handful of words? Why, he would probably stumble speaking English, just at first. "I shall be like that bird Stephanos gave me," he thought, "that fluttered in its wicker cage. But when I let it go free it beat from without on the bars, as though it would fain enter in again. In the very house I was born in, I shall carry an exile's heart, thinking of that immortal City, and how it passed away. And nothing will be simple for me, ever again."

The stars over his head were thick and brilliant; the waning moon poured silver on the ship's wake. With her delicately rigged moonshadow slipping along beside her, she sloped in the wind, and slid through the quiet Marmara, making for Western landfalls—for unconquered islands, and safe Christian anchorages, and so to far-distant Genoa, whence the Atlantic merchantmen embark their goods and men for England, in her cold northern seas.

AUTHOR'S NOTE

I have incurred many debts of gratitude in the course of writing this book. Pre-eminently to the classical archaeologist Dr. Themis Anagnostopoulos, who helped me to acquire a smattering of Greek, and to read the eyewitness accounts of the siege; and to the London Library without whose generous lending rules research would be almost impossible for me. Then, in a field in which my own learning is recent and thin, I have leaned exceptionally heavily on the two best accounts of the fall of Constantinople in English—Edwin Pears's *Destruction of the Greek Empire*, and Sir Steven Runciman's judicious and moving *The Fall of Constantinople*. I would also like to thank Mr. Michael Maclagan, whose eloquent words on the coronation of the Last Emperor at Mistra struck the first spark for this book. Then to many modern Turks, not known to me by name, and most of them children, who guided me through the labyrinth of Istanbul to find the monuments of the conquered City, many now ruined and obscure; and to my husband, my enthusiastic companion in these travels.

Lastly to Miss Gerrie Van Krevel, who with kindness and efficiency managed my household while I worked, and to J.V.H. for unendingly generous interest and moral support.

Finally I would like to say that it is impossible in a book written from the point of view of Byzantium and the West not to misrepresent the Turks. I hope to correct the balance in a second book on the same subject.

JILL PATON WALSH

Jill Paton Walsh was born in London and was educated at Oxford. She currently lives in Cambridge where, with John Rowe Townsend, she runs a small specialist imprint, Green Bay Publications.

She is the author of many award-winning books for children. She won the Book World Festival Award in 1970 for *Fireweed*; the Whitbread Prize in 1974 for *The Emperor's Winding Sheet*; the Boston Globe-Horn Book Award in 1976 for *Unleaving*; the Universe Prize in 1984 for *A Parcel of Patterns* and the Smarties Prize Grand Prix in 1986 for *Gaffer Samson's Luck*.